Praise for the Annie O'Hara & Claudius mystery series by Ann Campbell

"Sheer delight . . . the most original and funny book I've read in a long time. I literally could not put it down."
—Tamar Myers, author of *Gruel and Unusual Punishment*

"An amusing tale of mayhem and murder. [Claudius] is a joy to read about."   —*Romantic Times*

"Charming and funny. . . . A wonderful read."
—*Fitchburg Sentinel and Enterprise*

"A delightful tale."   —*Cozies, Capers & Crimes*

"A charming mystery starring amusing characters who deserve future appearances."   —Harriet Klausner

Other Annie O'Hara & Claudius Mysteries
by Ann Campbell

Wolf at the Door
Wolf in Sheep's Clothing

WOLF TRACKS

An Annie O'Hara & Claudius Mystery

Ann Campbell

A SIGNET BOOK

SIGNET
Published by New American Library, a division of
Penguin Putnam Inc., 375 Hudson Street,
New York, New York 10014, U.S.A.
Penguin Books Ltd, 80 Strand,
London WC2R 0RL, England
Penguin Books Australia Ltd, Ringwood,
Victoria, Australia
Penguin Books Canada Ltd, 10 Alcorn Avenue,
Toronto, Ontario, Canada M4V 3B2
Penguin Books (N.Z.) Ltd, 182–190 Wairau Road,
Auckland 10, New Zealand

Penguin Books Ltd, Registered Offices:
Harmondsworth, Middlesex, England

First published by Signet, an imprint of New American Library,
a division of Penguin Putnam Inc.

First Printing, May 2002
10 9 8 7 6 5 4 3 2 1

PUBLISHER'S NOTE
This is a work of fiction. Names, characters, places, and incidents either are
the product of the author's imagination or are used fictitiously, and any re-
semblance to actual persons, living or dead, business establishments,
events, or locales is entirely coincidental.

BOOKS ARE AVAILABLE AT QUANTITY DISCOUNTS WHEN USED TO PROMOTE
PRODUCTS OR SERVICES. FOR INFORMATION PLEASE WRITE TO PREMIUM MAR-
KETING DIVISION, PENGUIN PUTNAM INC., 375 HUDSON STREET, NEW YORK, NEW
YORK 10014.

To Claudius's canine pals, for sharing your lives and wonderful stories: Jimmy, Bunny, Ringo, Rasper, Jesse, Rex, Sika, Viper, Chloe, Pierce, Sam, Andy, Bosco, Baron, Duke and Gunny, Max, Sunny, Luke, Arsti, Abbie, Shadow, and Abby. And the goats, Milo and Otis. Thanks, guys. This one's for you.

Acknowledgments

Many, many thanks to my editor, Ellen Edwards, whose skill and endless patience helped bring Claudius alive on these pages. And to my friends who read chapters with a skeptical eye and a tart tongue. Not a bad combination.

CHAPTER

1

Annie O'Hara was feeling grumpy, and she knew why. It was mid-January, that time of year when temperatures plummet and it's as cold as a witch's you know what. The paper was full of doom and gloom: a Concord drive-by shooting, two more house fires—luckily everyone had gotten out alive—and no clues on last week's daring Boston motel robbery. Two New York jewelers ripped off. Half a million in diamonds gone.

What she wouldn't have given for half a million or even a quarter of that, Annie thought with a sigh.

Her feet were going numb. She stood up with an effort and pushed her curly red hair out of her eyes. Lord. Squatting in the snow on this January day, hammering nails into a run-down fence, wasn't exactly her idea of fun.

"I hope this repair job meets with your approval," she told Claudius, the dog on the other side of the fence, at the same time accidentally giving her thumb a whack that brought tears to her eyes. "Being such a brain, you'd know exactly how to do this."

The dog twitched his large ears and watched as she nailed up another board to cover the gap by the sagging gate. Three boards of varying lengths and thicknesses nailed up any old how.

"There," Annie said with satisfaction, putting down the hammer. "Looks good. What do you think?"

He woofed as if to make sure he had her attention, then hurled himself against the repair job, which promptly fell apart with a clatter.

He sat down as if to say she was to fix it properly.

"Thank you very much, dammit!" She counted to ten, picked up the boards, and started renailing them back into place.

The fence enclosed part of the yard behind the old Thurston Tavern, her bed-and-breakfast/antique shop in Lee, New Hampshire. If Annie could have afforded to hire a carpenter, she wouldn't have been out there making a fool of herself. As it was, her one semipermanent boarder, Kirk Dietrich, a professor of psychology at nearby Lester College, helped out when he could. The fence would have been his next project, but he'd gone to New York for a conference.

The gap by the gate was large enough for Claudius, the black German shepherd/husky mix watching from the other side, to squeeze through if and when he felt the urge.

Right on cue, he shoved his head through the opening, as if to say, *Hello? Don't you get it? Another board is needed, for crying out loud.*

"Hold your horses." She shoved him back, slammed another board against the fence, and nailed it in place. It was crooked, but at least the hole was covered. That was the good news. The bad news was that the nails weren't long enough. They'd never hold, not if Claudius really wanted to get loose.

Maybe he wouldn't notice.

Get a grip, she told herself. Did the Pope wear a long dress and live in Rome?

She took a deep breath. Never mind. She was in control here, not Claudius. He was just a dog. She hammered the rest of the nails into the last piece of scrap lumber, which was positioned as a crossbar brace. It wasn't long enough, but to the untrained eye, and she hoped to Claudius, it looked adequate.

What the heck. For the time being, it would have to do. She had other things to worry about—in particular, a phone call she'd gotten earlier that morning from her old English teacher at Fox Hill prep school.

Lucy Brennan, as Irish as Galway Bay, was by now well into her seventies. She'd introduced generations of students to the delights of Dickens, Shakespeare, and e. e. cummings and was still at it. In her mind, retirement was for sissies.

The indomitable Mrs. Brennan had had two requests. The first was fairly simple to fulfill: They needed donations for a silent auction to be held during the upcoming Winterfest Weekend. Did Annie have anything lying around the antique shop that would do? A Tiffany lamp or a table or two?

The second request was harder: How about giving a short talk to the senior honors class? Something about today's woman and achievement would be suitable.

Sure, just stand up in front of a roomful of teenagers and talk about whatever. The thought of it gave Annie hives.

Fox Hill. The name evoked memories of her own awkward adolescence, when she'd been a skinny, unathletic redhead with her nose in a book, any book. Twenty years later, nothing much had changed. She was still a skinny redhead who couldn't do a cartwheel without falling flat on her face. The only difference was that now she had no time for reading.

What had she achieved since Fox Hill and the University of New Hampshire? A succession of low-paying jobs, marriage and divorce weren't exactly equivalent to setting the world on fire. The Thurston Tavern and antique business was barely afloat, and she couldn't talk to schoolkids about her ill-fated marriage to Lenny, a.k.a. Lenny the Rat. Or could she? Anyone could make a mistake. Love was blind, after all.

Explaining the divorce a mere year later would be tricky. "We weren't suited" didn't do Lenny justice. The truth was she'd been an idiot to marry him. He was a pathological liar, and that was just the tip of the iceberg. He was also an accomplished check forger with a rap sheet a mile long. This last she hadn't discovered until she'd filed for divorce.

His record hadn't held any violent convictions. His brother-in-law, a Manchester cop, had managed to get those deleted from the computer. No wonder his family had looked so nervous at the wedding. They were terrified she'd get cold feet.

Not one of her finer moments.

Never mind Lenny. He was no longer her problem, thank God. Even so, she wouldn't mention marriage.

She eyed Claudius across the fence. Kids liked dogs. Maybe she could take him along and talk about their recent adventures investigating murders. Just last week a home video from Uncle Ira and Aunt Hortense had arrived. Uncle Ira had done himself proud with his new camcorder.

He'd taken twenty minutes of panoramic views of the land his church owned in Roswell, New Mexico, where at least one alien spacecraft had landed some years ago.

That wasn't the half of it. Uncle Ira had done a stand-up in front of the camera, detailing his experiences with aliens, whom he called "our friends beyond the Pleiades."

She could show the video to the class and segue into an explanation of her first murder case.

She couldn't help wondering how that would go over. Somehow a talk on murder investigations didn't seem quite up to Fox Hill standards. Well, if all else failed, she could talk about Claudius's former career as a prison guard dog.

Kids liked dogs, and they'd love Claudius.

As a matter of fact, Fox Hill had its fair share of resident dogs. Their owners walked them twice a day, no matter what the weather, be it a hot day in June or a frigid January night. Sometimes, they let them run loose on the school campus, and no one seemed to mind. For a new student far from home, a friendly dog could mean the difference between a sense of belonging and feeling isolated and alone.

Annie usually gave to Fox Hill's alumni fund, and a few weeks ago she had been asked by the scholarship committee to write a brochure for the school. Her research wasn't complete, and she was still working on a rough draft of Fox Hill's history. It was an old school, started in the 1600s as a boy's academy. Girls hadn't been admitted until the twentieth century.

There had been some serious trouble at the school a year ago. She remembered vividly what she'd read in the local newspaper and the alumni magazine. People had talked about the incident for months afterward. An elderly teacher had been found dead at the bottom of a stairwell. She'd suffered a dizzy spell and fallen over the railing or simply tripped at the top of the stairs. No one knew for sure.

Dr. Lawrence, the headmaster, had done the usual: sent letters to alumni and parents and everyone on the scholarship donor list, explaining the tragic circumstances. The student body had undergone counseling, and a memorial fund had been set up in the teacher's name. Life had returned to normal.

Claudius woofed, reminding Annie of more pressing concerns—how to keep him safely enclosed in the backyard.

"I need longer nails," she said. "They're in the barn."

He lay down and gave her a look of disgust.

"Hey," she said, "everything will be fine. Just stay there and behave. Don't touch the fence."

He stared back enigmatically, not promising anything. At one time his ancestry had probably been pure German shepherd, but recently, not far back on the family tree, someone had indulged in a dalliance with a husky, and the resulting union had produced a dog whose prominent characteristics were stubbornness and a razor-sharp intelligence.

The rule of thumb was that he did exactly as he pleased, period. As long as Annie let him have his own way, things were hunky-dory. If not, there was hell to pay.

He hadn't been her dog for long. She'd taken him into her home a few months earlier when her brother, Tom, had split with his wife, Lydia.

Lydia was spoiled and self-centered, charging through

life grabbing whatever she wanted. What she didn't want she heaved overboard—dogs, cats, husbands. Presently the town of Lee's most prominent interior decorator, she was making money hand over fist. Which, in Annie's jaded opinion, proved that life wasn't fair.

Enough obsessing about Lydia, she thought with a sigh. Like it or not, Claudius was now her dog. She had to deal with him. Forget the fact that he made her laugh at least a dozen times a day and that he insisted on being included in whatever she was doing. While she was working in the antique shop, he usually sprawled patiently next to the counter. If she was baking bread in the tavern kitchen, he snoozed on the rug by the stove. A few biscuits a day, an occasional rub, a daily walk or two—he didn't ask for much. She hated to admit it, but he was the best friend she'd ever had.

She stomped off to the barn and rummaged around in some old coffee cans, looking for longer nails. Four inches, enough to keep her best friend from heading for the tall timber. She found only a few rusty old screws and bolts, nothing remotely resembling four-inch nails.

Meanwhile, outside, Claudius had resumed barking. Annie didn't pay much attention; he was always sounding off at something. Suddenly she realized the noise level had risen—was a jogger running past the house, or some idiot taking his purebred poodle for a walk?

Because of Claudius's prison guard-dog training—which, after the better part of a year, the State of New Hampshire had seen fit to cut short due to his unbelievably stubborn nature—he might have decided the passerby was an escaped felon.

She heard a car drive down the road and around the corner, then a faint thud in the backyard—she had a sinking feeling she knew exactly what that was—and a black blur streaked across the clearing outside the barn window.

Claudius was out.

Already running, she made it around the side of the barn in time to see him hightail it down the road and through the woods.

She yelled her head off, but it did little good—naturally, he paid no attention. Still, she chased him for a half hour before trudging back home through the snowy underbrush with her hair full of burrs and no dog.

She told herself Claudius would come home when he was good and ready. He was a smart, well-trained tracking dog, and perfectly capable of finding his way home.

On the other hand, he might prefer life on the open road, and if so, there wasn't much she could do about it.

She yanked the last of the burrs from her hair, gave it a good brushing, then went back outside and jumped into her old Volvo. In a matter of minutes she was cruising up and down the back roads. She looked for him until nightfall.

By five-thirty, clouds had thickened overhead, and a shining drop of moisture hit the windshield, then another and another. It had started to rain. Well, it was January. She was lucky it wasn't sleet or snow. They'd had a fairly warm winter so far. Usually, by now they were knee-deep in snow.

When she got back home, it was pitch black out and raining hard. The temperature was dropping fast, and roads were turning icy. Tired and disgusted, she let herself in the back door.

The tavern seemed cold and empty with Kirk away and no dog to trip over, no cold nose nudging her for a biscuit.

She went around turning on lights after she dumped the keys on the kitchen counter and shed her wet coat.

First things first: She'd call the dog officer and let him know about Claudius's disappearance. Not that she was really worried. He was bound to turn up soon.

But he didn't.

By the third day, Annie was half out of her mind, having called dog officers in surrounding towns and learned that no one had seen Claudius. She made posters and put them up everywhere—telephone poles, trees, storefronts. All things considered, it was a good picture of Claudius. A profile shot, he looked noble, intelligent, sort of like Rin Tin Tin, she told herself.

This was nonsense. The truth was, he looked like the villain out of Little Red Riding Hood. People would be nuts to approach a dog like that. Still, they might call to say they'd seen him, especially if she offered a reward.

After some thought, she decided on a hundred dollars, all she could squeeze from the budget—and even that took some doing. They'd be eating peanut butter and jelly for the next month.

The very next afternoon, the phone rang. It was Lydia and she sounded annoyed.

"What's with the posters? Where's Claudius?"

"He ran off. So far he hasn't come back."

"So you were careless."

"No," Annie said, getting annoyed. What business was it of Lydia's how the dog got loose? She'd abandoned him months ago and adopted a little cockapoo, which fit better with her upscale, interior-design lifestyle. "I was fixing the backyard fence. I left him alone for two minutes to get more nails, and he took off. He must have caught the scent

of a bitch in heat. That's about the only thing that would affect him like that. He'll come back on his own, or someone
will see him and call."

"Have you heard anything so far—has anyone called?"

"Actually, no."

"No wonder. The reward's peanuts. He's worth a lot
more than a hundred dollars."

"Well, I thought—"

"Since my name's still on the license, he's technically
my dog. With all that training, he's worth at least eight
hundred. I saw a program on TV about guard dogs. They
paid five thousand for each dog and another ten thousand
for training."

"Are you offering to put up the reward?"

"Why should I? I wasn't the one who let him loose!"
She slammed the phone down with a decided click.

Annie stood there, fuming. When she got through with
mentally tearing Lydia limb from limb, there was still the
basic problem at hand: Claudius.

It'd be a cold day in hell before she'd up the reward.
One hundred dollars was plenty. People would keep an eye
out for him. He was a local hero of sorts. His picture had
been in the paper a few months ago, when he'd helped
catch a local woman and her lover who'd gone on a murder spree in Lee.

Understandably, Claudius was famous. Someone was
bound to see him if he didn't come home by himself.
They'd call.

But in the end, as the hours and days passed with no
word of Claudius, she gritted her teeth and reprinted the
poster. By Thursday, it read: $300 REWARD.

CHAPTER
2

The phone rang just after eleven o'clock, Friday morning. Hoping someone had found Claudius, Annie snatched up the receiver. "Hello, Thurston Tavern."

"This the number about the missing dog?" a man's voice said.

"Yes, have you found him?"

"There's a reward, right?"

"Yes, have you found him?"

"Well, I think I saw him a couple minutes ago, outside the postal annex on King Street."

She was already grabbing her coat and car keys. "I'll be right down. Five minutes. What's your name? If it's my dog, you'll get the reward."

"Seth Conroy. I'm the postal clerk at the annex. Sorry I didn't grab him, but I thought he might bite."

"I don't think he would, but he's probably hungry." Not the best choice of words perhaps. She rushed on. "If you see him again, put him in your car or tie him up. I'll be right there."

She hung up, hurried out of the house, and true to her

word, made the three-mile distance to the annex in about five minutes.

There was a black Ford Explorer parked in the lot, which she assumed was Conroy's. A bit pricey for a postal clerk, maybe, but what did she know. Could be he put in a lot of overtime.

After parking out front by the old horse trough and not seeing the hell hound anywhere, she yelled "Claudius!" a couple of times with no result, then looked in the Explorer. No dog. She went inside.

The current President of the United States smiled benignly from the wall behind the counter, along with a poster warning that theft from mailboxes was a federal offense which would earn the perp a lengthy stretch in a federal pen. The postmaster general smirked from the wall opposite.

Annie was the only customer. The annex serviced the south side of Lee, which consisted mainly of a trailer park of golden-agers, an industrial park that had gone bust two years ago, and a strip mall with a mom-and-pop convenience store and a used-computer outlet.

The computer store had few customers, but the convenience store did a roaring business, with a steady stream of taxi-ferried old geezers spending Social Security checks on keno and lottery tickets.

The dark-haired man behind the postal counter staring off into space wore a name tag that said he was S. Conroy, clerk.

Annie explained who she was and received a shrug for her pains.

"Last I saw him, the dog was sniffing around the old

horse trough out front. I looked around for him after I talked to you, but he was gone."

"Which way did he go?"

"Like I said, he was by the old horse trough, facing west. If he went that way, he'd head for the trailer park. He was skinny, probably looking for a handout."

That sounded logical. If there was a meal around, even in a garbage can, Claudius would find it.

Annie sighed and left.

The trailer park's location, cheek by jowl with the local R.V. emporium on the far side of the highway overpass, made it virtually impossible to get to without passing rows of unsold trailers.

The proprietor was a Desert Storm vet. An American flag and a black missing-in-action flag waved over the rusting R.V.s.

There was a curved driveway at the front entrance, where an old Chevy was parked. The storefront office looked deserted. Beyond was a Dumpster and the entrance to the trailer park. During the summer, the residents, most of whom had shrunk with age to the point where they could barely see over the steering wheel, drove in and out with scant regard for oncoming traffic. In the winter, those who could fled to warmer climes. Those who remained behind were mostly depressed and tended to drink. Everyone who could find a job was off working part-time, to pay for propane, cable, and booze.

Annie parked next to one of the trailers, crossed to the front door, and knocked. Surprise, someone was home: an elderly woman with a headful of pink curlers. Annie explained that she was looking for her dog. The woman grudgingly admitted she'd noticed a strange dog hanging around her trash can. She'd thrown a basin of water at him, and he'd run off, the nasty mongrel.

With that, the woman slammed the door.

About to leave, Annie noticed a man shambling down the steps of the trailer next door. She went over to talk to him.

A cigarette hung from his mouth. Unshaven and skinny, he wore a ragged black-wool jacket, grimy jeans, and a Grateful Dead T-shirt.

He squinted at her. "Yeah, I seen the dog. He ran outta here, 'cross the road down toward the industrial park 'bout five minutes ago. Big semi almost hit him."

On that cheery note, Annie drove to the abandoned industrial park. Again she called Claudius's name, this time across a wide, snowy expanse of dug-up dirt behind a fieldstone wall and a big sign declaring that Landmark Investments office park was to be erected any minute.

The paint on the sign was peeling.

The wind blew her words back in her face. No dog. She'd missed him by mere minutes. So what else was new.

She went home in a bad mood. About the only thing she'd learned was that Claudius was still in the area—maybe.

The next few days produced more of the same: harried phone calls, with Annie rushing off in all directions only to miss him again and again.

The problem was pretty clear. People were leery of approaching him. There wasn't much she could do about what he looked like, however. The best she could hope for was that some "doggy" person would find him and fearlessly offer him a Big Mac and jumbo fries.

A few calls Annie mentally classified as "semi-positives": a man who said his hens had quit laying because a dog had broken into the chicken coop at three a.m. Another claimed a big black dog had stolen a forty-pound bag of Hill's Science Diet from his garage. He didn't know if it was Claudius, but the dog food had cost him twenty-four ninety-nine, plus tax.

By now Annie was frantic with worry. In the few months she'd had Claudius, he'd driven her crazy, but the sobering reality was that she missed his keen intelligence and the uncanny way he had of talking to her. It was more than body language; she knew what he was thinking. The expression in his eyes . . . as if he spoke out loud. And since she'd never been one to keep her mouth shut, she talked back: Yes, she'd feed him. Yes, she'd let him out. Yes, there was someone at the door, she wasn't deaf, for heaven's sake.

When he came home, though, things would be different. Changes would be made. More training, and no more letting him get his way just because it was easier than taking time to correct him. There'd be a New Regime.

A well-trained dog was a happy dog. All she had to do was convince him of that fact.

No more of that self-serving whining when he sat himself in front of the fridge, acting as if he hadn't been fed in weeks. No more barking at anything and everything, or stealing food from the counter, table, and wherever he could reach standing on his hind legs.

No more midnight pantry raids when he devoured everything edible and a lot that wasn't. No more bouts of revenge whenever he felt slighted—chewed-up pillows, books, magazines, newspapers, and anything he'd sneaked from the trash.

She couldn't even sit down to a meal without him gnawing on the table leg.

By the next Friday afternoon, there was still no word of Claudius, and Annie was so upset she could hardly think straight. Then, as luck would have it, her second-best friend, Cary Goldberg, called about four-thirty from Dr. Harris's office in South Lee, where she worked as a receptionist.

"Annie, I need a favor. You doing anything right now?"

"No, I just closed the antique shop for the day. What's the matter?"

"I'm stuck at work—my car is in the shop. Could you give me a ride home?"

"Sure, no problem. I'll be right over."

Cary had helped her out plenty of times in the past, so it felt good to lend her a hand for a change.

Annie started the Volvo and drove downtown along River Road. Traffic was light in this direction when it was almost dark. Most people were heading home, going the other way.

It was quiet in the car without Claudius putting in his two cents' worth every time he saw something of interest. This was the way it used to be before Annie had adopted him—calm, civilized.

She blinked away sudden tears. Crying never solved anything. Either he'd come home on his own, or someone would see him and call. She had to believe that. Small comfort, but it was something to hold on to.

It didn't take long to get to Dr. Harris's office, located in his home at the junction of River Road and Route 50—

a brown-shingled Cape with white shutters and an oak tree out front with a big plastic tooth hanging from it. There was a two-car garage out back. The lot didn't have room for more than four or five cars, and now there were none.

Annie parked and ran up the steps to the cement stoop. The door was unlocked.

Cary sat behind the front desk, on the phone. She covered the receiver and said, "Just a sec. I'm calling Hemmer's garage." Her family hailed from Canada, and two generations before that, Northern Italy. She was gray-eyed and blond, fragile looking, but appearances were deceiving. In high school, she'd been a fireball softball pitcher. They'd paid Cary to pitch—twenty-five bucks a game— and she'd made out like a bandit. Annie had played right field and never had much to do. No one else on the team did, either. Cary had never lost.

She hung up the phone. "Unfortunately, Hemmer's won't get to it till tomorrow. This hasn't been my week." She locked up the office, and they went out to the Volvo. Eyeing the rusty fenders, Cary said, "You need a new car."

"I can't afford the payments," Annie said. "As long as this one runs, I'm happy." They got in and the Volvo started right up. You couldn't beat that, especially in cold weather. What a car.

"Any word about Claudius?" Cary asked.

"He's still missing."

"That's too bad. He's a great dog. He's got a wonderful personality." Of course, this had to be taken with a grain of salt, but it was nice of Cary to say it.

Annie swallowed hard. "I really miss him."

"How come he took off?"

"Who knows. He was chasing a car down the road. Then he cut through the woods, and I lost sight of him."

She backed up the car, turned around, and headed out onto Route 50. Meanwhile, Cary found a CD she liked and shoved it in the player. Pretty soon they were cruising along to Smokey Robinson.

"Hey, you hungry?" Cary asked. "My treat."

The Red Parrot was just ahead—specializing in burgers, spicy chicken, and ribs. This was the food-court part of town. Burger King, McDonald's, Taco Bell, and Chicken Lickin' bordered both sides of the street. There was even a Pewter Pot Muffin House, which no one under fifty was ever caught dead in. After some discussion, they pulled into The Red Parrot's drive-thru, and Annie told the ten-foot parrot they'd have two orders of burgers, Cokes, and fries to go.

"So what's wrong with your car?" Annie asked as they munched on burgers.

"You wouldn't believe me if I told you."

"Try me."

"Someone jimmied the door open—broke the lock. It won't even close now."

"You're kidding."

"I wish. You know where my apartment is, right? Goss Lane in the Elkhorn district. The house is my uncle's. He lets me live there rent free. The neighborhood is the pits. I don't care—after this, I'm moving."

The Elkhorn district was definitely the other side of the the tracks. Rundown buildings, most with sagging porches and leaky roofs. Originally the area had consisted of two- and three-family houses sprouting gimcrack additions that squeezed in as many as six apartments. Eight hundred a month for a two-bedroom walkup. Cary's uncle was doing okay for himself.

"Were they trying to steal your car?" Annie asked.

A couple of kids on skateboards rumbled down the icy sidewalk. Cary said, "Not exactly. Yesterday was my day off. I went to a flea market and got some good buys. Flowered pants, red sneakers, and a bomber jacket real cheap. And one of those Wonderbras. Almost brand-new."

Annie nodded. Cary spent peanuts and managed to look like a million bucks. Her secret was flea markets and yard sales. Everything she bought was coordinated. Colors matched, everything cleaned, pressed, starched—plus she was into accessorizing in a big way.

They drove on for a few more blocks, past a bar or two, a rental storage center, a pizza place that had never opened, and the Four-Square Church.

"After the flea market," Cary was saying, "I stopped home for a bite. I locked the car and left the clothes on the front seat. Five minutes. A glass of milk and a cheese sandwich. What could happen?"

"Sounds reasonable," Annie said. "What did happen?"

"I got robbed, that's what. Fifty bucks shot to hell. Some jerk jimmied my car door and stole everything—including my grandfather's World War II medal that I'd pinned to the bomber jacket in the store. I called the cops."

"And?"

Cary finished her burger and fries and stuffed the wrapper in the empty bag. "They laughed and said I should've known better than to leave clothes on the front seat in broad daylight. What's the world coming to when you can't go home for five minutes without getting ripped off?"

"That's terrible." Annie said.

Cary's apartment house was halfway down Goss Lane, on the right. Gray shingles, white trim, and an unpainted porch tacked on front behind a seedy-looking hedge. A Dumpster was permanently parked in the side lot. Laundry flapped on the backyard line.

They passed two kids on bikes whizzing down the shoveled walkways. Just ahead, a short, skinny man was strolling down the sidewalk. He was wearing baggy pants, a brown bomber jacket, and a yellow silk scarf—everything brand-new by the look of the tell-tale creases down the sides of the pants. He had gelled hair slicked back in a ponytail à la Steven Seagal, shades, and red sneakers on his feet.

The King of Cool.

Annie felt a twinge of amazement—she'd never have the nerve to wear a getup like that.

As they drove past, Cary took another look at the man and stiffened. "I don't believe it! That's my jacket, dammit! Right there on the lapel is my grandfather's World War II good-conduct medal!" She rolled down the window and yelled, "Hey, give me back my stuff!"

By now she was hanging out the window, shouting her head off. Annie stomped on the brake and pulled over. The man cast a startled look over his shoulder and spotted Cary screeching like a banshee. He took off down the street like lightning. Within seconds, he had zipped around the corner at the bottom of the hill and was gone.

"Damn!" said Cary.

Annie spun the wheel hard left, gunned the engine, and

raced after him. They drove up and down Elkhorn for the next half hour, but there was no sign of Cary's jacket or medal.

"Damn thief," she said.

Eventually, they gave up and went back to her apartment house. She was still mad. Annie threw the Volvo into park and left the engine running. They were both tired and frustrated.

"So what do we do now, call the cops?" she asked.

Cary sighed. "They'd laugh in my face. It's not like he robbed a bank, and I only saw him for a second. He looked Hispanic. He was wearing my jacket. I wish Claudius were here. He'd have nailed that little son-ofabitch in two seconds flat."

"Right. He'd have grabbed him, and we could have made a citizen's arrest and called the cops." They sat and thought about lost opportunities for a minute.

"Well, I don't care," Cary said. "I'm not letting that lowlife get away with it. What if I hire you to find him and get my clothes back?"

"Are you serious?"

"Why not? You're good at this stuff, Annie. You solved a couple of murders. Finding this guy should be a piece of cake. He's not exactly Einstein. I mean, who steals clothes and then wears them in the same neighborhood? Plus you can kill two birds with one stone: Ask about Claudius at the same time. Fifty bucks. What do you say?"

Actually, it didn't sound very difficult. Lee's current Hispanic population wasn't all that large, and it was a chance to question people about Claudius. "Okay," she said. "It shouldn't take long. A guy who dresses like that is bound to stand out. Someone will know him."

Cary thought a second. "Hey, the guy who lives out back, Ramirez Montez—he's Hispanic. Maybe the creep was visiting Ramirez."

"Hmm, could be. It's a start. But why don't you knock on a few doors and save yourself fifty bucks?"

"Huh. They all think I'm a snitch, that I report back to my uncle, which is true. I mean, that's why I don't pay rent. They won't talk to me, but they'd talk to you. Show that poster of Claudius. Make up something. Say someone saw him with the creep."

"Maybe," Annie said, wondering on second thought if this was such a good idea. She was fairly confident she could discover the man's identity, but did she really want to? Besides, as far as she knew, Claudius hadn't been seen anywhere on this side of town.

"It's the principle of the thing," Cary said angrily. "I couldn't care less about the clothes. They weren't perfect. The jacket had a hole in the pocket, which I hadn't gotten around to fixing, and yeah, I can buy more any day of the week. But why should he get away with stealing my stuff? Heck, he's done this before—count on it. He's probably got a closet stuffed with stolen clothing."

It was getting dark. Lights sprang on in the neighboring houses, spilling across fenced-in yards.

"Does Ramirez speak English?" Annie asked, figuring she'd talk to him first, then canvass the neighborhood.

"He rattles on in Spanish, but I suspect he knows English when it suits him."

Unfortunately, Annie's command of Spanish was limited. She could order Tex-Mex and count to ten, that was about it.

A small setback, but not insurmountable.

CHAPTER
3

After she closed up the antique shop the next day at three, Annie drove over to Goss Lane with a cup of coffee, a bag of blueberry muffins from McDonald's, and a fistful of fliers she'd printed up about Claudius. This was to get people talking, although she didn't think anyone in this part of town had really seen him. The Steven Seagal wannabe was another matter. By now she'd had more time to consider the likelihood of identifying him and wasn't feeling all that optimistic. Even if the residents knew who he was, it didn't mean they'd admit it. They didn't know her from a hole in the wall.

She chewed a muffin and started across the street. People in the Elkhorn district lived from paycheck to paycheck or with the help of Uncle Sam. Those who worked drove to and from in third-hand rattlebangers. Anyone home during the day was retired or getting by with the aid of inventive insurance scams.

Annie checked the time on her el-cheapo wristwatch—Indiglo Easy Reader with a Western-style woven wristband, a steal at nine ninety-nine. It lost the occasional half hour, but what could you expect from a discount chain special? It was just after three-thirty, more or less. People who worked the early shift would be straggling home about now, in the shank of the afternoon. Senior citizens and the chronically underemployed would be settling down in front of the TV for a cozy hour of Ricki Lake or *Supermarket Sweep*.

As Annie saw it, she had two choices: Plan A was to ring doorbells up and down the street, asking if anyone had seen Claudius. Once she'd caught them off guard, she'd slip in a few questions about Cary's missing clothes and Steven Seagal.

Plan B was less intrusive and more appealing. She'd hang out in the car, eat muffins, drink coffee, and watch who came and went. If Steven Seagal lived in the neighborhood, he was bound to show up sooner or later.

She'd brought along the paper. A little light reading to pass the time. She skipped the headlines about Boston's latest problems with The Big Dig. As long as she didn't have to pay for rampant graft and corruption, she figured it was no skin off her nose, and thank God for New Hampshire, the Granite State. Let's see, the comics. She checked out Zippy and Garfield, was reassured that they were fine, and glanced at the New England news.

No progress on the big jewel heist, but more details had come out. The New York jewelers had been fully insured. They'd thought, foolishly as it turned out, to outwit any possible robbers by driving up from the Big Apple in an un-marked van and staying at a Motel Six. The police theo-rized that this theft might be connected with several others that had taken place in New England in the past twelve months: one last spring in Rutland, Vermont; another in June in Concord, New Hampshire; and a third in October in Montpelier, Vermont. Ho hum.

Back to page one.

Well, well. Below the fold was an article about census workers being shot, bitten by large dogs, and otherwise set upon by irate householders irritated by intrusive government bureaucrats. In the present circumstances, this gave her pause.

On the other hand, she wasn't going to ask the residents of Goss Lane how much walking-around money or how many indoor toilets they had. Once she produced the flier, she'd bring the conversation around to men with ponytails and bomber jackets. She'd hardly break a sweat.

What the heck? She'd try Plan A, and if no one actually took a potshot at her or let loose a slavering pit bull, everything would be hunky-dory.

Maybe not, though. There was something to be said for patience. If she waited a little longer, ate another muffin or two, Steven Seagal might come skipping up the sidewalk in Cary's leather jacket.

She was still debating the pros and cons when an old red Buick rumbled down the street and slid to a stop by the curb. The driver got out. He looked about sixteen and sported six earrings, a nose ring, and a wispy Fu Manchu mustache. Annie rolled her eyes and earned a grin and a wave. He went into the house across the street. She finished her coffee and emerged from the Volvo.

The first house at the lower end of Goss Lane was a two-story, blue-shingled Victorian with a wraparound porch. Someone had done a half-ass job of shoveling snow off the steps. A bag of rock salt lay next to the front door. At head height, an empty bird feeder spattered with bird poop swung in the wind.

The card over the bell read: G. Chavez. She pushed the

bell once, then, when nothing happened, gave it another go. She stood, listening to icicles drip off the porch roof. After another minute, footsteps clattered downstairs and the door popped open. A skinny kid, ten or eleven years old going on thirty, stood there chewing gum and carrying a skateboard. He had on a winter jacket and boots. It looked like she'd caught him on the way out.

He smiled, his teeth even and white against olive skin. "Yo, what's up?"

By way of breaking the ice, she held up the flier. "Hi, have you seen this dog?"

He looked it over. "It says there's a reward."

"Well, yes. Three hundred dollars. Claudius is my dog. He's been missing for several days. My name's Annie O'Hara. What's yours?"

"Joey . . . Joey Chavez. So you're askin' around about this dog, right? Nothin' personal, but it must mean you want him real bad."

"Naturally. He's my dog."

"Tell you what. For a dollar a house, I'll take you 'round the neighborhood. We check it out, see if anybody's seen him. We get lucky, I get the three hundred. Deal?"

This wasn't a bad idea. Joey knew the lay of the land and probably spoke Spanish. "Okay. Do you want to tell your mom?"

"Nope, she's workin'. Nobody else is home. You gotta problem with that?"

"No."

He checked his blue Gore-Tex-strapped Ironman wristwatch. Big as a salad plate, studded with buttons, it probably cost more than her '93 Volvo. "I got time," he said.

"You wanna do this now?" Apparently he had a busy schedule. She was probably cutting into cartoon time.

"Don't you have any homework to do for Monday?"

"I don't do homework. Besides"—he coughed unconvincingly—"I gotta cold."

"Well, maybe you should go upstairs and put on a hat and scarf." He already had on a wool jacket and boots, but still. If he got sick, she'd be blamed, and there was nothing worse than a mother on the warpath.

"Jeez, you sound like my mother." He was three feet high and already a chauvinist, she concluded. It had to be a testosterone thing. He stuck out his hand, and she reluctantly forked over a buck. Maybe Cary would spring for per-diem expenses.

Having taken care of business, he dumped the skateboard in the hallway, closed the door, made sure it was locked, then led her around to the apartment in back. Upstairs were two apartments occupied by the Ngs and the McNeills, neither of whom were home. The card by the downstairs bell read: A. Figueroa. A sign in the window announced: *Salesmen stay away. Belgian shepherd guard dog on the premises can make the fence in five seconds. Can you?*

Joey noticed her eyeing the sign. "That's fake, they ain't got a dog." He rang the bell, then banged on the door. "Sometimes Tony don't hear so good. You gotta make a lotta noise."

The door snapped open. The lady of the house, stout with graying black hair and wearing a housedress and apron, gave them a sour look.

"*Sí?*" This she aimed at Annie, who showed her the flier.

"My dog's missing. I wondered if you'd seen him around the neighborhood."

"No comprendo . . . dog?"

Joey jabbed a grubby finger at Claudius's picture and rattled off a couple of sentences in Spanish. A look of comprehension crossed Mrs. Figueroa's face; then she shrugged.

"I . . . don' think I . . . seen him."

"He was seen with a man wearing a pigtail, red sneakers, and a leather bomber jacket with a World War II good-conduct medal on the lapel," Annie said. It sounded ridiculous, but she had to work his physical description in somehow.

Joey shot her a sly look. "No kidding?"

"Yes," Annie said, looking him straight in the eye.

She smiled at Mrs. Figueroa. Mrs. F. didn't smile back. Instead, she fired off a couple more sentences in Spanish, all fiery and mad looking, and slammed the door in their faces.

"She didn't see 'em," Joey explained.

"Okay, but what else did she say?"

"You don't wanna know. Look, we gonna stand around here all day? I'm busy, I got things to do." He accepted a blueberry muffin and led the way back to the sidewalk. From there, they proceeded from house to house, up the street, starting next door. Not everyone was home yet, but Annie managed to question a handful of kids and senior citizens. The kids weren't much help, but Mrs. O'Neill and Mrs. Juarez both looked as if they could have said a great deal about Steven Seagal if they'd cared to. Mrs. O'Neill's face reddened before she slammed the door, and Mrs.

Juarez sniffed and snapped something in Spanish that Joey said he wouldn't translate without a bonus.

Annie decided to skip it since she was running out of money.

Three houses and three dollars later, Annie questioned Tony Medeiros. Here clothes did not make the man. He was red-eyed and hungover and wearing what smelled like last week's sweats.

"Nada, no, él es loco, no damn perro," he said. Which, at a stretch, Annie figured meant that he knew Steven Seagal, the man was crazy, and furthermore, he didn't have a dog.

Somewhat cheered by this turn of events—this certainly sounded like Cary's clothes thief—she followed Joey as he trudged off up the snowy street. They worked three more houses and ten minutes later reached Cary's place. No sign of her Nissan in the parking lot. Presumably it was still in the shop. Cary didn't answer the bell, and four of the other five tenants were out, too.

The wind gusted around the corner. Annie shivered a little, tucked the fliers under one arm, and shoved her hands in her pockets for warmth. Still, for January, she couldn't complain. It wasn't half bad. The sun was out and it was almost above freezing. Plus it wasn't snowing, so things were looking up.

On the other hand, she didn't have all day. It was getting late; it would be dark soon. Maybe she'd finish canvassing the neighborhood tomorrow.

"Hey, kid," she said.

"The name's Joey, *comprende?* You got any more muffins?"

She gave him the bag. "Okay. Joey."

He munched. "How bad you wanna find the dude with
the ponytail? How 'bout ten bucks?" He kept walking, his
small booted feet crunching through half-frozen slush.

"Ten bucks? I don't think so!" She wasn't sure she had
ten dollars left. She didn't walk around with half her bank
account in her pocketbook.

"I don't do this kinda stuff for free. I ain't stupid, man. I
gotta live, don' I?"

"Don't do me any favors. I'll find him myself."

"Huh. That ain't gonna happen. Nobody'll talk to you."

"I'll take my chances. You're pricing yourself out of a
job."

He shrugged. "Okay, I'm feelin' generous. Five bucks.
Take it or leave it."

She set her teeth.

"Well?" he asked. This wasn't rent-a-kid, this was highway robbery. The little brat had her in a bind and he knew
it.

"Fine, but not one penny more. And if we don't find him
in the next half hour, you help me tomorrow for nothing."

"For nothing?"

"It's known as a liability insurance clause," Annie said.
"Standard business practice."

He thought this over. "I don't like it, but okay. Sounds
like this guy who hangs out at Moose Chiavaras's on weekends. He drives an old blue van. Shows up every coupla
weeks with a load of new tires and stores 'em in the shed.
A coupla days later, he takes 'em away. I seen him parked
over on Elm Street with the motor running, checking to see
if anyone's around. Once the coast is clear, he drives up and
unloads the tires. He works part-time at a big garage over
on High Street. Prob'ly stealin' the place blind."

Great, Steven Seagal was working his way up the criminal food chain.

"So where can I find this Moose guy?" Annie asked.

"Where's the five bucks?"

She ponied up with a sigh.

"That's more like it." Joey pointed. "That's him, over there."

Not thirty feet away in the side yard in front of the Dumpster, a fat man in overalls and a red-and-black checked wool hunting jacket was swearing a blue streak and chopping ice off the windshield of a red Toyota pickup. Moose Chiavaras in living color.

Just then a car pulled up by the curb. A man bailed out, heaved a couple of trash bags in the Dumpster, and took off.

Moose shook his fist. "Son of a bitch! Don' even live here and he's usin' my Dumpster!"

Joey flashed the flier. "Hey, man, you seen this dog?"

"*Qué?*"

"The dog's missin'. You seen him?"

"*No.*"

Annie nudged Joey. "Ask him about the man with the ponytail."

Joey translated. Moose stopped chopping. His little pig eyes slid to Annie. When Joey got to the part about the reward, Moose gave an elaborate shrug and suddenly was fluent in English. "Could be he's my brother-in-law, Rocky Martinez. He's got . . . problems. Alcohol. When he's drunk, he's kinda mean. Been in and outta detox more times than I can count, but he ain't got no dog. He don't like 'em. He got bit once." This sounded promising.

"I'd like to talk to him," Annie said. "Know where I can find him?"

Another shrug, this one no more convincing than the first. Joey popped a bubble, and Moose said, "Rocky's got a lotta irons in the fire. Nights, he drives a taxi. Weekends, he works as a mechanic, odd jobs, whatever. Although he said he had something real important to do this weekend in Peterborough." Moose hawked and spat on the sidewalk. "This time of day, he could be anyplace. Try Big Al's Sports Bar on Ruggles. He likes to hang out and play foozeball. I wouldn't mess with him. He's a real bad-ass. Don' like strangers. His ex is after him for back child support."

Hmm, this might mean that she'd have to revise her thinking. Rocky didn't sound like a man who'd walk around in women's clothing, but hey, it took all kinds.

For another five bucks, Joey said he had an idea. How about he went with her to Big Al's?

She decided to forego that pleasure. Ten-year-olds weren't supposed to hang around bars. Besides, another hour with him and she'd be in the poorhouse.

"Sorry, I'll check out Big Al's myself."

"Okay, it's your funeral. Here." He handed her a card.

Someone, presumably Joey, had run it up on a computer. *J. Chavez Enterprises.* Underneath: *No job too big or small, reasonable rates.* A phone number was listed at the bottom.

"You want to find your dog or Rocky, I'm the man. Gimme a call. Like today, we walk around, knock on some doors, make it happen."

"Hmm, I didn't realize I was dealing with a pro."

"Well, you're new around here. I'm 'vailable most after-noons after school. I gotta paper route on Friday, just around the neighborhood, but Mom and me go to early mass on Sunday, so I'm free all weekend."

She shoved the card in her pocket. "I'll keep it in mind

and maybe give you a call." This elicited a look that said he knew she wouldn't and that furthermore, she was a total loser. He strolled off down the street.

She jumped in the Volvo and cruised over to Ruggles.

Big Al's Sports Bar was located downstairs in an old brick building next door to the Ruggles Street Suds and Duds Laundromat. The building had once been a broom factory, but the neighborhood had since diversified. The storefront next door was now a temp agency. A sign announced that jobs were to be had, come right in. The storefront on the other side was the local AA meeting place. A woman inside was arranging folding chairs in front of a podium. The parking lot out front held angled slots. Annie pulled in between two pickup trucks and got out.

The bar had two big plateglass windows covered with neon beer signs and bowling league posters. Half a dozen dusty trophies were lined up under the posters. A guy who looked like Joe Pesci on a bad hair day came sauntering around the corner. Annie decided he was wearing a toupee tied down with a rubber band. He gave her a disinterested once-over and went into Big Al's.

So much for wowing the local studs. Maybe they weren't into skinny redheads in grungy pea coats and jeans, not to mention her cool Timberland boots, ninety bucks, half-price from the JCPenney catalog. Claudius had chewed the left boot some, but you could hardly tell.

As for Joe Pesci, he hadn't made her hormones pop either. So there. She entered Big Al's and stood just inside the door, adjusting to the fug and dim lighting. Unwashed men, beer, and buffalo wings. Big Al had a classy clientele. They got eats with their booze.

Feeling like a pro, Annie scoped out the place. Five or

six lowlifes were hunched over the bar, but no one in a bomber jacket. A jukebox thumped away in the corner, and several more of life's losers were playing pool in a back room.

She sat down at the bar.

The bartender gave the counter a swipe with his towel. By the hard look in his eye, she figured he was Big Al.

"You wanna order?" he asked.

"Coors Lite." She paid for the beer and took out the flier. "Have you seen my dog? He might have been with a man with a ponytail. Rocky Martinez."

Big Al's eyes narrowed. "Rocky Martinez?"

"Yeah." This was getting monotonous.

"I ain't seen your dog, lady. Sorry."

"What about Rocky?"

He stared at her, blank-faced. "He ain't been in since Monday. Try Henshaw Tires over on High Street. He works there part-time . . . when he feels like workin'."

She left the flier with Big Al, thanked him for his trouble, and asked him to have Rocky call her if he came in. Then she drove two blocks over to High Street and Henshaw Tire Emporium.

She parked in the side lot and got out, considering how to handle the situation. It wouldn't do to tell Rocky's boss about his little side line in stolen tires. She had no desire to get Rocky in trouble—that is, if his boss hadn't already discovered he was being ripped off. No, a few questions about Rocky's possible whereabouts, show the flier, and that ought to do it for the afternoon.

Cary was getting an awful lot for her fifty bucks. Counting expenses already incurred, Annie figured she was already in the hole big time.

Besides, it was getting late and she was hungry. She wanted to go home. If she'd gotten lucky, someone might have seen Claudius and left a message on the answering machine.

Two minutes in the garage, in and out. That seemed reasonable.

There were three bays, one of which was open. Four men were working on cars jacked up on lifts. New tires were stacked in back by an automotive computer analyzer. On the wall a sign informed patrons that no personal checks were accepted, only cash or credit cards. Eddie Henshaw, prop.

Eddie, a short, balding man with a little Hitler mustache, sat at a desk in the side office, clicking away on an adding machine. He didn't look happy.

Annie wondered if he was doing inventory.

She produced the flier and went into her song and dance. At the mention of Rocky's name, Eddie's mouth hardened. "Yeah, the little shit works here most weekends. Rest of the time he does odd jobs. Said he had some snowplowing gigs lined up."

"Do you happen to know where?"

"Matter of fact, Rocky said something about working over at that snot-nosed prep school, Fox Hill. Ask over there."

She thanked him and went back to her car.

It took fifteen minutes to get home. The first thing she did was punch the blinking answering machine button.

A woman's voice said, "This is Molly Houghton in South Lee. I think I have your dog. He went into my barn this morning just before I went to work. I'm the librarian at

Fox Hill School. My house is the old parsonage on Powderhouse Road . . . if you'd like to come get him."

She'd left a phone number, which Annie immediately dialed. They spoke for a few minutes, and Annie said she'd
be right over.

What a coincidence. Fox Hill School.

She jumped in the Volvo and started her up with a rumble. Snow had started falling. It looked as if it might snow
all night. The ground was covered, and daylight was fast
disappearing as clouds thickened and snow continued to
fall.

Even with the defroster on full blast, ice formed on the
wipers. They had trouble keeping up and clunked back and
forth, smearing snow like wallpaper paste. Driving was
treacherous, but the Volvo was like a tank, and a few weeks
ago Annie had remembered to put on snow tires and load
sandbags in the trunk for added traction.

Annie arrived at Fox Hill School in no time, in spite of
fishtailing a little around corners.

The parsonage stood at the top of Powderhouse Road,
right on the corner, a beautiful old Federal house painted
white with black shutters. The Episcopal church was next
door, with a gold weather vane atop the steeple. Assorted
school dorms, beautifully maintained, old Colonial homes,
and administration buildings lined the street.

As Annie pulled into the driveway behind fresh car
tracks—a black Mercedes hadn't been there long—she noticed a woman at the kitchen window. Probably Molly
Houghton. Typical preppy face, no makeup, strong bones.

Annie banged the door knocker—a brass clamshell—
and the woman opened the door. She pulled on a wool

jacket and came down the steps. "Did you go around to the barn?"

"No." But Annie could hear barking. It sounded like Claudius.

"I just got home. Sorry you weren't called earlier. My husband, Carl, was supposed to call this morning, but he started correcting exams and lost track of the time."

The barking, louder now, held a demanding note, as if Claudius knew Annie had arrived. Her heart started thumping like mad.

"At least he's been out of the cold," she said as Molly unhooked the latch on the barn door and shoved it back along its track. Annie barely had time to smell last summer's hay piled high in the loft before Claudius became airborne, his front paws slamming into her shoulders.

She reeled backward, laughing with relief, hugging him to keep from falling.

He licked her face and wagged his tail, every inch of his expressive face making his thoughts crystal clear: What had taken her so long? He'd tried to get home . . . he was hungry, thirsty. By now he was sniffing her hands, pockets, finding a cache of beef-basted biscuits.

She handed them over and he gobbled them up.

"All's well that ends well," Molly Houghton said, smiling. "Anyone could tell he's your dog. I hate to see homeless animals. It's heartbreaking. Last year one of the teachers here at the school fell during a terrible snowstorm. Coincidentally, there was a traffic accident on the main road—six cars involved. It took hours for the ambulance to arrive, and by then, it was too late. Stella had passed away. We had a difficult time finding a home for her dog, Trixie. A maintenance man finally adopted her. It would've been a shame if she'd had to go to the pound." She sighed and added, "I almost took her, but my husband is allergic to dogs."

Annie bent to snap on the leash, making a grab for Claudius's collar, but he took off across the driveway at a dead run.

"Come back here!" she yelled.

He halted a second, barked, and ran off behind the house.

"He's heading for the lake," Molly said. "I'm not sure the ice is safe."

Lowering her head against the driving snow, Annie raced after him, slithering every few feet. She rounded the side of the house and caught sight of him, a black shape down by the lake. She couldn't have missed him, actually, since he was keeping up his usual racket. His meaning was clear enough: Something was very wrong.

As if in slow motion, Annie slipped and slid downhill through the snow toward the lakeshore. It seemed to take forever to reach Claudius, but when she did, she made sure she had hold of his collar and got the leash on. He was still barking, staring out across the ice.

Damn. Had he heard someone out there crying for help? Or had an animal fallen in? The past few days had been warmer than usual for January, so even if the ice had been safe weeks ago, it wasn't now.

"What's wrong, Claudius?"

He stared out toward the middle of the lake and resumed his ear-deafening barking.

Her heart stopped. *Maybe a kid had fallen in. Kids played hockey and skated on the lake. . . .* But she couldn't see any footprints in the snow. If someone was out there, either they'd gone onto the ice before it started snowing, or they'd come from the opposite shore.

Maybe it was a dog or a deer.

She squinted through the falling snow. Yes, something was in the water way out there, a black blob.

By now, Molly had joined her. Annie pointed. "Someone's out there. He must have fallen in."

"Oh, God, I'll get help," Molly gasped. She ran back to the house.

Annie started praying. Whatever was in the water wasn't moving. "We're getting help!" she yelled, hoping he'd hear and take heart—but there was no reaction.

Her hands and feet were freezing. She stomped up and down and contemplated trying a rescue on her own. But if she ventured out on the ice, she'd fall in. They'd have to rescue two people, not one.

Claudius resumed barking, lunging forward, trying to drag her out onto the ice. Rin Tin Tin to the rescue.

"No!" she ordered and hauled him back. "Heel! Sit!" For once he did as he was told, although he didn't look happy about it.

What was taking Molly so long? She'd been gone at least ten minutes, plenty of time to dial 911.

Just then there came the distant wail of sirens, growing louder as they drew closer. Moments later, the woods were illuminated by flashing red and blue lights as a fire truck, ambulance, and two patrol cars roared up.

Car and truck doors slammed. Two cops, several members of the school faculty, and Tubby O'Connell came running.

Annie had known Tubby for years. As a kid, he'd been weird, overweight. Despite a stint in the army reserve, he was still fat, and now he was the local undertaker—O'Connell's Funeral Home, "We treat each client like family."

He spotted Annie as he raced through the snow. "Someone fell in?" he yelled.

Claudius put in his two cents' worth, and Annie told him to shut up. "Yes, I don't know how long he's been in the water."

Controlled bedlam reigned for the next few minutes. Firemen and paramedics raced to the shore with a small boat. Seconds later, they'd pushed it carefully out onto the ice and jumped in as the ice broke with a sound like a gunshot. They started rowing.

It didn't take long to reach the middle of the lake.

Feeling sick, Annie watched them haul a body out of the water. They wrapped him in a foil, heat-retentive blanket and began CPR. They were still working on him when they made it back to shore.

Tubby shook his head. "Damn fool should've known better than to go on the ice after the warm weather we've had. Well, I guess I can't complain. It means more business."

She couldn't look away from the foil-wrapped body. The dead man's head and shoulders were poking out of the blanket. His hair was black, pulled back in a ponytail. His face was gray and lifeless. He wore a silver earring, a brown leather bomber jacket with a medal pinned to the lapel, and red sneakers.

Good grief, he was Cary's clothes thief—Moose's brother-in-law, Rocky Martinez.

CHAPTER

4

"This ain't working, Sam," one of the EMTs muttered. "Better bag him. Keep up CPR while I get the kit." He jumped in the back of the ambulance and started searching through some drawers while the other EMT continued CPR.

Despite police efforts at crowd control, Annie had a pretty good view of what was going on. The two EMTs had worked with lightning speed, put an oxygen mask on Rocky, and gotten a saline drip going. Within seconds, they shoved him into the ambulance and took off, sirens wailing. One of the cops came over to tell Annie to move back, and Claudius started sniffing his boots and wagging his tail like mad. Cop boots. Wow. Old home week.

Annie hauled Claudius over by her left knee. Heel position.

With a huge sigh, he sat.

"That your dog?" the cop asked.

She nodded. "He let us know someone was in trouble."

"That was when?"

"Fifteen, twenty minutes ago. Will he be all right?"

There was still hope. They wouldn't have used the siren if Rocky had been dead.

"Doesn't look good. Sam McIntyre and Harvey Warren, the EMTs, really know their stuff, but the guy wasn't breathing. What was he doing out there?"

"How should I know?" She wondered if she should spill the beans and tell the cop, whose name tag read Sgt. Morris, that the man in the lake was Rocky Martinez. Who, furthermore, was probably a tire thief, and the bomber jacket he was wearing belonged to her friend Cary.

On the one hand, she'd already done the good citizen thing. Unless he asked, she had no obligation to tell him anything.

Besides, Cary wasn't likely to want her jacket back.

"How is it you happened to be around?" Morris wanted to know.

She explained about Claudius being missing, the posters she'd put up, and Molly Houghton's phone call. She left out the part about what she'd been doing all afternoon.

"Hmm," said Sgt. Morris. "Lucky you found your dog. As for that poor bastard in the lake, maybe he was ice fishing. Did you see any footprints? Did it look like he went on the ice from this side?"

"No."

The temperature was dropping. It was noticeably colder. Sgt. Morris stamped his feet. "Well, let's hope he was out there alone. It'd be a damn shame if someone else was under the ice. We wouldn't find him till spring."

On which sobering thought, Annie turned and headed back up to the parsonage with Claudius.

By now the fire truck had also gone. Behind her, she heard Sgt. Morris making his way from the lake. His walkie-talkie let out a squawk of static, then went silent as he reported in.

She knocked on the parsonage back door. Sgt. Morris was right behind her, kicking snow from his feet as Molly let them in.

A tall man was sitting at the table. He'd been among the crowd down at the lake. He had blond hair, unbelievably white teeth, flinty eyes, and a gold I.D. bracelet.

"Pete Lanza," Molly said, introducing him. "He teaches math here at the school."

Pete nodded. "Terrible thing, too bad. We've had a job keeping the kids off the ice."

"Hot chocolate?" Molly asked. "The kettle's on."

"Sounds good," Sgt. Morris said. A notebook and pen appeared in his hands. "Just a few questions."

They sat down at the kitchen table, Molly produced hot chocolate for one and all, and Claudius made himself at home next to Annie's chair. He'd already taken inventory. A fat Persian had hissed at him from the top of a wall cupboard.

"So you didn't see any footprints in the snow?" Sgt. Morris eyed Annie as if he were giving her a chance to come clean and admit she'd been lying.

She shook her head.

"Okay, what about his car? He wasn't dressed for a long walk in the snow. He probably drove down to the lake."

He owned a blue van, but Annie hadn't seen any sign of it.

Sergeant Morris's glance swung to Molly. "What about you, Mrs. Houghton?"

"I wasn't paying attention, sorry. Once I realized someone was in the lake, I ran back to the house to dial 911. That's all I know."

"Did you see anything?" Sgt. Morris asked Pete Lanza.

"Sorry, I got here after he'd already fallen in. Didn't see a thing."

Footsteps came down the hall, and a man appeared in the doorway. Molly's husband, Carl. He was of medium height with dark, curly hair. He had a long scar down one cheek, and his clothes were rumpled.

"My God," he said. "I just spoke to Dr. Lawrence, the headmaster. He talked to someone at the hospital. It's that man we hired to snowplow."

Molly gasped, Pete Lanza looked somber, and Annie eyed Sgt. Morris.

"That's right," Morris said. "Sam McIntyre, one of the paramedics, recognized him. Rocky Martinez. He lived in the Elkhorn district. Who hired him?"

Annie swallowed. Things were getting sticky. Sgt. Morris had used the past tense, so Rocky must be dead.

Carl lit a cigarette. His hands were shaking. "Actually, I recommended him for the job. Er . . . I bought new tires just before Christmas. Rocky was working at the garage where I got the tires. He mentioned that he was looking for more work, and I asked if he could drive a truck. We needed somebody to keep the school roads clear. Our maintenance man had just broken his leg."

"Well," said Sgt. Morris, "at this point we don't know exactly how Martinez fell in the lake, so I need to ask some questions. Routine follow-up."

Pete nodded and Molly looked shocked. "It was an accident," she said hurriedly. "What more is there to say?"

"Right," Carl added. In other words, here's your hat, what's your hurry.

"Martinez had a wound on the back of his head. Could be someone hit him before he fell in." Sgt. Morris looked around the table. "Any ideas about that?"

"No," Annie and Molly chorused. Carl merely shook his head.

Pete cleared his throat and said, "Couldn't the wound on his head have occurred when he slipped and fell?"

"That's what we have to find out," Morris said.

Meanwhile, under the table, Claudius made a big deal about licking his paws, sniffling and grumbling. Annie nudged him with her knee, telling him to shut up.

The policeman smiled at Molly, who was wringing her hands. "Were you here all day?"

"No. I'm the school librarian. I was setting up a display all afternoon. I'd just gotten home when I remembered the dog and called Annie. My husband was here all day."

Carl nodded. "I've no idea how Rocky fell in. My study windows face the street, not the lake. I was correcting calculus exams, so I didn't see a thing."

Claudius heaved a loud sigh, which Annie took to mean he'd heard that and didn't believe a word of it. She agreed with him. The Houghtons were nervous, as if they had dozens of bodies buried in the cellar.

"What kind of a car did Martinez drive?" asked Morris. He received blank stares from the Houghtons and Pete Lanza.

Annie frowned. Things were getting worse. Sooner or later she'd have to admit she knew more than she'd been telling. If she had a choice, later was better, and never better still.

"We really can't help you, Sergeant Morris," Molly said, giving him a tremulous smile. "I suggest you speak to the headmaster, David Lawrence. His office is just down the street in the administration building. He'd know what Mr. Martinez was driving." She glanced at her husband. "For security reasons we try to keep a strict eye on who comes and goes here at the school. Some of the students are quite wealthy . . ." Her voice trailed off.

And some of the students were as poor as dirt, attending on scholarships, Annie thought, thinking of her own situation.

Claudius stood up and woofed his opinion about the world at large. She gave him the hand signal to sit down—which she'd learned from reading a dog-training book that promised big changes in behavior in three easy lessons.

He ignored her.

"Shut that dog up," muttered Sgt. Morris.

Like magic, Claudius fell silent, and she wondered if he was responding to the cop uniform. The boots, no doubt. Maybe if she got herself a pair like that Claudius would instantly obey.

Sure.

The sergeant was busy jotting down notes. He looked up. "Was Martinez into ice fishing or skating?"

Pete shrugged his ignorance, the Houghtons looked blankly at each other, and then Carl said, "I hardly think so."

"Maybe he was taking a shortcut across the lake," Annie suggested. "If he was going to see someone on the other side, he could have slipped and fallen in."

"He'd take his car," Molly said. "Only an idiot would walk across the lake in all this snow."

"Maybe his car wouldn't start," Annie said. "Or maybe he didn't know it was a lake. Maybe he got disoriented. He could have wandered onto the ice." That stupid remark earned her a hard stare from the sergeant.

"Now that I think of it," Carl said, "I believe Martinez had a van. Yes, a dark blue one."

"We'll check it out." Sgt. Morris put away his notebook and stood up.

"Actually," said Carl, "it'd be best if we kept as quiet as possible. It was just a tragic accident."

"That hasn't been determined yet. I'll be in touch." With that parting shot and a grim smile, the sergeant let himself out.

Annie got out her checkbook. With some juggling, the check for the reward just might clear. "Shall I make this out to you?" she asked Carl, who, when you got right down to it, hadn't had anything to do with Claudius's return. But since when was life fair?

"Oh, the reward," said Molly. "Why not make it out to the Fox Hill scholarship fund?"

For a second it looked as if Carl was going to protest, then he nodded. "Yeah, why not. That'd be fine."

Annie wrote the amount and signed the bottom. It felt like letting blood out of her veins. Not that she wasn't glad to get Claudius back, but she was flat broke. As usual.

On a hunch, she asked to see the local phone book, and when Molly gave it to her, looked for a listing for Harvey Warren—but found none. The other EMT, S. McIntyre, was listed, however. He lived on Wamesit Trail, not far from Fox Hill School.

Maybe he could tell her more about Rocky's condition when he was dragged from the lake.

She'd pay him a visit on the way home.

Handshakes all around, thanks a lot, and she and Claudius trooped out into the still falling snow.

His tags jingled as he lifted his head and sniffed. His eyes gleamed, and Annie knew he was thinking, *This is the life.* What more could a dog ask for than ice and snow?

Annie stuffed him into the car and got the engine going. It was cold as hell. Her breath was already steaming up the windshield. She drove off down Powderhouse Road and braked at the bottom, turned left on Main, then right on Abenaki Trail.

The plow hadn't been this way in hours. There were two ruts in the road where the last car had passed a while ago.

Everyone with a brain in his head was snug and safe at home, watching reruns on TV, maybe one of those hospital shows. Blood and guts all over the place, people dropping like flies. Like Rocky Martinez.

It was six-fifteen, and Sam McIntyre's shift should be over. With any luck he'd be home by now.

She squinted through the smeary windshield and wished she'd cleaned off the wipers. Ice was building up as the wipers clunked back and forth. Houses were few and far between on this road. If she broke down, she'd have to walk.

Who said anything about breaking down? she told herself. Okay, the Volvo wasn't perfect. A stick shift with a hundred and fifty thousand miles on it. Lately, it had begun popping out of fourth for some reason she couldn't fathom. Certainly not because it leaked oil. She dumped in a quart of 10W-30 every ten days or so. The Volvo had plenty of oil. Maybe.

Some male in her past had told her she could nurse a sick transmission along for months, but when it wasn't happy about going into reverse, it was time to look for another means of transportation.

Uh-oh. She shoved the Volvo into neutral, back into fourth, and after it popped out again three more times, gave up. Third gear would do fine.

A new car would be just the thing. A Jeep. Dolby, CD, sub-woofers, heated seats . . . did they make those for Jeeps?

Speaking of which, she gave the heater a thump. It wheezed and belched forth cold air. Moments later it was barely warm. Great. The Volvo was heading for the big junkyard in the sky.

Occupied with her gloomy thoughts, Annie almost missed the sign for Wamesit Trail.

It was a short road that curled beside Wamesit Creek, which gurgled in the ditch to the left. On both sides trees drooped, heavy with snow, closing off the night sky. Sam McIntyre's house couldn't be more than a hundred yards down the road.

What if Sam McIntyre didn't want to talk? What if he suffered a fit of medical ethics and decided not to betray patient confidentiality?

No problem. She'd knock on his door and say she'd run out of gas. Maybe beg a ride back to town and a gas station—and pump him for all she was worth. That was Plan A. Plan B was to come right out and tell him the truth: that Rocky might have been murdered. So if he'd noticed anything, it might be a clue to whoever had killed him.

Claudius was thrilled to be slogging through eight inches of new-fallen snow, and why not. He was half husky. This was his kind of weather.

Sam McIntyre's name was on the mailbox three houses down on the right. A light shone from a back window, so Annie stumbled up the front steps and rang the bell. She waited a minute. God, it was cold.

It was almost six-forty-five. What if he'd decided to go out, maybe take in dinner and a movie? No, on a night like this, he'd come home.

Where was he? She punched the bell again.

There was a window to the left of the door. The shade was up, so she got nosy, hoping to see some sign of life. In the shadows, she could make out a lamp, an uphol-stered chair with a crocheted afghan, a table with a stack of books, and a spider plant with dozens of babies.

There was a sewing machine in the corner, and the win-dow curtains looked homemade, orange with tiny white flowers. Not Annie's taste, but that's what made the world go round.

From somewhere in the back of the house came the drone of a TV, and she saw a bluish light flickering in an-other room.

Just when she was wondering if they were going to sit through an entire Weather with Al, the door popped open. A man stood there. For the first time she got a good look at Sam McIntyre. He'd had his back turned to her down at the lake, but this had to be him.

He was tall and rangy with dark blond hair and thickly

lashed green eyes. In other words, a hunk. Her heart went pitty-pat.

His jeans and T-shirt were spattered with dark blue paint.

She introduced herself and explained that she'd run out of gas.

"Come on in," he said. "I have some gas in the garage—I was just . . . doing a touch-up job on my car. Let me get my coat."

"Thanks." Stepping inside, she told Claudius to heel, while Sam closed the door and hurried to get his coat.

Annie admired the way he filled his jeans, and Claudius sauntered to the end of the leash. His tail wagged. He raised his head and sniffed. Food, and roast chicken at that, Annie guessed. Yum.

"We'll be home soon," she said. "I'll feed you then."

Claudius rolled his eyes, his meaning clear: Who knew when that would happen? Anyone with half a brain would sniff out the possibilities of a home-cooked meal right here and now.

"Forget it." She scraped wet hair off her face, trying for respectability. She glanced around. A couple of framed color photographs on the wall. Four men in army gear next to a Jeep. Beside it, a photograph of mountains. Big ones. Several people bundled in brightly colored Gore-Tex, grinning and waving ice axes.

A knapsack lay on the floor in the corner near a window. Coils of rope were piled on top, and what looked like carabiners. Sam McIntyre was into mountain climbing.

He came back, pulling on a jacket. "You're lucky I was home. I'm a volunteer paramedic. I was on call today and just got in a few minutes ago. The name's Sam McIntyre."

His voice was low, his accent as Southern as blackstrap molasses. A definite 10.

"Small world," she said, flashing her best smile. Thank God for all those years in braces. "Actually, I noticed you down at the lake this afternoon. I happened to be there, too."

"Yeah, I thought I recognized you. The red hair." He shrugged. "Too bad about that guy in the lake—Rocky Martinez. It's a damn shame. I knew him slightly. He was in the army reserves the same time I was. A couple of months ago he started working part-time at Fox Hill School, maintenance mostly. He clipped hedges and mowed lawns. But he didn't stand a chance today in that freezing water. Kids do better. We can bring them back even after they've been under a long time. Their body temperature lowers in freezing water and slows the heart rate, like suspended animation." He led the way down the hall to the back of the house. A light was on in the kitchen.

A frying pan sizzled on the stove—hash browns. The scent of roast chicken was coming from the oven.

Claudius licked his chops and sat down. No way was he leaving without a snack.

"Your dog looks hungry," Sam said. Clearly he was a dog person. Things were getting better and better. He filled a pan with water and set it on the floor.

Claudius barked, sniffed, and decided it was worth drinking. Within seconds, he was into serious lapping.

"Sam?" an elderly woman yelled from upstairs.

"My mother," he explained, then went down the hall to the foot of the stairs. "It's nothing, Ma. Go back to sleep."

"Who are you talking to? Not that awful Eddie, I hope.

That no-good bum's bound to get picked up for driving drunk one of these days. I won't have him in the house!"

"It's not Eddie," Sam said. "Just someone who broke down on the road. They ran out of gas. I'm gonna give them a hand, so go back to bed."

"No, who could sleep through all this racket! Doorbells ringing, dogs barking." There was a series of thumps and shuffling sounds overhead as her feet hit the floor and she headed for the stairs. Mrs. M. was coming down.

"Sorry, my mother can be difficult," Sam said. "She's in the first stages of Alzheimer's and gets paranoid if she sees a stranger. Twice a week she calls 911 because she thinks someone's prowling around outside." He swept Annie and Claudius toward the back door. A blast of icy air hit them as he yanked it open.

Claudius, reluctant to leave, had to be dragged out. He shot Annie a look of disbelief. Was she out of her mind? Food was the first priority.

"Sam!" yelled Mrs. M. "What's going on?" She stumped into the kitchen and looked around. "Who tracked snow all over my clean floor?"

"Wait a sec." Sam poked his head back inside. "I'll be right back, Ma."

"Don't call me Ma. I hate that. What are you up to?"

"Nothing. I told you, someone broke down. I'm just taking them some gas."

Out on the back step, Annie was wondering how women TV detectives conducted interrogations. Like Abby Whatshername on those *Law & Order* reruns. Only she was a prosecutor. Well, it seemed pretty simple. First she'd gain his confidence. A little chitchat and then he'd spill whatever he knew.

Claudius sneezed and shook snow out of his eyes. He ambled over to Sam and planted himself at his feet. He was hungry. He hadn't eaten in a week, he seemed to be saying.

Which Annie knew to be false. According to one message on the answering machine, at some point in his adventures, he'd enjoyed a forty-pound bag of Science Diet.

The door opened suddenly, Sam jumped away from Claudius, and Mrs. M. poked her head out. She eyed Annie with suspicion. "Who are you?" she demanded in a querulous voice. "What are you doing with my son? I'm calling 911."

CHAPTER
5

There were a few awkward moments, but eventually Mrs. M. was convinced that Annie wasn't another lowlife like the despised Eddie. It was established that she lived in Lee and had run out of gas down the road.

Sam told his mother they had to be on their way. Chitchat was all very pleasant, but what mattered was gassing up the Volvo so Annie could go home.

He'd struck the right note. Mrs. M. was pleased.

"Right," said Sam, seizing Annie by the arm and hustling her down the porch steps. "Let's go."

On the way through the falling snow to the garage to get the can of gas, they talked about the prospects for a January thaw.

Sam pushed the garage door open and rummaged behind a stack of cartons. "The can is around here somewhere."

She stood in the doorway. It was a two-car garage. The air smelled of paint. A blue Toyota was parked in the shadows, beside it a spray painter and a large can of blue paint. It looked as if he'd done a lot more than a touch-up. The left rear door panel was still white.

He found the gas, and as they headed for the Volvo, Annie steered the conversation to Sam's job. He enjoyed EMT work, but it didn't pay enough so he was teaching part-time at Fox Hill—an outdoor survival course. The kids seemed to like it.

As they walked, she tried to keep Claudius from tearing her arm out of its socket. "That man you pulled out of the lake . . . do you think he just fell in? Or was he murdered?"

Apparently whatever comment Sam had been expecting, it wasn't that.

"Murdered?" he repeated. "What makes you think that?"

"I don't know," she admitted. "But the cops are asking a lot of questions."

"That's nothing. They always ask questions when someone dies suddenly."

"But why would he have gone out on the ice?"

"Who knows. He wasn't breathing when we got him into the boat. We worked on him on the way to the hospital, but he never had any vitals."

"Did you notice anything peculiar about him? Like if he'd been hit on the head, then dumped in the lake?"

"Nope," Sam said.

Annie wracked her brain, but couldn't think of anything else intelligent to say. She was so aware of Sam's attractiveness.

They reached the Volvo, and she brushed off six inches of newly fallen snow while Sam dumped gas in the tank. She drove him back to his house, then went home.

It was well past seven-thirty. Cary would be home by now at Goss Lane, probably fixing herself a fancy salad and deluxe pizza and getting ready to watch *The Naked Chef* on the Food Network. She was always saying she'd love to open a restaurant.

Annie phoned Cary as soon as she'd stripped off her coat and wet boots and fed Claudius supper.

"I have good news and bad news," she said, then explained that Rocky Martinez had turned up. Only he was dead, drowned in fact. A twin tragedy since the jacket was probably a total loss and Rocky had escaped the long arm of the law.

Considering everything, Annie had decided she'd only charge ten percent over for expenses. Her profit would be marginal, but that couldn't be helped.

"So the bill for my services comes to fifty-five bucks."

"Fifty . . . that's highway robbery."

"Ten percent over to cover expenses," Annie said. "The going rate is twenty, so I gave you a break."

There was a moment of silence while Cary dealt with the fact that she'd have to come up with fifty-five dollars and yet wouldn't get to press charges. "Damn," she said. "The creep got away with it. Of all the rotten luck."

"Well, yes, but he's dead," Annie reminded her.

"He probably got somebody mad. I bet it was murder."

"Maybe. The cops asked a lot of questions."

"Huh. He was nothing but trouble. Stands to reason sooner or later somebody'd put him away for good. Whoever did it deserves a medal."

"I wouldn't go that far."

"I would. And what *about* my jacket?"

"It's ruined. He was wearing it when he died."

"What about my grandfather's good-conduct medal? I want that back."

"Oh," This was getting complicated, but what Cary wanted, she usually got.

"So where is it?" Cary insisted.

"What? The medal?"

"Yeah."

"At the morgue, I suppose. Or the funeral parlor. Wherever Rocky is."

Cary thought about that for a minute. "He died today. That means they'll probably release the body to the funeral home tomorrow or the next day at the latest. O'Connell's does all the funerals in Elkhorn. Nobody in his right mind goes to Myer's Funeral Parlor. Although I suppose if you're dead, you don't have much choice."

"What's wrong with Myer's?"

"Mary Myer's crazy," Cary explained. "She runs the place. I knew a guy who worked there a couple of years ago. He quit because conditions were bad. It'd be just my luck if Rocky ended up there."

"Never mind," Annie said. "We need to find out who's handling the body. I'll do that. Then we'll go get the medal."

"I'm paying you, so you should get it."

"Oh, no. You're coming with me," Annie said firmly. "Besides, we went to school with Tubby O'Connell, remember? He was a year ahead of us at Fox Hill, so there shouldn't be a problem if he's handling Rocky's body. I'll get the scoop on Rocky's whereabouts and give you a call tomorrow. Or you can call me."

"Okay."

There didn't seem much more to be said about Rocky per se, so the conversation drifted to where he'd been found: Fox Hill, the scene of many a past triumph for

Cary, who, unlike Annie, had shone at everything while at school.

"Are you going to Winterfest?" Cary wanted to know. "The dinner dance? I'm going with Zack Henderson." Zack, local hotshot lawyer, was a stud, and, according to Cary, crazy for her. She anticipated a hot time the night of the dance.

Annie avoided the temptation to lie. It was embarrassing to admit she hadn't been invited to the Winterfest Dance. She made do with a simple no.

"Oh." Cary continued airily, "Well, there's the hockey tournament, ski races, snow sculptures—all the stuff we did as kids."

"I know." Annie sighed. She didn't want to ask the next question, but it was expected. "What are you wearing?"

"My red dress, the one with no back." And nearly no front, Annie recalled. Cary poured herself into that dress and looked like the cat's meow.

"I've been asked to give a speech to the senior class," Annie said.

"About what?" Cary asked suspiciously.

"Achievement. I thought I'd talk about solving crimes . . . murder."

"Are you taking Claudius along?"

"Yes, the kids will love him, and considering his past career in law enforcement, he'll be perfect."

After exchanging a few more pleasantries, Annie hung up.

Claudius was right there glowering at her. He picked up his full bowl and dumped it at her feet. Apparently dinner hadn't been up to his standards. Well, she couldn't afford Science Diet, thank you very much. He had to make do with whatever she'd picked up on sale.

"What's wrong with it?" She showed him the bag. "Look, chicken and lamb. It's good."

Claudius nudged the bowl. He wasn't eating this swill.

"Hey, I'm not made of money."

He gave her a beady stare and a low woof.

She tried staring him down and lost.

Well, he deserved a special welcome-home dinner, she decided, so she rooted around in the fridge and came up with leftover round steak, once destined for beef stew. She chopped it up, warmed up some gravy, and Claudius gobbled down a first-class welcome-home feast.

Afterward, while she was washing up, he nuzzled her leg—his first thank-you ever. She leaned down and scratched his ears, a warm feeling flowing through her.

Naturally, Claudius being Claudius, this didn't last. She had to earn *his* praise, not the other way around.

Never mind, Annie told herself. All he needed was a little training, a firm hand, and determination. She was still feeling her way with him. It would take time. Maybe she'd get a clicker. The dog training book she'd been reading was big on clickers. The idea was to teach commands using treats along with a small handheld clicker. After a time, one could dispense with the treats and simply use the clicker. According to various journals, it was a very effective method of training.

Next morning, after showering, Annie discovered that Claudius had made himself comfortable on a pile of sheets he'd dragged from the linen closet.

"Off!" she shouted.

He took his time about obeying, while she stood there,

dripping and fuming. Then she stomped around with a towel hitched up under her arms, dumped the sheets in the laundry, dressed, and read the local paper.

Headlines screamed: *South Lee tragedy. Local handyman falls through ice and drowns.*

An explanation of hypothermia followed, but no mention of the fact that Rocky Martinez had no conceivable reason to be out on the ice. He was described as a part-time maintenance employee at Fox Hill School. Period.

God forbid anyone should put two and two together and come up with four. Namely, that if Rocky's death wasn't accidental, someone at the prestigious Fox Hill School might just be a murderer.

"Hmm," Annie said to Claudius, who was curled up under the table. "What do you think?"

He yawned and gave her a long look, his eyes cool and assessing, seeming to confirm the obvious.

Outside, a light snow began falling. Annie had a second cup of coffee and checked her horoscope. "Listen to this, Claudius. Libras need to stay focused. That's me. The color white is unlucky today, but I can accomplish a lot with my charm, intellect, and knowledge." She left out the part where it said she shouldn't stick her nose in other people's affairs.

He let out a sigh.

"So you don't think I have charm, intellect, or knowledge. Fine. Be like that. Come on, let's walk off breakfast." She pulled on a jacket and boots, and they went outdoors.

Claudius wanted to inspect every bush and tree in sight, plus dive under the snow for mouse trails, so they

wandered around for a good half hour before he decided
he'd had enough and she could open the antique shop

Inventory was the first order of business—she had to
locate something to donate to the auction. She booted up
the computer and scrolled down the list of stock at hand:
cupboards, chairs, tables, oil lamps, bowls, sconces, tinder-
boxes, candlesnuffers . . .

Something special, but what? Pewter plates, a chocolate pot, old mirrors. Ah, this might do: a handmade quilt.

Blue and white, stitched in the Drunkard's Path pattern
in 1864 by a young New Hampshire bride whose husband
had died at Antietam. And worth about one thousand dollars.

If she sold it, she'd never get that much for it, and Fox
Hill's scholarship fund was a good cause. When she'd
been a student there, her scholarship had covered almost
everything, thank God. Her parents couldn't have afforded to send her there otherwise.

Customers came and went as the hours passed. It
turned into a fairly profitable day. Annie sold a pearlware
jug, some old prints, a wooden bucket bench, and a lovely
pair of oval, mirrored wall sconces. About three-thirty, she
wrapped up the quilt she intended to donate to the auction
and closed up shop for the day.

Claudius trailed after her as she carried the quilt back
to the house.

He sat down in front of the fridge, reminding her that it
was time for a treat. There was a pot roast inside, but she
didn't take the hint. Instead, she answered the phone—a
couple booking a room for next week—and planned the
menu: Italian dishes, steak, salads, soups, breads, pies,
tarts.

He nudged her leg.

"Okay," she said. "Here. It's good for you." It was a dog biscuit with a dollop of wheat germ on the side.

He bolted the biscuit, left the wheat germ in a lump, and stood there in an attitude of feigned supplication.

"Honestly, what did I tell you? Oh, well, here, have another. But this is the last, and I *mean* it. Watch the fingers."

He took it from her hand as slick as can be. Then, when she was distracted by the ping of the oven timer—she'd put bread in to bake—he stood on his hind legs and gave the cupboard where she stored treats a firm shove. As expected, and to his great delight, the bag of biscuits tumbled to the floor and burst open.

It was nip and tuck, but Annie managed to rescue most of the treats just as a knock sounded on the back door.

Gus Jackson peered at her through the window half of the door. He was laughing.

Of all the rotten luck. She hadn't seen Gus in at least a month. They were practically strangers, and if she had anything to say about it, they'd stay that way. A few months earlier, as the town of Lee's most senior detective, he'd tried his level best to pin a murder conviction on her brother, Tom. In Annie's mind, the fact that a mountain of circumstantial evidence had pointed directly to Tom didn't absolve Gus of blame in the matter. She'd known Tom was innocent right from the beginning and had worked hard to bring the real killers to justice.

Gus opened the door and came in, bringing with him the smell of snow, wood smoke, and breathless cold.

She put the biscuits back on top of the cupboard as Claudius trotted off to the living room. A stash of toys was hidden under the armchair: rubber balls, squeakers, bones, and what was left of Annie's hairbrush.

"That dog is driving me crazy," she said wearily.

"I noticed." Gus closed the door.

She straightened her shirt, which had crawled up around her midriff. "To what do I owe the honor?"

"Mind if I sit?"

She shook her head, and he took a chair at the table and sat down. He hadn't been in town very long. He'd been a Boston homicide cop—rumor had it he'd been shot and had traded in big-city action for a peaceful life in the country. He had a linebacker's shoulders and the touch of a Harvard accent. He wore L.L. Bean khakis and a sweater and an aura of innate competence like a second skin. She felt a flicker of attraction and wondered how he'd ended up as a homicide detective.

He stretched out his long legs and smiled. "We need to talk."

"About what?" But she already knew.

"You found another body."

"You mean Rocky Martinez?"

"How many other bodies have you found lately?"

She shrugged. "I didn't find him. Claudius did."

"The dog told you someone was drowning?" Gus's voice was expressionless.

"More or less. He was trained as a police dog."

"I see. Is there anything he can't do?"

"If there is, I haven't found it yet."

"Okay, forget the dog. Did you know the deceased?"

That was a tough one. Should she tell the truth and get into the clothes theft? That could be tricky—silly as it seemed, she might be giving Cary a motive for murder.

"Well, we'd never met, but I knew who he was. Sort of."

"The report doesn't say anything about your knowing Rocky Martinez, even sort of."

"I guess I forgot to mention it."

"Give me a break."

"I didn't think it was important."

"I'll decide what's important. That's my job."

"Fine."

"So?" Gus raised an eyebrow.

"Okay." She explained about the stolen jacket and good-conduct medal, downplaying Cary's outraged determination to get the medal back.

"Are you serious?"

"Would I make this up? He was such a loser. He stole her stuff and had the gall to wear it all over town." Despite everything, Annie was still indignant. "When they pulled him out of the lake, I recognized her jacket. By the way, which funeral home is handling the burial?"

"Why do you want to know?" Gus eyed her suspiciously.

"Oh, just curious."

"O'Connell's. His sister claimed the body."

Annie went to the fridge. Maybe he expected her to kill the fatted calf because he'd decided to drop by. Well, if so, he was going to be disappointed. "You want a beer or something hot? Coffee?"

"Beer's fine." At her raised eyebrow he added, "I'm off duty."

She got out two beers and opened a bag of pretzels. The way to a man's heart was through his stomach. Not that she was interested.

He sipped from the bottle. "About Rocky Martinez—"

"What about him? He fell through the ice and drowned. End of story. Unless you think someone gave him some help."

He smiled. "Did I say that?"

"No, but you wouldn't be here unless you thought his death was more than an accident."

He put the bottle down. "Call it simple curiosity. After all, I own a cabin on the lake, not far from where Rocky went in."

"Did you see what happened?" Stupid question. If he'd seen anything, he'd have been there in a flash.

"No, my nephew, Mike, plays hockey for Fox Hill. They had a game at Bridgeton Academy in Concord." He shrugged. "I decided to take in the game and drove over to Concord. They lost, four–zip. The goalie's a flopper. Unless they break him, they'll lose big time."

"What's a flopper?"

He sighed. "The goalie throws himself around like a dead fish, leaving the goal wide open. All the shooter had to do is lift his shot, and bingo."

"Oh, yeah, I knew that."

Gus chomped on some pretzels. "Sure you did. I bet you read the sports pages every morning."

"As a matter of fact, I do, now and then. So how do you break a goalie of flopping?"

"Tie him to the goal posts and shoot pucks at him for three or four hours."

She drank beer and gave that some thought. Brutal, but effective, and hockey players weren't known for being sensitive types.

"Is Mike staying with you?" Nosy, but you never found out anything without asking. Not that she cared, of course.

"He's living on campus at Wyndham House. Why?"

"Just asked. I went to Fox Hill. It's a good school."

"Well, Mike likes it. My sister, Shelly, lives in Manchester. Mike's her son. She thought it'd be a good idea if he went away to school. He's big, rebellious. She just couldn't control him."

"What about his dad?"

Gus shrugged. "He took off years ago. Mike's a good kid, but he gives his mother a tough time."

"So you're keeping an eye on him?"

"You could say that." He'd eaten all the pretzels. "Got any real food?"

"Leftovers," she said, hoping he'd take the hint and go home. She had things to do.

He leaned back in the chair. "Leftover what?"

"Clam chowder and turkey potpie."

"Mmm, sounds good."

She gave up and heated soup and potpie, then plunked both on the table along with French bread and a tossed salad. Gus got out plates, napkins, forks, knives, and spoons.

Claudius trotted in and parked himself strategically under the table.

Gus polished off the soup and picked up his fork. "That was delicious. Nice pie crust."

"Puff pastry. Store bought," she added to discourage him.

He helped himself to bread and salad. "Where were you last night? I stopped by and you weren't home."

Annie cleared her throat. He'd decided to stop by?

Baloney. Every instinct said he was investigating Rocky Martinez's death. "I ran out of gas," she said.

The phone rang. She went out to the front hall and answered it. "Thurston Tavern." The male voice on the other end asked for Gus. She handed him the receiver and went back to the kitchen.

Muttered conversation came from the front hall.

Claudius decided Gus wasn't eating and started sniffing his plate. Annie shooed him away and started eating her own potpie.

From the look on Gus's face as he stomped back to the kitchen and flung himself onto the chair, she guessed things weren't going well.

"What's wrong?" she asked.

"Everything! Mike wants to move in with me at the cottage. He says the dorm is haunted. Six-foot-two and he's scared of a ghost."

Annie looked up from scraping the last of the potpie onto her fork. "It's an old story. Wyndham is supposed to be haunted. Everyone knows what happened."

Gus frowned. "What?"

"The school's founder, Elijah Wyndham, was the chief jurist in New Hampshire back in 1700, when it was part of Maine. Anyway, Elijah married his daughter, Patience, to a horny old geezer with money—Joshua Barnes—who was murdered. Poisoned. Evidence pointed to Patience, poison being a woman's weapon, so she was tried in Elijah's court, found guilty, and hanged. Through the years students have claimed they've seen her ghost. Sometimes she walks in the attic, sometimes she's hanging from the tree outside the house. South Lee was the court seat for the territory, and Wyndham Hall is where Patience was tried. She was hanged from the big oak by the driveway."

He smiled. "You don't really believe in ghosts."

"Thurston Tavern's an old house," she reminded him. "Sometimes doors open for no reason. Stairs creak and no one's there. Who's to say there aren't ghosts?" She didn't mention that Thurston Tavern guests had said they'd seen an elderly gentleman in a nightshirt on the stairs. She'd never seen him, but that didn't mean he didn't exist.

"Well, I wasn't talking about the tavern," Gus went on. "Mike's determined to move out of Wyndham Hall. I'm damned if I'll have him move in with me. I don't have time to raise an adolescent." He frowned. "I just don't understand how this ridiculous ghost business got started."

"As it happens, you've come to the right person. I'm working on a brochure for Fox Hill, a compilation of the school's history—so I've done some research," she said. "Stories about Patience were handed down from generation to generation. She was beautiful and strong-willed, a lethal combination—especially in Colonial times. She even had a black cat. Word spread that she was a witch, but before they could try her, her husband was poisoned. So they hanged her anyway."

"It doesn't explain the ghost."

"The custom was to leave the body hanging for three days as an example to everyone. The story goes that when three days had passed, and nightfall came, Elijah ordered her cut down. They buried her in the family graveyard, next to her victim. But somehow that didn't sit well with some of the townsfolk, and they dug her up. She was buried again, this time in the town cemetery. But there was a fight over that—after all, she was said to be a witch.

They didn't want a witch in a respectable cemetery. So she was dug up a second time. They tried burying her again, and someone dug her up a third time. So they decided to cut her up and bury her all over town, secretly, in the dead of night. Her torso was buried at Gibbet Hill crossroads, so her heart could choose to repent and go to heaven, or not."

"My God." Gus shook his head.

"You can see why people got spooked," Annie continued. "Talk started that her ghost walked at night. Every time something weird happened, they blamed Patience. If crops failed or a cow's milk dried up, she was taking revenge. While she was being tried, they kept her locked up in a barred room in the cellar with no window. When the house was restored, they found the room. Elijah had had it bricked up. She must have been scared to death. Maybe what people sensed was her fear, a fear so terrible it never went away."

Gus snorted. "Surely you don't believe this stuff."

"Hey, she was a threat to the establishment. Her hanging served as a warning to every woman in the territory. Think about it. A meddlesome woman could expect to be put to death and even denied a decent burial. In fact, she could be hacked to pieces—all in the name of the law."

"Still, it's a horrible story. Why turn the house into a dorm for kids?"

She shrugged. "When Elijah died, the estate went to Paris, the nephew in Boston. As it happens, he married one of the family servants, but everything was entailed. At his death, it became part of the school. Even though it's a dorm, the house has been well preserved—the wideboard floors, even old wall stencils. As a matter of fact, a portrait of Patience still hangs in the front hall."

"No wonder the kids are scared."

"It's been part of the history of the school since the beginning. Generally, the kids ignore it."

"Except Mike. Just my luck." Gus forked up the last of the potpie. "This is excellent. I'll have to have you over for dinner one night. I cook a mean lasagna."

"Straight out of a can, no doubt."

He laughed. "My grandmother came from Sicily. I know how to cook."

Gus left, and Annie cleared away the dishes. She bolted the back door and turned out the light, then realized she was still hungry. More soup or potpie didn't appeal.

Maybe a cup of tea and toast would do. Poking around in the fridge didn't produce much. Good grief, she was getting as gluttonous as Claudius, who was burying his nose in the crisper drawer.

She gave him a good shove and stood there staring tiredly at the shelves. Hmm, yogurt with fruit at the bottom. Non-fattening. Half a dozen cups. Funny, she couldn't remember buying it, and as it wasn't the kind she bought ordinarily, she decided Kirk had picked it up before leaving for New York. The small mysteries of life.

She opened a cup of yogurt with peaches, took a spoon, and began eating it. She sat down, conscious of a weariness inside her—which was silly. What did she have to be so tired about? She'd had a successful day in the shop. Among other items, she'd sold a lovely pair of mirrored wall sconces. Hard to come by these days, they had been in fine condition, and a two-hundred-dollar profit was not to be sneezed at.

She sat there for a few minutes longer after finishing the yogurt. She was feeling better.

Suddenly, Claudius leaped up, ran to the back door, and began barking insistently.

Who could it be at this hour? She grabbed Claudius by the collar and looked out through the curtain. Light from the kitchen fell on the stoop.

Joey Chavez stood there.

She jerked the door open. "What are you doing here?"

He shivered. "Can I come in? It's real cold out."

Claudius wriggled free from Annie's clutches. He sniffed Joey's jeans and wagged his tail.

She hauled them both inside and told Claudius to go lie down.

Surprise, surprise. With a disappointed growl he did as he was told and lay watching while she parked Joey at the table and put the kettle on for hot chocolate. "Do you know how late it is? For heaven's sake, does your mother know where you are?"

"Mom went to see her sister in Portsmouth. Aunt Alida's real sick." He gulped down hot chocolate, leaving a mustache. He wiped his mouth. "Hey, you got your dog back. Cool. You prob'ly owe me the reward. Three hundred bucks, right?"

"I already paid the reward to someone else. You had nothing to do with getting him back."

"Oh, yeah?" Indignant disbelief warred with disappointment. His eyes narrowed. "Well, did you hear about Rocky?"

"Yes."

"Way cool. He's dead."

"Dead isn't way cool. Let's stick to the subject—your mom's whereabouts and why you walked three miles over snowy roads in the dead of night to knock on my door. We need to call your mom. She probably thinks you're home."

"It's okay. She won't care. She goes out a lot. I can take care of myself."

"What possessed you to come all the way over here?"

He shrugged. "I was home by myself, and I figured, why not see if you've found Claudius."

Hearing his name, Claudius wagged his tail like mad and went over to Joey to lick chocolate from his fingers. Annie shoved him away. "Cut that out."

"I'm hungry," Joey said, eyeing the stove. "Got anything good to eat?"

"Like what?"

He grinned. "Whatever. I'm real hungry."

She heated up more chowder and made scrambled eggs and toast. Joey gobbled down the soup, added catsup to his eggs, tasted, dumped on more, then downed the lot.

"Good," he mumbled through a mouthful of toast.

The phone rang. It had to be, of course, Cary.

CHAPTER
6

"I called O'Connell's Funeral Parlor," Cary said. "They're handling Rocky Martinez's body. How about meeting me there tomorrow around five so we can get the medal back?"

"Uh, I don't know. I might be busy." The thought of going over to O'Connell's filled Annie with dread. Rocky alive hadn't been all that appealing. Dead, he'd obviously be worse.

"Don't give me that," Cary demanded. "It's me, your best friend. You promised. You owe me."

Well, she *had* promised, but where did Cary get this "you owe me" idea?

Annie sighed. "How do you figure that?"

"Come on, Annie. Detective work is like meat and potatoes to you. Second nature. Admit it, you're dying to go to O'Connell's."

Annie glanced over her shoulder, back into the kitchen. Joey was making more toast, and Claudius was on his hind legs, eating leftovers from the table. "I've got to go," she told Cary. "There's something important I have to take care of."

"That's a crock. You're avoiding me for some reason."

"Don't be silly. Why should I be avoiding you?"

"Because you're mad at me."

Cary was a real pain when she got like this.

Annie attempted to retain some dignity by saying crisply, "I'm not angry. Just busy."

"Don't give me that. I know you, Annie. You're mad, all right. What is it—jealous because I'm writing a book about New Hampshire serial killers? Honestly, you're acting like a spoiled kid."

About to say "You're crazy," Annie stopped herself in time. Maybe Cary had a point. She'd gotten a modest contract with a local publisher. She was well on her way to accomplishing a big dream—getting published. Since working on the Fox Hill brochure for the past month or so, Annie had thought about writing as a second career. She'd even jotted down a few ideas: running a country inn, a woman's life in Colonial America, witchcraft trials, New England in the late 1600s . . .

"Well," Cary went on, "we've been friends too long for a thing like my book and getting my medal back to come between us. So I'll tell you what. You don't even have to drive. My car door's fixed. I'll pick you up right after work."

"Uh, no! I mean, thanks for the offer, but it's a bad time. I'm too busy—maybe later in the week."

"For heaven's sake, it won't take long. We'll be in and out in no time. I'll just snag the medal, and we're out the door. Please, Annie. I'm not asking much."

This was hitting below the belt, and they both knew it. Even so, if Cary hadn't been such an old friend, if she hadn't bailed Annie out of trouble numerous times—if she weren't, dammit, such a good friend . . .

But she was. Never mind, Annie wasn't about to give in too easily. She opened her mouth to protest once more, and Cary continued, "Okay, you twisted my arm. I'll let you read the first draft of my manuscript. You'll *love* it."

This wasn't happening, Annie told herself. But it was.

She glanced back to the kitchen in time to see Joey slap an inch-thick layer of jam on his toast.

"Marketing is everything," Cary confided. "It might be worth my while to work up some weekend graveyard tours. You know, where victims are buried. Or maybe where they were killed—a tour of the homes where they died. I'll have to think about it."

"That sounds like a good idea."

"So, tomorrow at five-fifteen sharp. Right?"

Annie knew when she was beaten. "Right."

That taken care of, Cary said she had to get back to her manuscript. "Chapter eight. I don't want the sagging middle syndrome, so I have to think of something to give it pizzazz."

Annie didn't want to ask, but curiosity got the better of her. "How?"

"I was thinking of dividing the book in two and making the first half about women, the second about men. I could use Pam Smart in the middle. You know, that teacher who persuaded a student to kill her husband? People hate her."

Annie could hear Cary typing in the background. "But Pam Smart's not a serial killer," she pointed out.

"Who cares. She's obviously crazy. A homicidal maniac. She would've gone on killing if she hadn't been caught. The important thing is that she sells. She's hot. So what do you think of it? Terrific, isn't it! There's a ton of material out there. You just have to know where to look." She paused, then gloated, "Think of the headlines if Rocky turns out to be a serial killer's latest victim."

Cary was getting carried away. To change the conversation, and because Joey was kicking off his boots and getting himself another hot chocolate, Annie lowered her voice and asked Cary what to do about him.

"He *says* his mom isn't home."

"Huh. Call up and see who answers. Kids lie all the time, especially Joey. He's a pro."

Well, she already knew that. To her cost.

"Okay, I'll try his number."

"Good. See you tomorrow." Cary hung up.

Annie checked the phone book for a listing for Chavez on Goss Lane. Yes, there it was. She dialed. It rang twice, then a woman's voice snapped, "Yes, who is it?"

She explained who she was. "Are you Joey's mother?"

"Yeah," Mrs. Chavez's voice rose. "Where is he? With you?"

"Yes, he's fine. I'll bring him home right away."

"That boy. I told him he could watch TV, and what's he do? Turns the sound up and climbs out the window. That's the last time he'll pull that trick!"

Annie cleared her throat. "Joey said you'd gone to visit your sister."

"Yes, but I wasn't gone long. Alida lives across town."

Another lie. Joey's stories were piling up like cordwood.

She hung up and told him he had to go home.

Five minutes later, they were in the Volvo, barreling

along the back roads. The headlights picked out a tunnel
of light in the night. A light snow was falling, enough to
make her use the wipers. Joey was sulking, and Claudius
was delirious to be riding in the car. He stuck his nose out
the side window and sniffed greedily at all the fascinating
smells.

In fifteen minutes, they were turning down Prospect
Street. Goss Lane was just ahead on the right. They were
within a block of Joey's home. She could see the houses
now. Good grief, there were cop cars and an ambulance
parked just up the street.

"What's going on?" she murmured.

"Wow!" Joey said, suddenly bright-eyed.

She pulled in at the curb, and Claudius barked and
jumped around in excitement.

Gus Jackson was coming out of the house next door to
Joey's, a red turtleneck visible beneath his overcoat.
EMTs followed with a stretcher. The face of the person on
the stretcher was covered.

"Wow, somebody's dead!" Joey cried, nose pressed to
the windshield.

"Maybe it was an accident or someone had a heart attack."

"Lemme out, I'll go see what happened!"

Annie grabbed his arm as he was about to launch himself onto the sidewalk. "You're going straight home."

He glared at her. "But I need to find out who's dead!"

"No, you don't." They got out, locked Claudius in the
car, and walked past the line of cars and pickup trucks
parked at the curb. The arrival of the ambulance had at-
tracted a large crowd. Back in the Volvo, Claudius kept up
a running commentary on the unfairness of everything.

If Gus saw them, he pretended not to. Apparently he had his mind on the business at hand, but he'd have to be deaf not to hear Claudius. She decided Gus was just being stubborn.

More curious onlookers were gathering in the falling snow, and as they walked past, Joey tried to squeeze through the grown-ups to get a closer look at the sheeted body on the stretcher.

Annie pulled him back. "No!"

"Jeez, I never get to do anything." Yanking his arm free, he turned and trudged off toward his house, though he kept looking over his shoulder at the ambulance. Annie felt her breath escape on a gusty sigh she hadn't realized she'd been holding.

About to follow Joey, Annie's eye caught the shifting movement of people near the ambulance. One man had turned his head away and pulled up his collar as if he didn't want to be seen.

She frowned. Maybe the man didn't want any cops to notice him. Maybe he had a stack of unpaid parking tickets.

Shivering a little, she followed Joey's snowy footprints. She knew her sudden chill came not from the blustery wind, but from the knot of people huddled near the ambulance.

One of the cop cars drove off, but Gus Jackson remained, talking to one of the EMTs. Annie bent her head and hurried after Joey. From the porch steps she heard Claudius bark again, a single staccato bark, followed by howls. The howls went on for a few seconds; then they stopped and all was silent. She knew what that meant. Claudius had sensed death.

Joey rang the bell, and seconds later Mrs. Chavez let them in, looking a little scared and more than a little angry.

"Joey!" she cried. "I can't trust you for five minutes. And look what's happened now. Maria Martinez is dead. Terrible. Hit and run, right here on Goss Lane. The cops don't even have a description of the car, and it's been more than half an hour since she got hit." The implication was clear: The cops were lying down on the job. She tweaked the curtain back and peered out the window. "They don't fool me. Probably some rich kid did it or a bank president. They'll look the other way. What's one more dead woman. Poor Maria always needed money. She lived with a man for five years. They just split up. He had a rap sheet eighty-six pages long. They never got married."

No wonder.

Annie suspected Mrs. Chavez was itching to go outside and give the cops a piece of her mind, but was reluctant to do so while she had company.

Annie cleared her throat. "Well, I'd better go."

Joey, glued to the window, turned around and gave her a long look. "Know who Maria Martinez was?"

"No," she said.

"She was Rocky's sister."

Annie swallowed. She didn't like that cold sensation creeping down her neck and back. Rocky's sister the victim of an apparent hit-and-run accident. Only maybe it wasn't an accident. Maybe someone had run her down on purpose.

Which probably meant that someone had lured Rocky out onto the lake ice, knocked him out, and shoved him into the cold, black water to drown. Maybe someone standing even now among the curious onlookers next to the ambulance—making sure Maria was really dead.

Annie said good-bye and left as Joey's mother was ordering him up to bed. He looked unhappy as the door closed behind Annie.

Outside, she threaded her way past the ambulance and people still standing around watching the EMTs slam the back door and prepare to depart. Much of the crowd had begun to clear, and she looked in vain for the man she'd seen turn away earlier. He was gone. She'd only seen him for a second, anyway. It probably didn't mean anything.

Gus was talking to one of the uniforms under the streetlight. She'd almost reached the Volvo when he turned and gave a cool nod in her direction. As if he hadn't been chowing down turkey potpie at her kitchen table a couple of hours ago.

Her hand on the Volvo door handle, she gave a polite nod back. He strolled over.

"We've got to stop meeting like this," he said. Snowflakes glittered on his eyelashes. He smiled, his blue eyes intent on her face. "What do you know about Maria Martinez?"

"Not much. I just took a kid home, that's all. His mother said there'd been a hit-and-run."

"And that's all you know?" he asked.

She stalled for time by opening the driver's side door and shoving Claudius to the back seat.

Gus waited.

Finally, she had to say something. "I never met the dead woman. Someone told me she was Rocky's sister. It's just a weird coincidence."

"I don't believe in coincidences."

"You already told me that."

"So I did. Well, I don't like having to repeat myself, so if you know anything else about this, you'd better tell me now."

She felt her face growing hot. He was treating her as if she'd been driving the hit-and-run, for heaven's sake.

"If you want to examine my car, you can get a warrant," she said haughtily.

Gus appeared to be enjoying their sparring. His lips twitched. "Maybe that's just what I'll do."

"Fine, go right ahead!" She climbed into the Volvo and started the engine up with a roar while Claudius put in his two cents' worth. "Quiet!" she ordered.

One look at her and he stopped barking.

Gus tapped his knuckles on the window. She cracked it a scant inch. "What is it now?"

"Who were you visiting?"

"Mrs. Chavez. I took her son home."

"You're sure you didn't know Maria Martinez?"

"*Yes*. Is that all? Can I go now, *sir?*"

He raised an eyebrow. "Touchy, are we?"

That didn't deserve an answer.

He shrugged, now seemingly intense and preoccupied. His interest had shifted back to the ambulance, which was pulling away from the curb. "Well, I know where to find you."

She snapped the car into drive and swung off down the street. That's it. She'd had it. He didn't deserve the time of day.

She started home on autopilot.

Forget the blue eyes and broad shoulders. Forget the husky voice, that elite accent, that air of old money somewhere in his background. He was just another policeman, and he didn't believe in coincidence. Neither did she, but there was always the possibility that just this once . . .

Goss Lane was snow-covered and slippery. It was dark, with no streetlights. As a money-saving ploy a few years back, the town had turned them off. Residents complained, but got nowhere. It was still as dark as a pit.

Maria's death could have been accidental. Some teenaged kid with more testosterone than sense could have nailed her and sped off.

Stuff like that happened all the time.

But suppose Rocky's and Maria's deaths were connected? His career as a petty thief could have earned him a deadly enemy. His boss at the tire place or a drug dealer someplace. Rocky had had fingers in a lot of pies. Annie had heard stories of people disappearing—that girl last year, for example. Rumor had it she'd been on drugs and owed her dealer. Unable to pay, she'd been stashed in a downtown Manchester construction site—in the foundation of a bank. It was all just rumor—but the girl hadn't been seen since.

Suppose Rocky was murdered. Suppose it had nothing to do with his being a petty thief, and there was no psychotic killer who'd shoved him in the lake for his own crazy reasons. What if Rocky had made some powerful people mad, and they'd murdered him, then his sister. But that didn't make sense, unless Maria had known something and they were afraid she'd talk.

Joey's mother had said Maria needed money.

Feeling a little sick, Annie drove on. It had been an exhausting day, and her conscience assailed her. Maybe she should have told Gus about Maria's financial troubles. No, he didn't deserve her help. Anyway, cops were relentless. He'd check Maria's background and find out all he needed to know.

Headlights appeared in Annie's rearview mirror and stayed there for several blocks. She turned a corner, hit a red light, and braked. The car behind her slowed to a stop, the motor idling.

Her imagination went into warp speed. Was she being followed? What if whoever killed Rocky and Maria knew she'd been asking about him? What if they'd been watching her, what if she was in danger? Had she put Joey and his mother in jeopardy, too?

Come on, get real, she told herself. Lee wasn't a hotbed of ruthless murderers. Okay, there'd been a few in the past—but the law of averages said Rocky and his poor sister dying like that was just one of those things.

The image of Maria's body being loaded into the ambulance flashed through her mind, followed by an abrupt memory of Rocky, sodden and dead.

A mile later, the headlights were still there, and Claudius had picked up on Annie's nervousness and was staring out the back window, growling.

She tried to tell herself it was someone going home who simply happened to live in her part of town. With no success. Okay, look on the bright side. The driver of that car had no idea she had a former police dog with her. Presumably, if it was Rocky's killer, or Maria's for that matter, he'd try and force her off the road, make it look like another unfortunate accident. Well, she wasn't going to make it easy.

She made sure all the doors were locked, then took the next left onto Harris Road. There wasn't much traffic at this time of night. Unfortunately, the headlights hung on behind her. Just ahead the road curved right. She was going too fast and hit the brakes just in time, then saw with a shock that the road was blocked by a fallen tree. Broken branches littered the snow.

What could she do? The car following would be upon her in a moment. But just there on the right was Golden Run Road, a shortcut home. Ordinarily, during the winter, she didn't use this route. Golden Run was narrow, winding, and almost all downhill. Thickly wooded on both sides, it remained icy and treacherous until late March. The town selectmen had limited the use of ice-melting chemicals and salt on side roads. As a result, Golden Run was basically a death trap.

She took it anyway. There was nothing else she could do.

Claudius swung his head toward her and let out a questioning growl. He knew a bad road when he saw it. The plow had made a cursory pass hours ago, one way. Snow had fallen since then. There was one line of tire tracks visible through the windshield—maybe one car had made it without ending up in a ditch.

"We're fine, trust me," Annie told him, shifting into first and keeping a steady foot on the accelerator. "I know what I'm doing."

He gave a huff of disbelief and lay down on the front seat without further comment.

Well, she couldn't go back now. It was too late to change her mind, and she'd forgotten to recharge her cell phone. She had no choice but to keep driving straight ahead.

The rearview mirror went momentarily dark, and she

prayed it would stay that way. Maybe the car had turned around and headed back toward Goss Lane. There was probably nothing to worry about, anyway.

It was very quiet, only the thrum of the engine and wind whipping falling snow into drifts. Annie didn't dare take her hand off the wheel to turn on the CD player, though she could have used a little soothing jazz, especially Ella Fitzgerald.

In the heavy silence, she knew without glancing in the mirror that something was wrong. A ghostly light flashed some distance behind her. Damn. That car. It had to be the same one.

Hands gripping the wheel, Annie felt the Volvo slither sideways, fishtailing. Wonderful. Why hadn't she turned around when she'd had the chance? The driver of the other car was probably perfectly innocent. She was getting paranoid.

But why was the car following her? When he'd seen the fallen tree, why hadn't he simply turned around and gone back to town over the main road?

She eyed Claudius—her protection, if and when he felt like remembering his training.

Snow was piling up on the windshield. Heaps of it. The wipers struggled, flapping slowly back and forth.

Claudius growled again.

"Look, we could do without the attitude," she snapped. "I'm doing the best I can under trying circumstances. Give me some support here."

No answer. Well, what did she expect? She gripped the wheel with a new sense of urgency. The headlights had grown larger in the mirror.

Snow-covered trees flashed by on either side. A few

houses were located well off the road, without lights. Sane people were safely tucked up in bed by now, not driving around in a blizzard.

The weather report that morning had lied. Snow showers, clearing by midday. Right.

The road beyond the Volvo's headlights stretched gloomily into the snow-driven night. A sharp left-hand bend, and Annie went careening along beneath low-growing trees. Then a small miracle as the rearview mirror went dark. Maybe she could get to the end of the road and lose her tracker.

But the car picked up speed, and seconds later, the mirror threw a reflected glare in her face.

They passed a plunging, narrow waterfall frequented in summer by picnickers and hikers. In January, the sound of falling water was a dull roar. Another curve, with huge maples too close to the shoulder. Scenic in autumn, blazing red and orange, but now they were just something she might slam into.

Despite her fear that whoever was following might take it into his head to ram her, she hit the brake and slowed to fifteen miles per hour, desperately looking for a house with lights, someone to answer the door and let her use the phone.

Beneath six inches of fresh snow, the road was deeply rutted. The wheels bumped and slipped in and out of potholes as the road dipped sharply downward. The headlights were larger now, not more than thirty or forty feet away.

She peered through the snowy windshield and flipped her lights on high. High didn't help. She went back to low beams. If the visibility improved, she'd try going faster. Her hands were sweaty inside her gloves.

God, she wished she had a weapon. Claudius qualified on that count, but who knew what he would do when they stopped? He might take it into his head to run away if he caught the scent of something interesting, a deer or fox. When and if he ever came back, she'd probably be stone-cold dead.

She shivered, thinking of what it would be like to be trapped here in the dark. Who was she kidding—she *was* trapped, and it was as dark as the inside of a mine.

More snow blew in blinding sheets. The road disappeared; even the ruts were gone. It was desolate, a no-man's-land, a frozen, alien world. She said a prayer of thanks that the Volvo's engine wasn't acting up and carefully guided the car around banks of drifted snow, nearly skidding into a big oak tree. She braked, missed the oak by the grace of God, heaved a deep breath, and drove on. As far as she could see, not more than fifteen feet straight ahead, it was sheer white. No gradations, no shading that could be someone's driveway. Just white.

Exactly what today's horoscope had warned about. White was definitely unlucky, and she'd tempted the fates by sticking her nose into other people's business.

Wondering how long she could keep it up, she pushed forward. At least she had plenty of gas, thanks to Sam McIntyre . . . oh, no, that funny engine sound she'd dismissed last week as just a dirty carburetor had returned. A stutter, almost. A hiccup.

She frowned, thoughts running around in her mind like squirrels in a cage. Maybe it wasn't the carburetor. In fact, she suspected she didn't even have a carburetor. No, the

Volvo had a stupid computer, which was always screwed up and costing her two hundred bucks a whack to fix. Progress was wonderful.

Claudius lay beside her, quiet, nose pressed up against her side. She suspected he might be making his peace with God. He didn't stir when she patted his head.

"We'll be fine, boy. Just a little longer."

The headlights behind them loomed larger, and suddenly she was rammed. Nudged, really, bumper to bumper. Then he dropped back. The Volvo lurched and slid toward the right shoulder. More trees, dozens of them, jumped in front of her windshield. She shrieked and yanked the wheel hard left.

God, she was panicking. No, she wasn't. She just wished Cary were here. Cary would know what to do, but Elkhorn was a long way across town, the other side of the world.

Headlights filled the mirror again, and this time she was hit so hard that her head bumped the roof. Claudius stood up and barked. The fur on the back of his neck went rigid. He meant business.

"Good boy," she whispered.

The Volvo inched slowly around the trees and slithered back onto the road. She recognized that last big maple. She'd almost hit it last summer and jokingly called it "the death tree."

It wasn't funny now. For some reason, her own headlights seemed dimmer—they were probably covered with snow. It was darker, or maybe it was just that she was terrified out of her wits.

She had a horrible vision of the Volvo crashing, windshield shattering, her body crushed and slumped over the wheel. Claudius wounded or dead, maybe finished off by the man in the other car. Shot in the head—the coup de grâce.

The thought of that happening to Claudius was enough to renew Annie's determination to get home alive. She forced herself to look in the mirror again. The headlights had dropped back. Maybe he hadn't meant to hit her. Maybe his tires were worn, bald . . .

The headlights brightened. The bastard had turned on his high beams. The forlorn hope that this was all a mistake vanished, and she knew. He was giving himself a flying start. This time when he rammed her there'd be no way to stay in control.

She was so tired. Would the cops know her death wasn't an accident, or would they write her off as one more casualty of the storm? Gus Jackson would forget her in a week or two. She'd become someone he once knew. Life would go on.

She'd never subscribed to the adage "an eye for an eye," but the bastard in the other car had made her mad. If she could have figured out some way to get even, she would have. A bazooka would be helpful.

White-faced, she hunched over the wheel and hit the accelerator. The Volvo leaped forward, and the headlights behind her faded a little. She'd taken him by surprise. Good.

She thought hard. Golden Run Road didn't go on forever, and she'd been driving for quite a while. A few more curves, another sharp downhill stretch, and then the stop sign at the bottom. Sugar Road. If she made it that far, she could take a left and, hopefully, drive down the road until she was out of sight. A right on Sugar Road would eventually bring her onto the main road.

She had a feeling the bastard would think she'd turn right. Any sensible person would head that way, especially a frightened woman whose car had been rammed . . . which was why she planned to turn left.

She picked up speed and gained precious seconds as the headlights behind her disappeared. Her confidence increased. Two more curves, always heading downhill as fast as she dared. Then the stop sign. She didn't stop, but veered left, hard. Now the straightaway, fifty, one hundred yards. This road saw more traffic, so there were tire tracks in the snow, thank God.

She made it around a big curve, saw a narrow road leading off into the woods, and pulled in. She switched off the engine and lights and sat very still, not breathing. She'd have given anything to have been back home at the tavern.

She put her arms around Claudius and hugged him hard.

Probably, she decided later, she sat huddled in the dark for only ten or fifteen minutes. When she decided it was safe to go, she backed out slowly, half expecting to see him in the mirror at any moment.

She drove home, roared up the driveway, and scoped out the yard. No one had followed them. No strange cars. Nobody with a baseball bat or a gun hiding in the bushes by the back door. She let herself in and turned the bolt. The click was loud in the silent house.

No messages on the answering machine. No one had called, wondering where she was all this time.

Claudius stayed by her side, as if he understood they'd escaped a close call with death. When she went upstairs, he followed like a shadow.

Everything looked the same when she turned on the lights and went through every room. Nothing was out of place; no one was hiding in the closets.

She undressed and went to the bathroom to brush her teeth. Her face stared back at her in the mirror, filthy with black streaks where her mascara had run. She didn't remember crying.

The bedroom curtain rings rattled as she yanked them shut. Her fingers trembled. She was ashamed of herself. Anger, simmering all this time, popped to the surface. She was a coward. She should have thought of something to do other than running like a scared rabbit, but the attack had been so sudden. He'd thrown her off balance.

Next time she'd be prepared. Not that there'd be a next time.

The headlights had been set higher than normal and annoyingly bright, even the low beams. Maybe it had been a truck.

That, at least, was something, a clue. She could call Gus Jackson and tell him she'd been rammed by a truck on Golden Run Road. Someone had tried to kill her.

She reached for the phone, her hand hesitating in the air.

Would he believe her? She could hear him now, all cool and authoritative. "Oh, come now," he'd say. "It's a bad night to be out. The roads are all but impassable by this time. Icy as hell. Besides, Golden Run is the worst road in town. Someone probably ran into you by mistake. Chalk it up to experience and stay off the back roads until spring."

What proof did she have? A few new scrapes on her rear bumper, that's all. Since the Volvo was an eleven-year-old rattletrap, it already had more than its share of dings and dents.

She let her hand fall. Calling the cops wouldn't do any good. They wouldn't appreciate having to come out to take her statement. She could call in the morning if she felt like it. It wouldn't make any difference.

She climbed into bed and pulled up the covers. Claudius dispensed with any pretense of sleeping on the floor and jumped up beside her. For once she didn't scold him.

Okay, sleep. She closed her eyes tight and listened to herself hyperventilating.

Stop it.

This was silly. She was tired. She needed sleep. But all she did was stare at the ceiling. Minutes passed. Claudius made himself comfortable by taking more than his fair share of the bed. She turned over and decided she wasn't going to fall asleep no matter how hard she tried.

She groped in the dark for the TV remote on the bedside table and flipped on the set. Animal Planet, a program on cats. A black-and-gray striped tabby stalked a mouse.

Claudius woke up and eyed the screen.

A man's voice explained that cats were natural hunters. The striped cat proved it by ripping the head off the mouse and eating it. The rest of the mouse jerked around disgustingly.

Claudius yawned.

Annie flipped off the TV. With determination, she

closed her eyes and let a wave of fatigue wash over her. In minutes she fell into a restless sleep.

She dreamed she was at Fox Hill School. The portrait of Patience Wyndham Barnes stood before her, and somehow she'd stepped into the picture just as if it were real. Patience was being led to the gallows tree. Her dress was ripped and dirtied, her face sallow from weeks of incarceration. Two men in Puritan hats held her by each arm.

Patience said, "Have the courage to do what is right." She repeated this line and stared straight at Annie. It was a warning. Then, as Patience stopped speaking and the noose was lowered around her neck, she disappeared. Annie was in another place. It was dark. A man whose face she couldn't see was holding a candle and standing next to a casket. She was afraid to look, but he gestured her forward, his eyes glowing orange. She gazed into the casket.

Patience lay there, the noose still around her decaying neck. Even as Annie watched, the face disintegrated, mold forming, maggots wriggling, flesh dissolving. The skull was exposed with bits of hair still attached. The overpowering stench of death rose all around and choked her.

Nauseated, she backed away.

The man with the candle pointed to a second casket. It was empty, but she knew it was hers.

She woke up, sweating, disoriented, tangled in the covers, which were all but wrapped around her neck.

The next morning, a hot shower brought Annie back to life. Patience's words returned to her as she was scrubbing her legs: *Have the courage to do what is right.*

She dried off and pulled on wool slacks and a heavy

sweater. Outside, the snow had stopped but the thermometer by the window said it was below freezing.

Claudius gulped his usual breakfast while she made do with coffee and a muffin. It wasn't until they were outside in the bright morning air that she began to feel like herself again. On the chance that she might stop at Fox Hill, she put the wrapped quilt in the back of the Volvo, then let Claudius into the front seat and paused as the snowplow roared down the road in a cloud of flying snow. At least the roads were clear.

Her first stop was the police station. Why call on the phone and listen to a disengaged voice on the other end when she could look some officer in the eye and tell her story face-to-face.

She drove straight there and pulled into a spot reserved for the handicapped. Well, why not. There was no one else around and the sign was covered with snow, anyway. The station was located on the ground floor of an old Victorian building. Upstairs was the town hall, where guest speakers held forth on whatever subject took their fancy. The town held an annual mixed-bag lecture series: authors, a puppet theater troupe, folksingers, and storytellers.

Downstairs it was all business. The tax collector, dog officer, and through the side door with the blue light outside, the police station.

She brought Claudius along. As the door closed behind them, cutting off the winter chill, she let out a slow breath. They stood in a narrow hallway. To the right a flight of stairs led to the second-floor auditorium. To the left was a waist-high counter with bullet-proof glass. On the other side, the female dispatch officer slouched in front of a computer. A mug of coffee steamed at her elbow. She typed in a few lines and gazed laconically at Annie.

"Can I help you?"

"Is Gus Jackson around?"

"Hey, Charlie, is Gus around?"

A faint "no" echoed from down the hall.

"He's out. You want to see someone else? Officer Choate is on duty."

Annie decided it wouldn't hurt to talk to Officer Choate.

She was ushered into a small back room. Officer Choate was young and good-looking, but not enough to distract her. He offered her a chair and coffee. She sat, but declined the coffee with thanks.

He listened quietly and wrote everything down as she told him about last night's wild ride home. Even to her own ears she sounded like a walking, talking nutcase.

She'd been followed and rammed by another car, except she couldn't prove it. He might have slid into her by accident, the road being treacherous and ice-covered. No, she didn't have another witness to the alleged rammings. Except Claudius, and his word wouldn't stand up in court.

Officer Choate grinned and sipped his coffee. He made a face and put the mug down. "Too much sweetener. Now then, what about the make of the car?"

"It might have been a truck or an SUV. The headlights were sort of high up, even when he lowered them."

"High . . . up. Maybe . . . a . . . truck or SUV." He wrote that down. "Could've been kids driving around, raising hell. A lot of kids get their kicks scaring people on the road."

He put his pen down again and said he'd file the report.

They'd let her know if they came up with anything. Then he suggested she go on home.

She was angry, but kept it under control. It wasn't his fault she didn't have a more convincing story to tell. Still, she hated being patronized.

He ushered her to the door, more to make sure she left, she suspected, than from small-town politeness. When he saw where she'd parked, he wrote out a ticket.

"Why am I getting a ticket?" she demanded.

"You parked in a handicapped space. There's a twenty-five-dollar fine."

"Great. You're more concerned about a snow-covered sign than the fact that I was chased all over town last night and damn near killed." She stuffed the ticket in her pocket and glared at him.

"I told you, Ms. O'Hara, there's nothing we can do without some leads. As for the handicapped sign, you've been here before; you should know that space is here. It's the law."

She had no choice but to leave. Claudius wasn't offended. Far from it, he'd oozed slavish affection all over Officer Choate.

Annie gave him a sour look as he jumped up on the front seat. Cary's grandfather wasn't the only one who'd won a medal. So had Claudius. According to the citation for bravery that he'd received, he'd been patrolling the prison wall. Snow had been driving down, and a dangerous felon had crept across the yard with a sheet over his head, invisible to the guard up in the tower. But Claudius had padded silently after the crook and taken him down with one lunge just as he'd been about to scale the wall.

They'd given Claudius a well-deserved medal of

honor. The accusation that Claudius was arrogant and hardheaded, which had culminated a short while later in his separation from the service, was something she preferred not to dwell on.

She eased the Volvo out of the parking lot, ignored Officer Choate's cheery wave from the station steps, and headed for Dover. She'd had an idea: Joey's schooling, or lack of it, was bothering her. She decided to stop at Fox Hill and pick up a brochure and scholarship application. The school had classes from third to twelfth grades. With any luck she might persuade Joey's mother to let him board. He was smart, but if he started running the streets, he'd be lost. She knew this as surely as she knew her own name.

He wore the uniform of the streets, his self-image already of the criminal class: studded leather bracelet, dog chain around his neck, oversized watch that he'd probably shoplifted, baseball cap turned backwards, hundred-and-fifty-dollar sneakers and jailing pants, baggy around the ankles to make it look as if he had no belt. It was a wonder he could walk at all.

She had a feeling of having accomplished something positive when she arrived at the school and ten minutes later, having dropped off the quilt, emerged from the administration building, application and brochure in hand.

With any luck, she'd have no trouble convincing Joey's mother that he couldn't afford to pass up a chance like this. The school had plenty of money. The applications officer had said they looked for children like Joey, bright, motivated. With a promise of "We'd be delighted to see him anytime" ringing in her ears, Annie emerged into the cold morning sunlight.

She wasn't sure about Joey's reaction to the news, but it was the chance of a lifetime. At first he might be apprehensive, but with a little persuasion, she was almost certain he'd come around.

She had no trouble recalling the afternoon years ago when she'd arrived for her own interview. She'd been so nervous. She'd thought she'd never get in. The kids she'd seen walking on campus had looked as if they came from wealthy families. How surprised she'd been to learn that many were there on scholarship.

Prepared to leave, she noticed Wyndham Hall on the corner. It might be worth a visit, just to see that portrait of Patience. At the very least, it might put her nightmares to rest.

A couple of teenaged boys emerged from the building. Shouts echoed as they tossed snowballs at each other.

Annie pulled the Volvo into the side lot and sat watching for a minute. The kids were of many different races—more so than when she'd been a student—and they looked as if they led charmed lives, with the right clothes, doting parents, prep school, then college and careers ahead of them.

They looked happy . . . as she'd been happy here twenty years ago.

She had to wonder if Joey would fit in. The last thing she wanted was to make him miserable, but he was just a kid. His mother would make the final decision.

Annie and Claudius walked up to Wyndham Hall. The original portion had been built in 1690, with additions made through the years. A carriage house stood at the end of the curving driveway, with a big red barn out back.

January sunsets turned the snow-covered fields pink, and herds of deer routinely grazed at the edge of the woods.

The hanging oak still stood by the front door.

Annie went inside.

You couldn't miss the portrait over the fireplace. Patience, gray-faced in death, stood before a large oak tree. A black cat curled around her ankles, and a noose dangled from the branch over her head. The legend beneath told the story: "Patience Barnes, daughter of Elijah Wyndham, head of the Supreme Judicial Court. She was arrested in 1710 for the murder of her husband, Joshua Barnes. She was tried, convicted, and hanged, July 7, 1710."

Patience had been in her early twenties when she died. What a waste, Annie thought, and wondered if she'd really been guilty.

Her second thought was that this was one murder Cary hadn't mentioned including in her book, although she could probably whip up an engrossing if blood-curdling account of the goings-on back in 1710. It was a really good murder—two, if you counted Patience's execution. It had everything. A beautiful woman, money, power, witchcraft. Rich old man poisoned by his wife. It would sell.

And Cary could conduct a tour of the very place where Patience had been incarcerated, tried, and hanged. With the permission of the school authorities, she could exploit Patience's story for all it was worth.

Annie knew there were other houses like this one in Lee. Old houses like the Thurston Tavern, which had been part of the Underground Railroad. The Tory house on the green was the site of a Presbyterian minister's death in 1775. He was shot by angry militiamen—he hadn't answered fast enough when asked if he was joining the revolution.

Then there were the private tragedies—people who'd committed suicide for one reason or another, like that farmer who'd shot himself after killing his wife and her lover several years ago.

She sighed and decided she had enough on her plate, what with Rocky's and Maria's deaths, without worrying about past crimes.

She drove back to Lee, stopping at Burger King for a couple of Whoppers and large fries. Claudius chowed down contentedly, had a quick walk around the parking lot, and they headed for Goss Lane.

Few reminders of Maria Martinez's death remained. The plows had been up and down the road several times. Kids played outdoors, building snowmen, having fights. She pulled up in front of Joey's house.

A beat-up Chevy was parked in the driveway. It had been there last night too. Maybe it was Joey's mother's.

Annie got out, told Claudius to stay, and walked up the front steps. She rang the bell.

Mrs. Chavez opened the door. "Yes? What do you want?"

"Could I talk to you for a minute?" Annie produced the brochure and application. "Is Joey around?"

"He went to the store."

"I've got something that might interest you." She was ushered inside with reluctance, but when she explained to Mrs. Chavez what she had in mind, the woman nodded.

"That would be wonderful. I can't always get him off to school on time. I gotta work or we don't eat. Joey's a smart kid, maybe too smart for his own good. I'm afraid of what he'll get into one of these days." She shrugged. "Maria Martinez dying like that makes you think. One minute she's alive, next she's dead. That could've been Joey. He's always running across the street without looking." She read the brochure and frowned. "This school looks awful expensive. You sure they'd find scholarship money for Joey?"

"Let's fill out the application, take him for an interview, and see what happens."

CHAPTER
7

When she got home, Annie called Fox Hill and set up Joey's interview for the next day at three p.m. He'd get a tour of the school, an interview, and have a chance to check out the place.

It occurred to her that Joey might have to be talked into going along with her plans. What if he didn't want to live away from home at a boarding school where he'd actually have to attend class? A pep talk was in order, and she hoped she could think of one that would work.

She dialed Mrs. Chavez and told her she'd pick him up at two-thirty, then phoned O'Connell's Funeral Parlor and said she'd drop by later to pick up Rocky Martinez's clothes. Specifically, a leather jacket.

The man at the other end, one Henry Spelling, said he'd just been hired and didn't know the procedure for picking up the deceased's effects. He said he'd pass her message on to Mr. O'Connell.

Annie said fine, she'd be over later, hung up, and went upstairs to make sure the front bedroom looked okay. A couple had booked for the coming weekend. She smoothed the bedspread and plumped up the pillows.

That done, she opened the shop at ten a.m., as usual.

Business was brisk—she'd hung out her January sale sign. By two o'clock, she'd sold a hooked rug, a school slate, and early leather-bound books, one printed by Benjamin Franklin's brother, as well as some transfer-painted creamware with an amusing satire: The pitcher depicted a rake's inevitable progress to the gutter, and the two mugs bore scenes of marital discord.

Just after one o'clock, Fred Ogilvie arrived with a truckload of country furniture and "smalls." He was one of several "pickers" who cruised around rural New England, picking up odds and ends to resell to area antique dealers. Today he had great stuff: a tavern table with original paint; six mismatched chairs; a child's chair with the original rush seat, blue paint, and well-scuffed front stretcher; and an old tavern sign that had come from Nashua, New Hampshire.

Best of all was a drop-leaf desk that was to die for.

It was pure country Queen Anne—brown-painted pine made to look like mahogany, with a deeply scalloped apron, tombstone arches over the pigeonholes, and carefully shaped drawers that fit the curve of the inner compartment.

The desk spoke to her. *Buy me.* She had to have it.

They dickered over price—Fred knew Annie was a sucker for painted furniture. Finally, she talked him down to a price she could afford, and he helped her move the desk into the tavern.

"Where'd you get it?" she asked.

"Oddly enough, right here in Lee. Someone found it stored up in a hayloft with a bunch of old junk. The owner said he thought it came originally from the Wyndham house up at Fox Hill School. Belonged to Patience Wyndham. You know, the witch."

Annie was intrigued. The desk might well be a family piece, and she had no intention of selling it. It fit beautifully right in her front hall beside the corner cupboard. With a sigh of delight, she hung an old sampler above it.

"Looks perfect," Fred said.

She smiled.

At approximately five-thirty, Cary picked up Annie in the Nissan. It was snowing again, the temperature just below freezing. They made the journey to O'Connell's in under five minutes, which was a good thing because the Nissan's heater was on the fritz. Cary hit it a few times to get the blower going, but you could still see your breath.

At this time of night, most of the traffic was headed in the other direction. O'Connell's Funeral Parlor was a mile outside the center of Lee. It had originally served as the rectory for a pastor to a small church, which had been destroyed by fire in 1870.

The house was large, ramshackle, and rambling, with formal viewing rooms downstairs. Tubby O'Connell lived upstairs, and the business end of things was conducted in the basement. A semicircular driveway led in from the street.

At five-forty, Cary pulled in at the funeral parlor and parked round back beside a silver Lexus.

Claudius, along for the ride, was told he'd have to stay in the Nissan—but not for long; they wouldn't be inside more than five or ten minutes. Cary was sure he couldn't get into trouble in that length of time.

He stood up in the back seat, then lay down again with a sigh.

Annie patted his head. "Good boy."

"He'll be fine," Cary said.

"He'd better be," Annie added darkly.

One small light burned by the back door at the rear of the funeral home. There was also an entrance with a ramp, for rolling caskets in and out, and to the left a three-car garage. Two doors were open. A hearse was parked inside.

They got out and, while Claudius watched from the car, his nose pressed to the window, they tried the back door beside the entrance with the ramp. It opened with a creak. They went inside.

The walls were painted gray. The floor was plain linoleum tile. In some ways it looked like the back hall in any large house, but it wasn't.

There were four doors in the hallway, plus a back stair to the right. As they hesitated, a door opened, and Tubby O'Connell emerged. He wore a rubber apron and gloves. A blue mask hung from his neck.

"I called earlier and spoke to Henry Spelling," Annie said. "About my friend's medal."

"Yes, I want it back," Cary waved the jacket's bill of sale as proof of ownership.

Tubby narrowed his eyes. "Why? It's not really worth anything."

"It was my grandfather's," Cary said. "Rocky Martinez stole it from me."

"Well," Tubby said dismissively, "I don't recall seeing it. Maybe the police have it."

It wasn't a very believable lie, considering that he'd already said it wasn't worth anything. Why would he want to keep it for himself? Maybe he planned to give it to someone else, although that seemed highly unlikely.

"Clothes are sent along with the body," Annie said. "You have Rocky, so you've got his effects."

"Ordinarily, that's so," Tubby began.

"Ordinarily, nothing," she snapped. "It's simple. Rocky's dead. He's here. Hand over the medal, and we'll be on our way."

"Yeah," Cary put in. "Are you the boss?"

"Yes, I'm the director. I take care of most of our clients. Normally my father would be helping, but these days he's retired. It's a small business. We handle mostly local trade."

"Rocky's sister, Maria, is probably here, too," Annie said.

"Yes." He stripped off his apron, gloves, and mask, tossing them on a nearby table, then pulled on his suit jacket. "As a matter of fact, she is here. Very sad. Yes, uh, Maria Martinez's boss, Armando Hernandez, a very generous gentleman, is taking care of the final expenses."

Son of a gun. Annie had seen Armando Hernandez mentioned in the paper and in the police log more than once. He was a pimp, which meant that Maria had probably been, as they say, on the stroll.

She stared at Tubby. He stared back and smiled.

"What do you know," Cary said, looking around uneasily. "Um, where do you keep the . . . clients?"

"Downstairs," he said. "Were you interested in a casket for a loved one?"

"No, we just want the medal," Annie said.

Clearly disappointed, he led the way upstairs to the front hall. "We have a special plan that allows you to pay for final expenses in advance. Small monthly payments.

The price varies, of course, depending on the model casket chosen."

"Huh," Cary sniffed. "Sounds like a scam. Bad enough trying to come up with the gas bill every month, let alone pay for a casket you don't even need."

"Fortune smiles upon the wise," he said with dignity. "Those who buy early get a cut rate."

"How much?" Annie asked. Not that she was really interested, but you never knew.

"Twenty percent. You won't find a better deal anywhere."

"Too rich for my blood," Cary announced. "I'm gonna get cremated when the time comes. It's cheaper."

"Way cheaper," Annie agreed.

Tubby looked pained.

They'd reached the front hall, and Annie was peering into the viewing rooms. In the Sheffield Room vases of flowers were placed at either end of a casket by the far wall. Chairs were arranged in a semicircle, with a satin-striped settee off to one side, for the bereaved family.

A tag in the slot by the door read: Fred Marsh. Purple ribbons decorated the flower vases. A large wreath of carnations and roses bore a ribbon reading, "Farewell, Fred, from Bentley Auto. Have a good trip."

Annie shivered a little. Obviously, oil prices being what they were, Tubby had cranked the heat down.

Maybe corpses looked better cold, Annie found herself thinking. It wouldn't do for makeup to run, and once the viewing room filled with family and friends, things were bound to get warm. A wake would generate a lot of heat.

The tall case clock by the front entrance chimed six o'clock. The front door opened, and Fred Marsh's family

entered. Everyone wore black or dark blue. Several
elderly women looked as if they'd been weeping. The
others were mostly middle-aged or white-haired men,
who looked as if they'd taken a few snorts of the hair of
the dog to keep out of the night air.

Tubby stepped forward and got busy greeting the
Marsh family, while Annie made a discreet check of the
other viewing rooms. Three more wakes tonight. Flemming's, Lally's, and Kemp's. Tags were up next to all four
viewing rooms. Business was booming.

"Would you care to sign the Marsh guest book?" Tubby
asked unctuously. The question was meant for Fred's
nearest and dearest, but Cary grabbed the pen and dashed
off her flowing signature.

"You didn't even know Fred Marsh," Annie whispered.

"It'll make the family feel good if they get a lot of sig-
natures."

"Please. They'll see a strange woman's name and think
he was fooling around."

"Too late. I already signed." Cary handed the pen to a
middle-aged woman who eyed her with dark suspicion.

More people came in. Annie could see Tubby out of the
corner of her eye. He looked as if he had his hands full, so
she hustled Cary down the back stairs. "There's got to be
a room where someone does the makeup. Tubby wouldn't
want anyone to see."

At the bottom of the stairs Cary looked around. "Where
do we go now?"

Annie wondered what Tubby had been doing when
they'd arrived. He'd come out of that room just ahead.

It wasn't locked. Inside, a woman was bent over an
open casket. She looked around and frowned. It was

Yolanda, the office manager/assistant from LaKeisha's Salon of Beauty. Short and caramel-skinned, she had a well-earned reputation for having a bad temper. At the moment, to the casual eye, she looked fairly approachable. To anyone who knew her better, she looked menacing. Yolanda did not put up with frivolous interruptions. "What do you want?" she snapped.

"We're looking for Rocky Martinez," Annie said.

"Don't be touching nothing. I'm working on him. I'm almost done."

"Where are his clothes?"

"I don't mess with stuff that's none of my business. Talk to Tubby." Yolanda went back to dabbing Rocky's face with makeup.

Annie peered into the casket. Yolanda had arranged a white towel under Rocky's carefully coiffed head so she wouldn't mar the aqua-blue satin pillow.

Rocky was dressed conservatively in a dark gray suit, white shirt, and red-and-gray striped tie. His hands were crossed over his chest.

"What do you think?" Yolanda asked thoughtfully, stepping back to get a panoramic view. "Does he need more eyeshadow? You gotta be careful not to put on too much."

Cary took a quick glance. "He looks better than I do."

"Girl, you got a point," Yolanda said. "Your lashes need more definition. Try a gray or brown eyeshadow. Don't use blue. These days, only old ladies and 'ho's use blue."

"Thanks," Cary said.

Annie made a mental note about eyeshadow, then

cleared her throat. "Look, we need to locate Rocky's clothes. What he was wearing when he drowned."

"That's right," Cary said. "There was a medal on the jacket. It's mine."

"I told you, I don't mess with stuff that's none of my business," Yolanda retorted. She dabbed Rocky's cheeks again and touched up his eyebrows with a black pencil.

Annie heaved a tired sigh. This was taking all night. "Come on, where does Tubby keep the clothes?"

"I don't have time for this," Yolanda said loudly, sending her malevolent look. "Oh, all right. I've seen him stick the damn things in that closet." She gestured vaguely with the eyebrow pencil toward the far side of the large room.

The closet door was unlocked. Annie turned on the wall light and rummaged among the shelves full of brown and black plastic bags marked: Marsh, Flemming, Lally, Kemp, and lastly, Martinez. Congratulating herself, she opened Rocky's bag, and his belongings fell out: trousers, shirt, belt.

She dug to the bottom of the bag and produced the red sneakers and the bomber jacket, both much the worse for wear.

"You found the jacket—great!" Cary exclaimed. She turned it over, and there on the lapel gleamed an old World War II army good-conduct medal. "Thank goodness, here it is. Let's go." With deft fingers, she unhooked it and slipped it in her pocket.

"Let me see the jacket for a sec," Annie said. She searched the pockets and came up empty, then poked around down by the hem and felt something small and hard. A quarter probably. Cary had said there was a hole in one of the pockets.

When she pulled the hard thing out and unwrapped it from the damp cloth covering it, she discovered it was an antique miniature—a portrait of a young woman with green eyes and dark hair parted in the middle and pulled back in a tight bun. She had a cleft chin and looked intelligent. Good grief. Where could Rocky have gotten it?

She showed it to Cary, who looked mystified. "It's not mine. Must've been something Rocky stole. It looks valuable. Maybe there's a reward."

"Maybe. Let's stick around a little longer," Annie said, thinking hard. "I want to ask Yolanda something." She walked back to Yolanda, who was busy packing up her makeup kit.

"I was wondering about something," she said. "When you first started working on Rocky, did you see a bruise anywhere on his head, like in the back somewhere?"

"A bruise?" Yolanda wrinkled her brow. "Yeah, there was a place on the back of his head where the skin was broken. You can't see it the way he's laying now. I brushed his hair over the spot." Her eyes narrowed with suspicion. "Why'd you ask about the bruise? I didn't do anything to him!"

"I think someone hit him and dumped him in the lake."

"Get real. People die from accidents all the time. That lake is dangerous. The ice is always thinner out in the middle. Damn fool just fell, hit the back of his head, and drowned."

"The cops don't think so," Annie said soberly. "And his sister died in a hit-and-run accident last night. What are the odds of that happening?"

Yolanda bristled. "It ain't none of my business. I don't want to hear 'bout it."

"About one in a million," Annie informed her. "There's a murderer running around town. He's already killed two people, and I don't know why."

"Oh, well," Yolanda began, backpedaling like mad at the thought of being dragged into an ongoing police investigation. "I think I saw a bruise on the back of his head, but I wouldn't swear to it. I mean, it ain't something I could testify to in court."

"If it comes to that, you won't have a choice." Annie smiled.

Yolanda gaped at her, outrage and contempt oozing from every pore, and Annie made a mental note to patronize a different hairdresser in the future.

In the car on the way back to the tavern, she told Cary about being rammed on Golden Run Road.

"Well, what do you expect?" Cary said promptly. "It's your own fault. You got the murderer mad. You set the whole thing in motion."

"I did not!"

Claudius leaned his chin on Annie's shoulder and licked her ear, expressing canine support. Absently, she scratched his muzzle.

"Maybe the murderer connected you with Rocky," Cary went on thoughtfully. "You canvassed the neighborhood, asking questions. It could be he thought you were a threat. Maybe he read about Claudius in the paper. He thought you were onto him, so he tried to run you off Golden Run Road."

"Maybe," Annie admitted.

"Watch out, he could decide to try again." Cary glanced in the mirror and said nervously, "It's okay. Nobody behind us. Hey, this is kind of exciting. In a weird way."

"Sure, like playing with a pit viper," Annie muttered.

"You're not really scared, are you?"

"What do you think?" she snapped. "Of course I'm scared. How would you like it if somebody was after you?"

"Well, nothing happened. You're okay, thank goodness. Just be careful, and make sure you take Claudius along when you go anywhere."

Cary slowed at Annie's driveway and pulled the Nissan up by the carriage house. They got out and went inside.

The lights were on, Annie noticed with a sigh of relief. Kirk had arrived back from his trip.

They opened up a bottle of good red wine and celebrated his return. Kirk was a college professor who taught psychology and always had a sensible view of life. "Don't worry about things you can't affect," he often told her. "Don't make other people's problems yours."

Easier said than done.

Tonight he looked a little tired, but it wasn't that late, and he was willing to talk for a while.

"Thank goodness, the doctor is in," Cary said. "You won't believe what's happened. Annie might be mixed up in two murders."

"It could be a coincidence." Annie explained. "Rocky drowned, and then his sister was killed in what looked like a hit-and-run accident." She showed him the miniature she'd found in the bomber jacket pocket and went on to describe the events of the past few days: Claudius's running off, then her canvassing of the neighborhood with the flier after Cary's clothes had been stolen.

Kirk shrugged. "The miniature is clearly valuable. Take it down to the police station first thing in the morning and let them figure out who it belongs to. As for everything else, it sounds as if you were in the wrong place at the wrong time. If you two hadn't driven down Goss Lane when you did, you wouldn't have seen Rocky in the stolen jacket, and you wouldn't have gone door to door asking about him. If he was murdered, and there's still some doubt about that—"

"I don't think so," Annie insisted.

"Okay, let's assume it was murder," Kirk said. "No one in his right mind would kill someone because some woman was asking if he'd been seen with her lost dog."

The dog in question, who'd made himself comfortable at Kirk's feet, grunted his agreement.

"Still, you might be wrong," Annie said stubbornly.

Kirk put down his glass of wine. "I don't think so. Listen, not to change the subject, but my sister, Leah, is driving up from New Haven. She's at Yale, doing her thesis on landscape architecture on New England's old graveyards. She plans to research Lee and several other New Hampshire towns. She should be here in a day or two. Would you mind putting her up for a week or so?"

"Of course not," Annie said and thought for a moment. "I wonder if she'd be interested in the Wyndham family graveyard. It has a peculiar history."

"Such as?" Kirk asked.

"It's missing," Annie said. "Somehow in the past hundred years, the gravestones were removed. People forgot where it was located. If Leah did some research, maybe she could find it."

Kirk nodded. "That would be great for her thesis."

Cary glanced at her watch. "It's getting late. I've got to go. Listen, thanks for everything tonight. I'm so glad to get the medal back. It means a lot to me. I don't have anything else from that side of the family."

At the door, Cary remembered she hadn't paid Annie for sleuthing and dug sixty bucks from her wallet. "This will cover all your expenses, too. Right?"

"Right. Thanks." Annie nodded and shoved the money in her jeans pocket.

"If there's a reward for the miniature, we split it fifty-fifty, okay?"

"Okay."

The temperature was dropping to the low twenties. Everything was freezing hard outside, and Cary's footsteps across the snow-covered driveway sounded unnaturally loud and crunchy.

"Don't drive too fast," Annie yelled.

"Don't worry, I'll be careful." After clearing accumulated snow off the windshield, Cary jumped in and started her up. A cheery wave, and the Nissan disappeared down the road, red taillights winking out as it rounded the corner.

Annie closed the door and headed down the hallway. The only bright spot in the long day had been the Queen Anne desk. She gave it a satisfied pat in passing.

The telephone answering machine light was blinking. She pressed the button, and Sam McIntyre's Southern drawl emerged. "Annie, hope your car's running okay. I called because you left a glove at my house the other night. At least I think it's yours. Blue, with a white border. I'd like to drop by and return it, or better yet, maybe we could go out for dinner some night soon. Give me a call when you get in."

She looked up his number and dialed. When he answered, she said, "Hi, it's Annie. Sounds like my glove, all right." Even if it hadn't been, she'd have said it was. Just hearing Sam's warm voice was a tonic.

He laughed and said he'd been sitting there watching TV, thinking about her. Small world.

She imagined being curled up on his couch, engulfed in his warm embrace . . . but she was getting ahead of herself.

"I just had supper," he said. "A ham sandwich. We'll have to try that new Italian place out on River Road. How about tomorrow night?"

Annie hoped she sounded reasonably calm as she said, "Sounds terrific. Want me to pick you up?"

He laughed again. "No offense, but your Volvo's seen better days. I'd rather take my car. What if I come by around seven?"

"Great, see you then." She chatted a little more, then hung up feeling as if her entire day had just turned around. Silly, but he had that effect on her.

She wandered back to the kitchen, smiling.

Kirk was still there, yawning. "Promise me you'll drop that miniature off with the police in the morning."

"Okay."

"Good. So what's really got you scared?" he asked.

"Other than almost getting killed the other night?"

"Which could have been an accident."

"But it wasn't."

"You don't know that for sure. Don't borrow trouble. From what you've told me, you've got enough on your plate as it it. Anyway, things will look better in the morning. They always do." His voice was reassuring, but his face was grave.

Annie took Claudius and went up to bed, wondering if Kirk was right and the morning would bring a better day.

Unfortunately, it didn't.

CHAPTER
8

Annie's first suspicion that something was wrong came the next morning, when she saw the look on Kirk's face. He was outside, heading for the back door and frowning. He came in, closed the door behind him, and opened his jacket. "The snowblower won't start. I'll have to shovel out the driveway."

"Give me a minute, and I'll come out and help," Annie said.

He nodded. "Want me to take Claudius out?"

"Yeah, he'll enjoy it."

Claudius rushed to the back door and got his leash down off the wall hook before she could change her mind.

Ten minutes later they were shoveling like mad while Claudius ran around having the time of his life.

Methodically, Annie and Kirk worked their way down the driveway, shovelful by shovelful, piling snow on either side of the driveway and clearing an eight-foot-wide strip so they could get their cars out.

Kirk uncovered a Frisbee and tossed it a few times to Claudius, who leaped around, getting in the way, reveling in the icy snow and wind. After a time he dropped the

Frisbee by the back door and rolled around deliriously in the snow.

Annie and Kirk kept shoveling, scooping the heavy snow and throwing it to the side. The driveway slowly cleared. Every once in a while Annie stopped to stretch her aching back and blow on her numb fingers. She'd found a pair of gloves in a kitchen drawer, but they weren't as warm as the glove she'd left at Sam's. She'd be glad to get that back.

And glad to see Sam again, and listen to that wonderful deep drawl, that husky laugh.

"Annie, you all right?" Kirk asked.

She realized she'd been standing there daydreaming. She felt her face go red. "I was taking a break."

"Oh." Satisfied, he went back to work.

She shoveled a few feet more and frowned. The road looked as if it were a hundred yards away, although she knew it was more like ten or fifteen feet. The sun was out, although there wasn't much warmth. A cold easterly wind blew, picking up snow and swirling it in glittery drifts.

Annie felt as if she were frozen solid. She glanced at the back door and thought about a hot cup of tea, but reality was deferred for another ten minutes of back-breaking labor.

Finally they went back inside, and Kirk lit a fire in the kitchen hearth while Annie peeled off her jacket and kicked off her boots. This was the life. She'd sit there with her feet stretched toward the flames, damp socks steaming, until spring came or hell froze over, whichever came first.

Slowly but surely she thawed out.

Claudius had been brought in, protesting but philosophical. He knew Annie would have to go out again. She wouldn't have shoveled the driveway otherwise. Well, she wasn't going anywhere without him. He lapped up about a gallon of water and lay down to wait.

The phone rang.

It was Mrs. Chavez. She said Joey wanted to talk to her.

"Yo, what's with this stupid school deal?" he demanded.

"You're going for an interview this afternoon," Annie said firmly.

"Why? What's in it for me?"

"A good education."

"Huh, like I really care."

"Your mother has a hard time making ends meet. If you're safe at school, she won't have to worry about you all the time."

"What if people at this school don't like me?"

"What's not to like? You're bright, a good kid. You can handle yourself." Cleverly, she appealed to his male ego.

"Damn right."

"Don't swear."

"Well, I can handle myself. I'm smart, too. Get mostly A's at school . . . when I go. Okay, I'll check the place out." He acted as if he were doing her a big favor.

Encouraged, Annie thanked him and said she wanted to speak to his mother.

When she came on, Mrs. Chavez said she'd have him dressed and ready to go at one-thirty. Was this okay?

"Fine," Annie said. "I'll have him home by four or so."

She hung up, and Kirk said, "First things first. You're taking the miniature to the police, remember?"

"In a minute. I'm just thawing out."

He tossed her jacket to her. "Do it now before you forget."

Grumbling, she pulled her boots back on, buttoned her jacket, and grabbed the miniature from the desk drawer where she'd put it for safekeeping.

Despite the new snow, the drive downtown to the police station took only a few minutes. The Volvo's heater had just warmed up as she pulled into the parking lot. She clambered out, slammed the door, and yelled through the glass at Claudius to stay where he was in the back seat—an order he obviously hadn't the least intention of obeying since he'd already made himself at home in the front seat.

"Get in the back!"

He didn't move. His eyes smiled.

She gave up and went into the station. When she explained how the miniature had come into her possession, the female dispatch officer—Officer Winifred Donnelly, short, blond, and sharp-eyed—handed her a manila envelope and a form to fill out. Annie scribbled the details, put the miniature in the envelope, and signed at the bottom.

"Who will handle this?" Annie asked.

Officer Donnelly didn't answer at once. She looked as if she were considering whether to answer at all. Finally, she said, "I'll see that Detective Jackson gets it."

"Which means exactly when?" Annie inquired.

"When he comes in."

With that Annie had to be satisfied. She scooped up her purse, nodded good-bye, and headed back to the car. As she opened the door, Claudius jumped into the back seat, sat down, and grinned.

She told him what a good boy he was and wondered why she had this feeling of having been had.

Later that afternoon, as she drove to Fox Hill School, Joey—unusually neat and clean, even his pants fit properly—grumbled, "This is a stupid waste of time. They'll think I'm a geek." But he cheered up some as Claudius licked his hand.

Pet therapy. It was a good thing she'd decided to bring Claudius along, Annie thought as she pulled into the parking lot. They got out and entered the administration building.

"The minute they tell me I'm not gettin' in," Joey said sourly, "I'm takin' off this stupid sweater. It itches."

The navy sweater served to cover his patched shirt. His mother had warned Annie not to let him take it off.

They sat down in the waiting room. A low table held brochures, *The Boston Globe*, and a glossy picture book of the school.

The headmaster's golden retriever wandered in, and Claudius merely yawned and closed his jaws with a snap. Whereupon the retriever beat a hasty retreat.

"It's a good thing that dog left," Joey whispered. "Claudius would've killed him dead."

"No," Annie said, "he's not like that."

"He used to be a police dog, right? They're trained to kill."

"Where'd you hear that?"

"I watch The Learning Channel. While I do homework," he added virtuously.

"Well, despite what you saw on TV, Claudius isn't a killer."

"Yeah? Then what good is he?"

She could tell by the way Joey scanned the office and the dean of admission's office door that he was extremely nervous.

"Everything will go just fine," Annie said. "Mrs. Adams, the dean of admissions, is looking forward to meeting you."

"Sure," Joey said gloomily. He kicked his worn boots on the parquet floor. "Look at this place. They got megabucks, big time. Why would they want me?"

"You have a lot to offer. You're bright, intelligent. You have personality and enough energy to light up the whole state. They're lucky you're even considering Fox Hill. Don't be scared."

"I ain't scared!" He swallowed. "Okay, so maybe I am a little." He eyed his feet, where a puddle of melted snow had formed on the floor. Finally, he said, "I changed my mind. They can't stand me, I can't stand them. I ain't goin' through with this."

Just then, thank goodness, Mrs. Adams emerged from her office, smiling and saying she was sorry for the delay.

They all went into her office. Annie and Claudius stayed for fifteen minutes or so, then left Joey alone with Mrs. Adams.

In the waiting room again, Annie read the paper, not really taking in the details of the latest police log. With her peripheral vision, she noticed Claudius sniffing the contents of the basket on the table.

"Don't even think about it."

With a sigh, he sat down on his haunches.

Annie patted his head. Something was working—her firm tone of voice, no doubt.

"You're my dog, so start acting like it."

His large ears twitched. He yawned. He looked at the office door and whined low in his throat.

"He'll come out soon. You like Joey, I can tell." She patted his head again. "Good boy."

Ten minutes passed. As they sat, waiting, she hoped the interview wouldn't drag on much longer. How many questions could you ask a nine-year-old and expect intelligent answers? Longer than fifteen or twenty minutes would mean—what? That Joey was telling his whole life story, complete with amusing anecdotes about skipping school?

No, he had common sense. His mother must have told him what to say—or maybe not. A depressing thought.

Maybe, Annie conceded, she should have wised him up herself about how these things usually went.

Another ten minutes passed; then the door opened, and Mrs. Adams and Joey emerged. Mrs. Adams was smiling and had her arm around his shoulder.

A good sign? Annie hoped so. Then Mrs. Adams said, "I have several discretionary acceptances, and I've told Joey we'd be delighted to have him join the fourth grade here at Fox Hill as soon as possible. I gather his mother is working today and couldn't be here."

"Yes," Annie said.

"In that case, I'll send the rest of the paperwork home with Joey, and she can fill it out. We have a scholarship that will take care of tuition, books, room, and board. Also a stipend for clothing and incidentals. I've asked one of our fourth-grade boys, Tyler Moulton, to take Joey on a tour of the school—ah, here he is now."

On cue, a boy about Joey's age came through the front door and shuffled over to Mrs. Adams. "Hi," he said.

Annie was silently amused by his somewhat scruffy appearance. Freckle-faced, snub-nosed, he looked like a bumptious puppy. Mrs. Adams introduced the two boys, and they left on the two-dollar tour.

Annie took Claudius down the street to check out the Founders' display at the library, this being preferable to spending half an hour trudging through the snow around campus with two ten-year-olds. Besides, she could take notes for the brochure she'd been working on and talk to Molly Houghton about the miniature. If it was Patience Wyndham's portrait, Molly might know where it had come from.

As Annie entered the library with Claudius, Molly Houghton looked up in surprise from the papers she'd been sorting at a long wooden table.

"How are you? How's Claudius?" she asked.

"Fine," Annie said, smiling as Molly leaned down to shake his outstretched paw. "I heard you have an interesting Founders' display—I'd love to see it."

"Certainly. It's in the reference room." As Molly ushered them down the hall, they passed the massive staircase that curved upward toward the domed roof. A lovely old quilt had been hung over the banister. Annie glanced at it, taking in the faded colors and intricate stitching. She paused with Claudius at the foot of the stairs. Along the back wall, windows stretched from floor to ceiling and reflected her own image in the glass. Her expression was grave. She placed her hand on the balustrade; then, after a moment, she followed Molly to the reference room.

"In the far bookcase," Molly said, "we have a collection of books bequeathed by Stella Danforth. She taught senior English and died tragically last year in a fall. She was an example to everyone. She was well into her seventies, yet walked three miles a day and watched her diet. She looked years younger than you'd expect."

"How did she happen to fall down those stairs?" Annie asked.

Molly sighed. "It was a double tragedy. She was found at the bottom of the stairs about a week after the library had been broken into. It was so upsetting. At first there was talk that the two events might in some way be connected, but I can't see how that is possible. Stella Danforth was a very moral person. She'd never have had anything to do with the library robbery. In fact, Stella had helped to organize the display cases, and when the robbery was discovered, she was absolutely devastated."

"But her death was an accident?"

"Well, yes. She was getting on in years. It could have been a stroke. I'm afraid I don't really know. That sounds awful, but I was upset, and reading all the grisly details in the newspaper wouldn't bring her back."

That last statement seemed to close the subject. Molly's face assumed a shuttered expression, and Annie nodded.

"As a matter of fact," she said, "I happened to come across a miniature the other day. A portrait of a young woman with dark hair. I didn't know the owner, so I gave it to the police."

Molly frowned. "One of the stolen items was a miniature of Patience Wyndham. The police have a complete description of everything. If by some miracle you found our miniature, we'll be informed. Wouldn't that be wonderful!" Her face brightened. "Where did you find it?"

"It's a long, complicated story," Annie said, preferring not to go into detail. "It turned up at the funeral home, in Rocky Martinez's jacket pocket."

"My goodness," Molly said. "I don't know what to say."

She was, Annie noticed, watching her steadily and thinking hard.

"Well," Molly said, "let's hope it *is* our miniature." She glanced at her watch. "Actually, I have to make a phone call. Why don't you look around? I'll be back in a few minutes." Not waiting for an answer, she rushed off down the hall.

Annie's initial impulse was to follow Molly to see what she was up to. Was she making a phone call about the miniature to her husband, Carl? Even if that were the case, it was hardly an admission of guilt in the robbery or Rocky's death. Upon reflection, Annie decided to stay where she was and wait for Molly to return.

Various paintings and photographs of the school through the years hung on the walls, while underneath, glass cases displayed objects associated with Fox Hill's history. Elijah Wyndham's kid gloves, his top hat and cane. A book printed in 1865, the headmaster's admonition to tardy students in 1737: "Anyy students arriving after morning prayers and the tardy bell will be required to run around the perimeter of the school grounds, approximately one and one half miles, thrice before the noone bell."

There was also a list of students who'd joined the revolutionary army and died. Annie got out a notebook and pen and started taking notes.

The nearest case contained an 1854 list of infractions sure to earn the unfortunate miscreant suspension if not expulsion from school: alcoholic drinks, cheating, consorting with bad companions in the town . . .

There was also an interesting clipping from the *Boston Spy*, the newspaper of the day: "A British soldier, Lt. Lloyd Montague Digby, recently stricken with the poxxe, perished due to the perilous nature of his fatal disease." His body had been transported as far as possible from Boston, to be buried in Indian territory.

According to a hoary school legend, the soldier had been buried in the field beyond the cow pasture. There was no marker on the grave, but generations of Fox Hill boys believed the very spot lay beneath the lilac hedge near the science building.

Each spring, the lilac hedge bloomed with wondrously fragrant flowers. The hedge had never needed fertilizer. Indeed, it required extensive trimming.

Annie moved to the second glass case. Here were more possessions of the Wyndham family: antique pewter utensils alongside a small oaken chest dated 1679, handblown glassware, a few pieces of jewelry, and an empty space with a card indicating that a gold brooch and a miniature belonging to Patience Wyndham had been stolen during the previous year.

Annie reread the card. It didn't describe the miniature, but every instinct said the one she'd found had to be the missing portrait. Miniatures were valuable. They didn't come on the antique market very often. What were the odds of two different miniatures coincidentally being stolen or otherwise misplaced and turning up again?

It didn't make sense. The one she'd found in Rocky's pocket had to be the one missing from this case.

Probably Rocky had yielded to overwhelming temptation and stolen it.

Why had he held on to it for so long? A year later, and he'd still had it in his possession. Had he had problems fencing it? Well, antique dealers and auction houses were warned about various items that had been stolen around New England. Presumably, the brooch and miniature were on the current list. That she didn't recall reading about it didn't mean anything. She could easily have missed it.

A thought occurred to her: There was a big antique show in Peterborough this weekend . . . and Moose had said Rocky planned to be in Peterborough! Maybe Rocky planned to try to sell it there—which would explain its presence in his pocket.

With a sense of having come close to the truth, Annie continued browsing the display cases.

Across the room, she noticed a leather-bound copy of the school history, privately printed in 1949 by the board of trustees. It contained old photographs and interesting faces of long-ago students. She flipped through the volume and came across an engrossing account of the hurricane of 1938. South Lee and Fox Hill School had suffered great damage.

She replaced the book on the shelf and examined the other display cases: a butterfly collection, shells, birds' nests and eggs, bequeathed to the school in 1890 by Ethan Francis Webster.

On a nearby wall was a sampler stitched by Patience

herself. Some of her cooking receipts were displayed in the case below: One for roasting eel and one for roasting lobster. "Strech ye lobser & tey it upon ye spit a live & if you do not wash it before you spit it you must do it after wt water and solt. Yn set a plate uner to catch ye gravey and bast it with eather butter or clarid & put ye gravey to best butter for ye sauce. Let it be prety thicke & send it on a plate by it self. A large one will take a qutr of an houre."

The bookcase to the left was locked. According to the list on the door, it contained first editions, first folios, and assorted rare volumes.

The top row held sixteen calf-bound volumes, with the same number on the middle row.

It was overwarm in the library. Annie put away her notebook, yawned, and decided she might take a nap when she got home—after all, she had a dinner date tonight.

She reread the list of books. A very old King James Bible, Henry James, Dickens, Wordsworth, all first editions, signed, notated, valuable.

It seemed careless to leave books worth a small fortune lying around with only a tiny brass lock to prevent their theft. Molly Houghton was very trusting and naive. Or maybe they had a great security system. Annie wondered if it had been in working order when the miniature and brooch were stolen.

A loud bang—the library front door opening—announced Joey and Tyler's arrival. They rushed in, laughing and stomping snow from their feet.

Annie turned with a smile. "Hi, ready to go?"

"I'm gonna be in Tyler's dorm," Joey cried. "Same floor, too!"

Patiently, she listened to him enthusing about Fox Hill. It was cool, way cool. They'd had donuts and apple cider in the cafeteria, where a real chef presided over the cooking.

"Wow!" she said.

"I had three donuts," Joey confided. "Chocolate with cream inside."

Tyler nodded. "I had French crullers." He burped. "Sorry, gotta go. Hockey practice."

They went outside, and while Tyler slogged off toward the ice rink, they piled in the car and headed home. Joey babbled about Fox Hill, the fun they'd had, and how the kids were pretty much okay. Then, as they neared Goss Lane, he fell silent.

"What's wrong?" she asked.

"I like it there, but it's, uh, kind of ritzy. What if I don't fit in?"

She noticed he hadn't expressed any reservations about his ability to do the schoolwork.

"You'll fit in fine," she said and talked for a few minutes about her own experiences at the school as a student on a scholarship grant. "My family didn't have much money. My brother was at Fox Hill on a scholarship, too. He played varsity lacrosse and had lots of fun."

"Yeah, well, I ain't wearin' geeky clothes."

"Nobody's asking you to." Usually he dressed Goss Lane style. Presumably, Fox Hill would change that.

She took him inside, and Mrs. Chavez made tea while Joey stomped off to his room to change.

"Do you think he's happy?" Mrs. Chavez asked. "Maybe I'm not doing the right thing. We're not in the same class as those people."

"My brother and I both went there on scholarships," Annie said. "We didn't have much money, but it didn't matter. We did all right. Tom graduated and went to M.I.T., and I went to the University of New Hampshire."

Claudius gave a low woof and sat down by the door.

She picked up his leash. "Okay, you win. Time to go home."

In the car, he flopped on the front seat with an air of complete exhaustion—he'd put in a hard day's work.

Annie patted his head absently. For good or ill, Joey was going to Fox Hill. With luck he'd achieve his potential and go on to college. With his drive and intelligence, there was no limit to what he could achieve.

The sky was darkening to black, stars were twinkling through the trees, and a gusting wind blew snow on the windshield as Annie drove home. Her teeth were chattering, and it took forever to get the heater going. Claudius's body warmth as he leaned his head on her lap was a blessing.

Ten minutes later the heater was asthmatically wheezing lukewarm air, Claudius was snoring, her leg was numb, and she pulled up the driveway. What a relief to drive straight in without getting stuck in snow.

All that shoveling had been worth it. Not like that awful winter three years ago, when people had repeatedly slid into her snowbank and stayed there. She'd had to call a tow truck for one couple from Rhode Island who'd booked Astronomy Weekend—distant galaxies, nebulae, Saturn's rings, and Jupiter's moons on display through the telescope up in the cupola.

Two hundred dollars per couple: two nights lodging,

two breakfasts, Friday and Saturday dinners, plus Sunday brunch and a fifty-dollar refund if clouds spoiled the view.

New Hampshire winters meant snow and ice, and Annie had learned the hard way to stockpile sand and salt near the barn. By spring, it was always gone.

But tonight Sam McIntyre was coming. She had a date. She smiled in anticipation. She would spend a few hours with an eligible bachelor, enjoying a meal someone else had cooked. It sounded like bliss.

Breathing deeply of the cold night air, she tried to damp down her feelings of excitement. It was just a dinner date, for heaven's sake. He was good-looking and single, but so what. Half the appeal was that blackstrap-molasses accent of his.

Lights were on in the kitchen—Kirk was home. She let herself and Claudius in and closed the door. It smelled like Kirk was busy making supper.

"Mushroom pizza?" he called.

"Nope, I've got a date."

"Anyone I know?"

"I don't think so. Sam McIntyre, an EMT. Teaches part-time at Fox Hill School—rock climbing, mountaineering."

"The outdoor type." Kirk grinned from the doorway. "And how is he, romantically speaking?"

"It's the first time we've gone out, but he seems really nice."

Kirk thumped pizza crust on the bread board, and Claudius ambled in and leaned against his leg.

"How are you, boy?" Kirk gave him a quick scratch between the ears and glanced over at Annie. "What happened with the miniature?"

"I dropped it off at the police station. They didn't call, did they?"

"Not since I've been home, and there's nothing on the answering machine. I heard from Leah. She'll be here tomorrow."

"Wonderful!" Annie said, smiling. She was looking forward to meeting Kirk's sister. If she was anything like her brother, she'd be very interesting, indeed.

Kirk grinned and went back to making pizza.

An hour later, when Sam rang the bell, Annie shot downstairs and opened the door. She'd been ready for a good half hour.

It was too cold for anything but pants, though she'd thought twice about it. Her legs weren't bad. Still, there was no sense freezing to death, and besides, casual was better. No point in scaring him off.

She'd pulled on wool pants and a nice wool sweater. Blue, embroidered with snowflakes. On sale from Lands' End and a steal at twenty-nine-ninety-five.

"You look nice," Sam said. It was pure flattery, but she ate it up. He could have called her ugly in that delicious drawl, and she'd still have loved it.

They were on the main road to town, and already Annie's thoughts were occupied with later on, perhaps a romantic clinch or two at the tavern's back door. She'd ask him in, and then . . . no, not on the first date. No sense in rushing things.

Sam mentioned that he was in the mood for Italian food. What about Annie?

"Sounds good," she said.

His mouth widened into a beguiling, crooked smile.

She relaxed and really began to enjoy herself.

Mario's was a small restaurant located just past the main drag. Sam pulled around back and parked. They went inside. At that time of night, still early, Mario's was only half full. In another hour, there'd be more than a dozen patrons waiting for tables.

The zucchini-and-mushroom pie and arugula salad were delicious.

Annie sipped red wine and felt every bone in her body warm with delight. She glanced at Sam, who'd dropped his napkin and bent to pick it up. "You're into climbing? I noticed photographs at your house," she said.

"I've been climbing for years," he said, placing his napkin on his lap. "Expensive hobby, though. Like everything else, you pay your dues and work your way up. Lone Peak, American Fork Twins, McKinley. I got a chance to do some climbing in the Alps a few years ago when my army reserve unit was sent to Europe. I'd like to tackle the Himalayas, Everest, and mountains in South America someday, but we'll see." He looked up with a smile. "So what do you do for fun?"

She thought about that. "I'm writing a brochure for Fox Hill," she said. "They'd like to have it ready for Founders Day in May." It sounded feeble compared to conquering walls of stone and ice.

"You have lots of time, then."

"I don't know about that. I have the inn to run and an antique business, too. What about you? Seen any good plays lately? Boston usually has something worth a trip. A revival or Andrew Lloyd Webber's latest?"

A forkful of salad halfway to his mouth, he paused and gave her a long look. "Afraid not. I go into Boston every few months on business. I was there last fall. Then again a week ago, but it was in and out. Sometimes I take a run to Vermont or down to Rhode Island, but I don't like to leave my mother alone too long. The Alzheimer's, you know. She forgets to take her medication."

"Oh."

"What about you? Anything exciting going on in your life?" When she didn't answer right away, he continued, "Did you hear that the sister of the man who drowned in the lake was involved in a hit-and-run the other night? She died of a fractured skull. Her head was cracked open like an eggshell. I wasn't on call, though." His dark eyes probed.

"I did hear about it, and it's terrible. But let's not talk about it now, okay?"

Why discuss violent death in the middle of a romantic date?

Whether they were appropriate or not, Sam's questions were understandable. His job as an EMT afforded him a practical view of life and death, so it had to be routine to him. She was probably lucky he hadn't launched into a technical discussion of Maria's fatal injuries.

Annie ate her zucchini-and-mushroom pie, wondering a little at the somber tone the evening had taken. All of a sudden she was tired and felt deflated.

It wasn't really Sam's fault, but what had happened to that delightful champagne fizz of half an hour ago?

She grasped for something interesting to talk about. "I found an antique miniature that might be part of that robbery at Fox Hill School last year."

"You're not serious," Sam said, giving her a sharp look.

"No, it's true."

"Where is it . . . do you still have it?"

She shook her head. "I gave it to the police. It might be stolen property."

. "You're right," he said. "But how did you find it?"

"Antique dealers see a lot of things," she said, sidestepping his question. "We have to keep up with lists of stolen property printed in trade newspapers."

They ate in silence for another few minutes before he said, "How long have you had Claudius?"

"Just a few months, why?"

"You don't see a woman with a dog like that every day. Big, tough to handle. How'd you happen to get him?"

"His former owner couldn't keep him. He needed a home." She didn't want to spoil a wonderful evening by even thinking about her former sister-in-law, Lydia.

"So you adopted him?"

"It was one of those things. I got involved."

"I read something about him in the paper a few months ago," Sam said. "Didn't he catch a murderer?"

She put down her fork with a sigh. Candles, music, great food, and who were they talking about? Claudius.

"He's a police dog, but he's been socialized."

"So he doesn't bite?" Sam raised an eyebrow.

"Only criminals."

"How does he decide who's bad and who's good?"

"He's smart."

Sam sipped his wine. "A dog that size is a big responsibility. You can't just let him run around loose."

"It's not like owning a chihuahua," she admitted. In fact, she'd spent long hours daydreaming about just that—owning a small dog that didn't eat you out of house and home. A dog that wasn't smarter than you were. A biddable dog, lovable, cuddly . . .

"You've had a few problems with him?"

A few?

She helped herself to garlic bread. "I'm still learning how to handle him."

"Oh, right. Didn't I see a poster recently—"

"Yes, he was missing. I suspect he caught the scent of a female dog in heat. I can't prove it, but that's probably why he took off. Nothing else makes sense. The sex drive is so strong, they'll follow a bitch in heat for miles. Luckily, someone spotted him going inside their barn, and I got him back."

He nodded. "A friend of mine adopted a poodle named Trixie about a year ago. She came into heat. Drove him nuts. There was a battle royal every time he took her outdoors. I thought I'd seen everything, but you wouldn't believe it. He couldn't take her out to do her business without a dozen dogs trying to jump her."

"That must have been awful."

Sam chuckled. "I sound like I hate dogs . . . but what I'm really trying to say is that it was tough."

"Must have been," she agreed. "But there are things your friend could try next time Trixie comes into heat. He could have her spayed, or if he's thinking of breeding her, there are products that mask the scent—"

"That's an idea," Sam said thoughtfully. "He might want to breed her, and he likes walking her in the street."

Where, no doubt, the poodle peed on every snowbank, advertising to one and all that she was ready, willing, and able.

Annie began to wonder about Sam's friend's common sense.

She cleared her throat. "About climbing. Are you planning another trip anytime soon?"

"No, it takes considerable funds and months of preparation. Maybe next year."

"Sounds exciting."

He chuckled. "Spending summer vacations freezing your tail off at eleven thousand feet with seventy pounds of food, camping gear, climbing ropes, helmets, crampons, ice axes, and other winter gear for survival on your back? It helps to be a little crazy."

"How did you get into climbing?"

"When I was a kid, my dad and I hiked the Wasatch Mountains in Utah. Then we did some climbing in Wyoming's Wind River Range. I had to learn it all, extreme weather survival, glacier travel skills, crevasses, ice walls. That lit my fire."

Their conversation grew desultory after that. It was almost ten o'clock. They drank coffee, and Sam's face was shadowed in the candle glow. She admired his thick, curling lashes and his firm jawline. She wondered what he was thinking. Years of climbing had given him a great physique, with no trace of fat. His shirt stretched across broad shoulders, accentuating the strong muscles beneath.

He had strong hands, she thought. Nails clipped short, no rings . . .

"Shall we go?" he asked.

They drove back to the tavern in companionable silence. After they pulled up the driveway and stopped, he turned off the ignition and gave her a brooding look.

She reached for the door handle, and his warm breath

fanned her cheek as he stretched across to stop her. "Wait. I'd like to see you again. Soon."

"That would be nice," she got out huskily.

"Good." His voice was low, and at the look in his eyes, she felt as if she couldn't breathe. He still hadn't moved back, and his detaining arm pressed hard across her midriff, the sleeve of his jacket brushing her breast.

His mouth was inches from hers, and she had an almost overpowering urge to kiss him. After all, what could it hurt? They were both consenting adults.

Reaching up, she slid a hand around his warm neck and pulled him close. His mouth was warm, hard, and sweet.

Ten minutes later, when he walked her to the back door, her knees were weak and her senses were spinning.

CHAPTER

9

The red answering machine button was blinking when Annie went inside. It was Gus Jackson. Would she call him when she got in. It was more of a demand than a question. So what else was new where Gus was concerned?

She dumped her purse and looked up his number. Two rings, and he said, "Jackson here."

"Annie O'Hara. You called me?" She sat on the stairs and kicked off her boots. Claudius wandered down the hall and sniffed them to see where she'd been and what she'd been up to. Seeing no doggie bag, he trotted back to the kitchen.

"You dropped off a miniature at the station with some cockamamie story about how you found it."

"That's right," she said. "Although that's not exactly how I'd have phrased it."

"Finding the damn thing in a corpse's pocket is a little peculiar, you'd have to admit," he snapped. "Do you honestly expect me to buy that story?"

"It happens to be the truth. My friend Cary was with me when I found it. I put her name and address down in my statement. Call her if you don't believe me."

"I already did," he admitted. "She backs you up."

She let a second or two pass, then said, "Is it the minia-ture stolen from the Fox Hill School in last year's rob-bery?"

"Yes, but that's not the only reason I called."

"Oh? What else did you want?"

"An explanation for the complaint you filed at the sta-tion the other day. I wish I'd been there; unfortunately, I was busy."

"So they said." Silence.

"Well, let's have it. What happened?"

"Nothing much. I was rammed on the way home the other night. That's all."

"What, another car slid into yours?"

"No, the other guy deliberately rammed me. I'm lucky I'm still in one piece. I could have ended up like Maria Martinez."

"Please. Your Volvo's a tank. You weren't in any dan-ger."

"That's a relief," she told him. "I feel so much better."

"Don't get nasty. Did you get a look at the other driver?"

"No." She peeled off her jacket. "It was dark."

"Have you driven anyone beside me crazy lately—to the point that they might want to see you dead?"

"No." Well, except Lenny-the-jerk, her ex. She hadn't heard from him in months, and actually, the last time they'd been in touch, he hadn't called in person. Instead, New England Mountain, formerly Bell Atlantic, even more formerly Ma Bell, had sent her a bill for nine hun-dred dollars. Someone had been jaunting around Ten-nessee making lots of long-distance calls. Annie had never been to Tennessee, which she'd told the phone company. Lenny-the-jerk was a big country-music fan. No doubt he'd jetted down to Nashville to take in the sights and sounds of Ole Opry and charged half a zillion calls to her number.

The phone company had hemmed and hawed, said they'd look into things—but could she see her way clear to pay the bill in the meantime?

She'd told them no and returned their dunning notices.

As far as she knew, New England Mountain hadn't caught up with Lenny, so he had no reason to be mad at her. Besides, Lenny wasn't the violent type. He was just a sleaze.

"Have there been any other incidents?" Gus asked. The question was routine. He was going through the motions and didn't expect her to say yes.

"Like what? Car wrecks? No. And before you ask, yes, I look in the rearview mirror all the time, and so far I haven't seen anything suspicious."

"Well, that puts what happened into context. Relax, it was an accident or kids raising hell."

"Oh, right. Like Maria's accident, I suppose."

She heard a blender going in the background along with a loud burst of rock music. His voice muffled, he said, "Hey, put the lid on—it's going all over the kitchen—and turn that damn radio down! Clean up the mess when you're done!" Gus had company. His nephew, Mike, she guessed. Ha ha.

"Oh, dear, am I keeping you?" she asked.

"No." He sighed. "Mike's here."

"Spending the night?" She could almost hear him grind his teeth.

"Just for a few days, then he's moving to a new dorm. He's driving me crazy."

"Hey, I was just thinking," she said. "While we're on the subject, anything new about the hit-and-run?"

"No, and do me a favor. Stay out of police business from now on, and that includes the Fox Hill School robbery."

"I have every right to ask questions." Who did he think he was—God?

"Don't give me that. I've got enough to deal with without you poking around, playing detective."

"If that's all, I'm hanging up," she snapped.

"No, wait! I have a favor to ask. It's Mike. He's . . . well, he's not doing well in history. He has a big project due in two weeks, and I wondered if you'd be willing to help him with it."

"What's the project about?"

"He has a choice, actually. Seventeenth-century New Hampshire life or Fox Hill School during that time. What life was like for students, that sort of thing. Mike's a good kid, Annie. I'd appreciate it if you'd give him a hand."

Put like that, how could she refuse?

"All right. I'm working on a brochure that might have some bearing on his project. Why don't I talk to him about it?"

"Sure. Wait a sec." Gus's voice faded, and she heard him put the receiver down.

Moments later, a younger male voice spoke in her ear. "Annie? My uncle said you'd, uh, help out with my history project."

"It's Mike, right?"

"Yeah, Mike Rawlings, and I sure could use some help. The teacher's a hard marker. You'd be saving my life."

"Why don't you come over tomorrow afternoon after school? Maybe your uncle can give you a lift. We can discuss the project and come up with something really impressive."

"Great! I'm done around two, so I'll be there by two-thirty. Okay?"

"Sure, see you then." She hung up. As soon as she did, she wondered what she was getting herself into. Oh, well. Mike's project would probably be fun. Maybe the rough draft for the brochure would spark his creative genie.

She locked up the tavern and went upstairs to bed. In the morning, she was occupied with last-minute cleaning and baking. Kirk's sister, Leah, was due to arrive sometime in the afternoon, and on Friday Sophie and Rex Farraday, from Newton, Massachusetts, were expected for the grand Astronomy Weekend. The weather predictions were good: clear, cold, and no cloud cover, indicating a fine weekend for stargazing.

January nights in Lee, New Hampshire, were something special. Far from city light pollution, Lee was nestled in a secluded valley. Stars shone so bright, you could almost reach up and touch them.

After enjoying a cup of tea and a bowl of vegetable soup, Annie realized it was time to open the shop, so she unlocked the carriage house door and let herself in.

Claudius trailed behind her, looking positively glum. She noticed his dragging tail and decided he was bored. Well, maybe Mike's visit later on would cheer him up.

Annie booted up the computer and started work on the Fox Hill brochure. It would be interesting if she could actually find the old Wyndham family graveyard with Leah's help. Hopefully, she'd think it worthwhile investigating and include it in her thesis, and Mike could take photographs and get some extra credit for his history class.

Annie told Claudius the plan, although he didn't seem in the least interested. He yawned and stretched out for a nap.

Customers stopped by and browsed, and the January sale went well. By the time Annie was ready to close, she'd sold several hooked rugs, a Rockinghamware Toby jug, an octagon bird's-eye maple sewing box, and a pine corner cupboard.

She'd just locked up the shop and gone back to the house when a yellow VW Bug with Connecticut plates pulled in, a tall young woman with curly brown hair at the wheel. Annie opened the back door and called out, "Hello, you must be Leah. I'm Annie O'Hara. Welcome to Thurston Tavern."

Half in and out of the car, Leah extricated herself and her backpack, and waved. A few moments later, she stepped into the kitchen and looked around. "Wow, what a house! It's charming—"

Claudius sniffed her shoes and wagged his tail.

"That's some dog," Leah said, edging away slightly.

"Claudius is a sweetheart once you get to know him," Annie explained. "If you let him ride in your car, he'll be your friend for life."

Leah's face brightened. "Oh, Kirk told me about him. He's a retired police dog."

"Yes." Annie winced inwardly, wondering if "retired"

was quite the word for Claudius's permanent separation from the police force.

Leah set her backpack down on the floor. "You wouldn't have a cup of tea handy, would you? I haven't eaten anything since breakfast."

Annie made a pot of tea and a roast beef sandwich, and set them on the table before Leah. Her eyes, Annie saw, were sharp and intelligent, besides being bright blue. And she had the Deitrich family straight nose.

Over tea, they discussed Kirk's and Leah's choices of career. From the courses Leah described taking over the past year and a half, Annie realized that landscape architects had to know a lot more than how to choose foundation plants and where to put a driveway.

Leah finished her sandwich, but still looked hungry, so Annie fetched a loaf of carrot cake from the refrigerator. "Eat."

"Real cream-cheese frosting," Leah said. "I'm in heaven."

"Did Kirk mention anything about a missing graveyard when he spoke to you last night?" Annie asked. What if Leah wasn't interested in the Wyndham cemetery? If so, Annie decided, she'd look for it on her own. If she did manage to locate it, it would be perfect for the school brochure. And if she didn't, well, the research would still be interesting.

As it turned out, Leah *was* enthusiastic about locating the graveyard. "Many old New England cemeteries have been sadly neglected," she said. "In the past, they used marble—a soft stone. It cracks and doesn't weather well. After the Civil War, we see a lot of granite being used. Metal markers, especially for veterans, came into vogue in the past century. I gather that's not the case with the Wyndham's?"

"No," Annie said. "This cemetery goes back well before the 1860s, to 1690 or so. Evidence suggests it might be somewhere on Powderhouse Road, at the Fox Hill School. That's where the old Wyndham house is."

"Sounds as if it would be right up my alley," Leah said. "Count me in." She was just finishing a second piece of carrot cake when Gus's car arrived.

With him was a boy—young man, Annie corrected herself. He was about seventeen, tall and angular, with blue eyes and a lot of thick, curly dark hair. He was dressed in jeans and a Fox Hill hockey jacket.

Claudius was already barking a loud greeting. Annie grabbed his collar with her free hand and let the visitors in.

"Annie," Gus said. "Mike."

Annie introduced Leah, who smiled. "Hi."

"Thanks for helping me," Mike said as Annie shook his hand.

Claudius sniffed him all over, wagged his rear end, and decided Mike was a friend, while Annie asked if they wanted a Coke, coffee, or hot chocolate with carrot cake, and motioned them toward the table. They both refused refreshment, and she joined them.

"Before we get started, I'd like to run some ideas by you," she said to Leah and Mike.

She told the long, involved story about how Patience had died, been buried, dug up again, and reburied. "Since the location of the Wyndham graveyard has been lost through the passing years," she said, "wouldn't finding it make a great idea for a project?"

Lean nodded agreement, Gus shrugged, and Mike said, "Yeah, that'd be pretty cool." He took a deep breath. "Think we could really find it?"

"The school library has old letters that describe the location in detail. If we put our heads together, I bet we could do it." Annie pushed her chair back and stood up. "I'm going to make hot chocolate after all. You guys sure you don't want anything? Cold drinks are in the fridge. Help yourselves."

Leah poured another cup of tea while Gus helped himself to a beer and handed Mike an orange soda.

Annie busied herself with the hot chocolate and returned to the table. "Okay," she said. "What we need to do is check out the letters in the library. Molly Houghton will help. Then we figure out the most likely locations. It's got to be somewhere on Powderhouse Road, probably not far from the church."

Leah nodded. "That makes sense. Family graveyards were often located near a church, if at all possible."

A gloomy look settled on Mike's face. He chewed a piece of carrot cake, then said with some reluctance, "Okay, but what about the snow?"

"I'll bring along a couple of shovels," Annie said briskly. He looked startled, and she went on, "Don't worry, this isn't an exhumation. We'll just dig around and see what we can find. I'm giving a talk to the senior English class on Monday. If you have some free time Monday afternoon, we could do it then." She looked at Leah. "Is Monday okay with you?"

"Fine," Leah said.

Mike nodded. "Okay, I'll be free. No problem."

Leah patted his arm. "Good. Be sure to bring your camera. We'll want shots of the actual search and whatever gravestones we turn up."

"And maybe I can talk a friend of mine into lending a helping hand," Annie said, thinking of Cary.

Mike ate more cake and said thoughtfully, "Maybe Mrs. Houghton will let me take shots of the letters in the library. I've got a digital camera and a scanner. I can run the pictures off with my computer. It'll be easy."

Annie brought out the rough draft of the brochure and the notes she'd been working on, and Leah quickly read them through. Soon they were deep in a discussion of seventeenth-century customs and the Wyndham family in particular. Time passed, and Gus got himself another beer.

While they continued talking, Gus leaned down to scratch Claudius behind the ears. Claudius rolled over and Gus rubbed his belly. The mutual admiration society continued for a time, then suddenly the dog jumped up and ran to the back door.

It opened, and Kirk Deitrich came in. Leah jumped up and hugged him as he shrugged off his jacket. "Great to see you," he said with a wide smile. "How was the drive up from New Haven?"

"Not bad," she said. "The turnpike's well plowed."

He leaned down and patted the dog on the head. "Hi, boy."

Annie didn't know where the time had flown. It was already dark outside, way past dinner time. She fed Claudius and said to Gus, "How about staying for supper? Steaks in five minutes."

Gus murmured something to the effect that they didn't mean to impose, but she assured him it was no bother and in moments had the table cleared of papers and notes.

Kirk had already taken Leah upstairs—she was to have the room next to his. When they returned to the kitchen minutes later, Mike was already setting out plates and cutlery. Gus fixed a salad, and Leah made the dressing while Kirk fired up the grill.

The steaks were superb. Gus asked for the name of the butcher or grocery where she'd bought them. The supermarket where he'd been shopping didn't have meat like that.

She told him about the market in Dover, where the butcher was willing to cut meat to order.

Mike and Kirk were talking about the Wyndham dorm and ghosts. Mike's face reddened as he admitted he was uneasy about staying there.

"If you haven't seen or felt anything peculiar, perhaps that's because there's nothing there," Kirk suggested.

Leah rolled her eyes. "A lot you know. I've been in graveyards—"

Mike shot her a worried glance. "Haunted graveyards?"

"Not really," Leah said. "I was just kidding."

"Sometimes people make up stories about old houses. Graveyards, too, for that matter," Kirk said quietly. "I wouldn't let it bother you."

For the past few minutes Gus had been silent. Annie caught him glancing from Kirk and Leah to Mike and saw a glint in his eyes as he reached some kind of conclusion.

"So far no one's seen any ghosts in the dorm," he said with a shrug. "Mike's worried about nothing. I told him he could stay at my cottage, but it's a mess. I'm renovating it." He glanced at Mike, who looked embarrassed. "Hey, you keep telling me how awful it is, but you knew the kitchen was torn up."

Mike applied himself to his steak and didn't say a word.

Kirk and Gus started discussing handyman projects and how to know if a task was beyond one's capabilities— the ethics of calling in a professional plumber or carpenter.

"Right," Gus said. He pushed his plate back. "Dinner was great."

Mike looked up guiltily. "Yeah, thanks for dinner. Uh, I guess maybe I'll go back to Wyndham after all. It'll be easier to do my research after class if I'm staying on campus."

There was a small silence, broken when Gus rose and put his plate by the sink. "I'll check and see if coffee's ready," he said, his voice sounding strained.

Belatedly, Annie realized he was trying not to laugh. "I'll help," she said and followed him over to the coffeemaker.

"Very clever," she whispered.

He shook his head. "You haven't lived until you've shared a cottage with a truckload of lumber and a teenager."

When he and Mike left, Claudius escorted them outside with a friendly woof and a wave of his tail. As they drove off, he came back inside and flopped on the rug by the stove with an air of having done his duty as the tavern greeter.

Annie and Leah loaded the dishwasher, while Kirk disappeared upstairs with a week's worth of exams to correct.

When the kitchen was tidy, Leah yawned and said the

long drive had tired her out. She was going to shower and head for bed.

Annie checked the doors, set the alarm for the night, and went up to bed, too.

In the morning, she drove downtown for milk and bread and noticed that signs had sprouted all over the town green, announcing nature talks at the library, some sort of folk song fest at the town hall, and lastly, a dog birthday party at the local pet shop. It seemed that Sunny, a yellow lab/husky, was two years old on Thursday. Everyone was invited.

"Today's the party. Want to go?" Annie asked Claudius, who yawned his disdain and glowered out the window at a little Yorkie being walked by his two owners.

For some reason known only to himself, Claudius decided not to alert the world to this invasion by one small dog.

Counting her lucky stars, Annie decided to celebrate by taking Claudius to the dog birthday party. She drove downtown to the strip mall where the pet shop was located right beside a small mom-and-pop store. She picked up bread and milk, stowed the plastic bag in the car, and took Claudius for a quick walk.

The original building had been two stories with a peaked roof, but wings had been added to accommodate a video store and the mom-and-pop grocery. The pet-store windows were plastered with advertisements for various dog and cat foods, and an announcement that a greyhound rescue showing was set for the next Saturday afternoon.

A signboard festooned with red and white balloons on the front walk welcomed one and all to Sunny's birthday party.

The parking lot was already half full.

"Just try and behave," Annie warned Claudius. "If you're a good boy, there'll be cake and treats."

His ears pricked at that, and they joined the throng of dogs and owners heading for the pet shop.

Nearby, a long-haired dachshund whose name tag said George was dragging his owner down the rows of cars. Several more car doors slammed. Two handsome yellow labs trotted by with name tags: Sam and Pearce.

Claudius sighed.

"Okay, so you don't have a name tag. Who knew? We'll get one inside."

She told him to *stay* as a little Yorkie trotted past, whereupon the owner shot a horrified look at Claudius and snatched up his dog. "It's all right, Jasmine. Daddy won't let that big dog eat you."

Even as he spoke, Claudius smirked and tried without success to look the perfect gentleman.

More dogs streamed toward the pet shop: several black labs, a golden retriever, and a happy-looking shepherd mix with a name tag that said Baron.

From the bored expression on Claudius's face, it was obvious that he'd already concluded they were all beneath his notice.

Sunny, wearing a party hat on his head and a red ribbon under his right ear, met them at the door. His entire body wagged with delight as Annie patted him.

"Happy birthday, boy." She scribbled Claudius's name on a stick-on tag, attached it to his collar, and then steered him around the milling crowd toward the table with the birthday cakes. There were two. Chocolate for people and turkey loaf for dogs.

It was a madhouse. More than a dozen dogs sniffed noses and tails, while the cash register behind the counter rang gaily as people bought collars, books, treats, and anything even vaguely related to the delights and responsibilities of owning a pooch.

Near the grooming room, a piñata had been hung from the ceiling. In due course, small children were blindfolded and took turns trying to break the papier mâché puppy with a long pole. Soon scores of dog treats showered the crowd.

Annie had a piece of cake and Claudius wolfed down some turkey loaf. He continued to be his usual confident self, aloof, superior, striding around without a care in the world.

At least two other dog owners expressed the strongest determination to keep their dogs as far away from him as possible—which Annie thought was unfair. Claudius hadn't even growled in their direction. In fact, anyone could see that he regarded himself as a dog of consequence who couldn't be expected to hobnob with lesser breeds.

Annie squared her shoulders and hauled him past a display of treats shaped like hapless mailmen off to the relative obscurity of the birdseed aisle. Before she knew it, she was eavesdropping on a conversation taking place on the far side of a line of hanging Droll Yankee feeders and assorted squirrel-proof contrivances.

"Is this any good?" a woman said.

Annie peered past a clear plastic feeder and saw Marnie Pearson, Fox Hill's French teacher. Marnie was a stuck-up bottle blonde with thick ankles and an attitude.

At the moment, she was holding a white tub of Canadian catnip. Evidently Marnie was a cat fancier.

"It says it's organically grown," Marnie added. "Sweetie has a sensitive stomach. I wouldn't like to give her anything too strong."

Pete Lanza, beside her, mumbled something to the effect that he didn't give a damn, and why didn't she make up her mind so they could go. There was something tense about the set of his shoulders and the way he'd shoved his hands into the pockets of his old army jacket.

Marnie suddenly noticed Annie on the other side of the bird feeders. "Oh," she said, "you gave me such a start. I didn't see you, and suddenly there you were." She gestured with the catnip. "Think this is any good?"

Annie shrugged. "I don't know. I'm not into catnip."

Something had upset Claudius—the fur on the back of his neck was stiff, and he was staring intently at a stack of cat carriers. Annie prayed Marnie hadn't brought Sweetie along for an afternoon's outing.

It seemed she hadn't, for after another moment, Claudius relaxed and Annie wondered what he'd been worried about. She ordered him to sit, and he obeyed at once.

Marnie turned her attention to a display of cat food. Rummaging around the shelf, she came up with two cans. "This isn't exactly cheap. I wonder if Sweetie would eat chopped veal. She throws up when I change brands, but—"

"Sweetie's a Persian," Pete told Annie.

"Oh."

Marnie replaced the cat food and dug into her purse. "I

have pictures of Sweetie that go way back to when she was a kitten. I bet you'd love to see them."

"Maybe she doesn't like cats," Pete said. "She's got a dog."

"I like cats," Annie protested. "I'd love to see your pictures." This was a big fat lie, but she had another reason for chatting with Marnie, who'd taught at Fox Hill for several years. She would have been there when the library was robbed and Stella Danforth died. All Annie had to do was get her talking.

Pete shook his head. "Don't say I didn't warn you."

Marnie produced a folder filled with Sweetie's snapshots. Sweetie, long-haired and fat, eating, sleeping, playing, looking annoyed—Marnie had obviously stalked the poor cat.

"In some of them she has red eyes, but that's just the photos," she explained. "Her eyes are really emerald green."

"My," Annie said admiringly. "Just like jewels."

"Yes." Marnie held up a picture of Sweetie snarling and cooed, "Isn't she beautiful?"

"My, she certainly is," Annie agreed. "Speaking of jewels, I heard that Fox Hill was robbed last year." Clumsy, but at the moment it was the best she could do.

Pete shrugged. "Yeah, thieves broke into the library and took some valuable odds and ends. Antiques, I think."

"Didn't that happen around the time Stella Danforth died?" Annie asked.

Marnie frowned. "A couple of weeks earlier, I think."

"Stella wasn't robbed, was she?" Annie probed.

"No, not that I know of." Marnie thought, then went

on, "She wasn't rich. Well, maybe she wore a few rings, but nothing special."

Annie nodded. "Did she usually carry a lot of money around with her?"

"You mean in her handbag?" Marnie asked. "Well, I don't know, but I wouldn't think so. If she had money, she didn't let on. In fact, she was rather stingy. Watched every penny. Stella was old. She just fell down the stairs. Old people fall all the time. It was an accident. If you're thinking she was robbed, you're wrong."

"I was," Annie admitted. "Not seriously, though."

"What made you mention Stella Danforth?" Marnie demanded suspiciously.

"Oh, you know how it is," Annie said airily. "People talk. I heard something about it the other day."

"Like what?"

"Oh, just that she might have had money. And that maybe her death wasn't an accident, but a robbery gone bad."

For a second, Marnie looked as if she didn't know quite what to make of this idea. Then she said, "Well, Stella didn't spend a lot on clothes. You can tell if something's tailor made. As far as I know, she didn't have anything worth stealing. Which, if she was pushed down the stairs during a robbery attempt, would rule out a casual thief. So . . . if she had something valuable and was murdered for it, it'd have to be someone who knew she had something worth stealing. Presumably, someone who knew her."

Pete didn't look convinced. "If you remember, Stella died during that big snowstorm we had last year. There was a terrible accident on the main road through town that night. It was blocked for hours. No one could get in or out. We had students stranded at Logan Airport down in Boston until the next morning."

Marnie gave him a long look. "So, what are you thinking?"

"Well . . . it's interesting," he said mildly.

"Yes," Annie agreed. "If Stella's death wasn't an accident, then the list of who could have done it narrows itself to the people at Fox Hill that day."

Marnie frowned and stuffed her cat pictures back into her purse. "You're forgetting the lake," she said. "Someone could have walked across the lake. It could have been anybody. A total stranger."

"Nonsense," Pete snapped. "This is all conjecture. Think how exposed a murderer would feel, walking across the lake. What time did Stella die—just before six o'clock, wasn't it? All those cottages overlook the lake; they turn their lights on at dusk. People glance out while they're having dinner. He'd have been taking a terrible risk."

Annie had already worked that out in her mind. "Not really. You're in a lighted room, looking out at a darkened lake. If you see anything, it's just a blur. You'd never be able to identify anyone." She paused, then added, "Just like Rocky Martinez, as a matter of fact. He went out on the ice and died."

Marnie's face had gone pale.

Pete shrugged. "This is all a crock. You don't have proof either one of them was murdered."

"But in both cases it would have been simple enough," Annie said flatly. "All the killer had to do was shove Stella down the stairs and take off. Rocky was even easier. He was lured onto the ice, then hit on the head, and drowned. It was dusk, almost dark, so even if the murderer was seen, he didn't have to worry."

During this conversation, Claudius, bored out of his mind, eyed the cake table, located just beyond the stack of motorized wind-up vermin guaranteed to drive any cat crazy. The store owner was handing out doggie bags, and Claudius wanted one. He sighed.

Annie looked from Marnie to Pete. "Who exactly was on campus the night Stella died?"

"Let's see," Pete began. "It happened on a Sunday. I remember because I'd just come back from skiing, and the snow was coming down really hard. I had trouble getting my car up Powderhouse Road. A couple of students had to give me a push. Most of the staff was already there, I'd guess. We had classes as usual Monday morning." He frowned and added, "Surely, you can't suspect us of having murdered Stella. Not Marnie or me, anyway. I went over to her place and stayed there all night."

Marnie glared at him. "Oh, sure. Blab it all over town, why don't you?"

"We had no reason to want to harm Stella," Pete continued, ignoring Marnie's outburst. "Or Rocky either, for that matter."

"Maybe, maybe not," Annie replied.

There was an awkward pause. Then Pete said, "Of course, anything we can do to help . . . I've read about you and your dog in the paper. You work with the cops."

Marnie's face went even paler.

"Once in a while," Annie said.

"Well." He took a deep breath. "I mean, anything we say is in the strictest confidence and off the record."

"That's right," Marnie put in firmly.

"I don't know," Annie said, exasperated. What good was it worming confessions out of suspects if you couldn't tell the cops?

Pete, busy mulling over the ramifications of a police grilling, had obviously come to the conclusion that this was to be avoided at all costs. "Look, we'd be willing to cooperate, but—"

"Speak for yourself!" Marnie exclaimed. "No way am I talking to the cops without a lawyer. *I didn't do anything!*"

"Gee," Annie said cheerily. "I'm in a very awkward position. I don't see what else—"

"Give me a break," Marnie snapped. She stared at Annie with fury in her heavily mascaraed eyes. Then, grabbing Pete's arm and with blond hair flying, she stomped off down the aisle and out the door.

With a sigh, Annie let herself be dragged to the cake table, where Claudius gleefully received his doggie bag. Most of the treats inside were biscuits of the chicken or beef variety, but some goodies were individually wrapped, and while she was disentangling the plastic wrap from what looked suspiciously like a chocolate kiss, but wasn't—chocolate being bad for dogs—a woman happened by with a springer spaniel.

She noticed what Claudius was chomping. "Heavens, I hope they're not real chocolate. Shadow ate fifteen last year, with the wrappers. He vomited up the foil, but I had to take him to the vet's to have his stomach pumped."

At the sound of his name, Shadow pricked up his ears and attempted to look noble.

Claudius, intent on gobbling the goodies, shot him a

look that seemed to say, I am your worst nightmare, while Annie wound the leash around her wrist a few more times. No sense in risking an incident—they wouldn't be invited back to Sunny's next birthday party.

Wasting no time, she marched Claudius back to the grooming corner, which at the moment seemed to be relatively dog-free.

Claudius spent the next few minutes sniffing around for piñata treats that had escaped detection under the shelves. He would have happily spent the next half hour continuing to do just that, for he'd come across a mother lode, and after all, the party was still going great guns. But Annie decided she'd had enough and took him home.

CHAPTER
10

Friday morning, Annie came downstairs and found the trash basket overturned in the kitchen. Someone had been rooting around discarded egg cartons and empty cans. Claudius, of course.

He strolled in as she picked up the last of the mess. "I don't know if I can find the words to tell you what I think of you," she told him. "You are a very bad dog. Arrogant, stubborn—look at you, you don't even care!"

Unperturbed by her ranting, he sat down and watched her shove the basket back under the counter. Then, as a peace offering, he got up and licked her hand.

She glared at him. He gazed back.

What was the use?

Several things were crystal clear. Claudius made no apology for his behavior. He was happy. What was her problem?

Unfortunately, she was stuck with him. And there was no point in even thinking about running away, because one, she'd have to take him along since no one else would have him; and two, the only person who'd take her in was her mother in Florida, and that was totally out of the question.

Her mother was impossible to live with. Nothing pleased her. Ever. Last, Annie didn't have enough money to run away on, even if she'd had somewhere to go.

What the heck. Life went on. Annie made a cup of coffee and booted up the computer.

By then, Kirk had come downstairs and was making breakfast. Annie got up and went to say good morning—a bad idea, since Kirk promptly burned the toast, and when Leah wandered in still yawning, he grumbled that they were late. If she wanted a tour of Lester College campus, she'd better get a move on.

They gobbled the burned toast and eggs, gulped down coffee, and dashed off in Leah's car.

Annie went back to the computer. Let's see, the inventory list: sold stock, unsold stock, alphabetically sorted. She scrolled down, looking for a listing of a pair of brass candlesticks. She'd sold them last week, but carelessly hadn't entered a notation.

She typed in the date and amount and saw, farther down, the listings for quilts. There was the one she'd donated to Fox Hill and another she'd sold to a woman from New York—a child's quilt stitched from bleached feed bags in the 1860s. They'd recycled just about everything back then.

That thought triggered another: the upper hall stairwell in the Fox Hill School library. She'd seen another lovely old quilt on display there, an intricately stitched patchwork in muted colors, dated 1803.

She wondered how long it had been on display—since

last year? It was the same staircase from which Stella Danforth had fallen to her death.

Had the quilt been a silent witness to murder?

It seemed peculiar that three people connected to Fox Hill School had died violently in the space of twelve short months: Stella, Rocky, and his sister, Maria. Well, Maria's connection with the school was tenuous at best, but as Rocky's sister she might have been to the school a few times—or maybe not.

For the sake of argument, Annie decided Maria might have picked up Rocky once or twice if his car had broken down. Anyway, what were the odds of three people being dead, just like that? Was Fox Hill turning into the Bermuda Triangle of prep schools?

Later, just after eight, Joey Chavez's mother called with the wonderful news that he was starting school there next Monday. Annie offered to drive them over on Sunday afternoon and see him settled in. This arrangement being agreeable, Annie said she'd pick them up around two p.m. and went into the kitchen to wash the floor.

Later, out in the shop, she glanced up at the sound of an engine and realized a car had pulled in. A customer.

After that it was wall-to-wall business until four. Happily, she made enough profit after expenses to justify closing early. She had things to do at Fox Hill: that speech to give to the senior class and Joey to check on.

First, she got dinner ready for the weekend guests, Sophie and Rex Farraday, who turned out to be sixty-year-old newlyweds. Sophie was slim and gray-haired, Rex balding and hearty. A retired airplane pilot, he confided they'd been married all of two weeks.

Sophie sported a baseball cap with BRIDE embroidered

on the visor. Rex beamed, puffed out his chest, and managed to look like the cat's meow.

Annie showed them up to their room, and after they'd unpacked, served them a quick meal of chicken stir-fry with homemade five-grain bread and goat-cheese salad.

"What a lovely old tavern," Sophie said. "The stories these walls could tell! Must have seen a lot through the years."

"Yes, and Lee seems to be a nice town," Rex said. He helped himself to seconds of stir-fry.

Claudius was on his best behavior, rolling over to let them scratch his belly. The Farradays were dog people. He'd sensed that right away.

He lay down near the stove and waited for leftovers.

"Are you from Boston?" Annie asked.

"Actually, we're from Medfield, just outside the city," Sophie said.

Rex snorted. "Boston's great—if you like congestion and traffic. I'll take the country life. You're lucky to have this place."

Sophie lifted her wineglass and said she'd drink to that.

Annie poured herself a cup of tea and stirred in milk and sugar. "How did you hear about the tavern?"

"We were planning a ski trip to Maine," Rex explained, "so we picked up a guidebook with a complete listing of bed-and-breakfast inns. There was the Thurston Tavern— three and a half stars, by the way. We decided to give it a try."

"Yes," Sophie said. "Rex's hobby is astronomy, and when we saw that you offered this wonderful star-gazing weekend, it seemed perfect!"

Rex sipped his wine. "I'm really looking forward to

this. The winter night sky is special. Jupiter's moons, Saturn's rings, Mars. Nebulae, galaxies. What about the weather?"

"Looks good so far," Annie said.

Rex rubbed his hands with enthusiasm. "Great! The guidebook mentioned that you have a fair-sized telescope—"

"Right," Annie said. "A previous owner was interested in astronomy. He even ground his own lenses and installed a telescope in the cupola."

Kirk was in charge of the astronomy part of the weekend. Annie's contribution was making sure the guests were fed and housed in country-inn style.

Sure enough, when a short while later Kirk arrived and it grew dark—and cloudless—he and the Farradays trooped up to the cupola for several hours of prime viewing.

Annie cleared the dinner dishes away, set the dishwasher going, and sat down, wondering why she was beginning to feel unproductive. Okay, what had she done lately? A short list: She'd found Cary's jacket and medal, but it didn't seem fair to count that since Rocky was dead. So her only real accomplishment was getting Joey Chavez enrolled at Fox Hill School, and even that wasn't her doing. She'd set things in motion, that's all.

As for Rocky and Maria's murders—and no way had their deaths been accidental, no matter what people said—unfortunately, she had nothing in the way of proof.

Physical clues were scarce. Nonexistent, in fact. Maybe if she looked at the murders from another angle, she'd come up with something the cops had missed.

Nothing psychic—she'd never had any luck there, and

she had a pocketful of losing lottery tickets to prove it. No, simple concentration might provide an insight to the killer or killers' motivation.

The cops had had plenty of time to collect forensic evidence in Maria's hit-and-run. Maybe even time enough to come up with a suspect and run down a few leads. Maybe they'd found paint chips from the car or tire tracks in the snow.

She phoned Gus Jackson and invited him to lunch.

"Tell you what," he said. "Mike's got a hockey game tomorrow afternoon. Fox Hill's playing Manchester Academy at home. Let's take in the game Saturday and go out for a bite later."

"Even better," she said, "I'll meet you at the rink and bring a picnic lunch."

As Annie sat watching both teams skate around the rink during the warm-up, Gus, beside her, bit into a meatball sub and said, "This is great, but why do I feel it's a setup?"

"You're a cop. You've got a suspicious mind," she said lightly.

"Huh, I'd like to think my big blue eyes and manly charm had something to do with it, but somehow I don't buy it."

Annie chewed her vegetarian sub and decided to change the subject. "Anything new on the miniature?"

"We're working on it, and yes, it was part of a robbery right here at the school a year ago."

Annie waited a moment, then said, "Rocky must have been mixed up in the robbery."

"Maybe."

"Maybe?" She was indignant. "That has to be why someone murdered him."

He shrugged. "Maybe."

"What do you mean? He stole it by himself, or he was working with someone else. They had a falling out and he was murdered. Logically, that's what must have happened."

"Logic isn't your strongest point. Better leave this to professionals."

Of all the nerve. Annie seethed while, at the far end of the rink, Manchester Academy took turns shooting on goal. Fox Hill was doing the same thing at the near end, and the rink resounded with booming echoes.

Claudius, sitting between Annie and Gus, stared at the door. A couple of dogs had wandered in and out—two golden retrievers and a little terrier. Annie knew that Claudius considered them nonentities. Goldens were congenitally stupid, slavishly adoring their owners no matter how undeserving, and Claudius had scared the pants off a terrier about that size just last week. Still, he kept his eye on them.

"Look," Annie said, "I could help with the investigation if you'd give me a chance."

"Thanks, but no thanks." Gus selected a sugar cookie in the shape of a dog bone. Annie had also brought along a few homemade dog cookies made of potatoes, whole wheat flour, wheat germ, and carrots—Claudius's favorite.

"These are good," Gus said absently. "I need a new oven. Nothing bakes evenly in the one I have."

"Turn the temperature down and move the baking pan

to a lower shelf," Annie said. She noticed that his attention was on the maintenance man just entering the rink.

He ate another cookie and said thoughtfully, "Rocky drove the Zamboni machine here at the rink."

The Zamboni machine groomed the ice surface, putting down thin layers of freezing water, which turned immediately to ice.

Rocky had run the Zamboni? This was news to Annie, although when she thought about it, it made sense. The job Rocky had had plowing the school's roads meant he'd only been needed when the weather turned bad.

The maintenance man left the rink, and Gus turned his attention to the hockey game that was about to start. "Last couple of games we got beat bad," he confided. "Too many goals one on one. It's damn near impossible to get back into the game if you're down more than two goals. You can't depend on power-play goals. You need other things, strategy, defense."

"What position does Mike skate?" she asked, scanning the Fox Hill skaters' red-and-white uniforms in search of him.

"Defense, number six."

She spotted Mike just as he wheeled and shot on goal. He skated with a skill born of long years spent in various New England ice rinks. He lifted another lazy shot into the net over his goalie, making it look easy.

Gus chose another cookie and took a bite. "Last game, we got thrashed, although we skated pretty well. We got a few bad calls and lost momentum."

Annie sipped hot chocolate from a thermos and wondered about Rocky. He might have groomed the ice for all the games. The school rented ice time to various area youth teams, too. It was a busy place. So he might have spent quite a lot of time here.

She stared unseeing at the ice. Why would he take a job like that? At first consideration it didn't suit his character, but the job had given him a reason to be here on campus, and not just when it snowed.

Gus eyed her with suspicion. "You look thoughtful. What's on your mind?"

"I'm right about Rocky. He was murdered because of something here at the school, probably the robbery."

"Is that so—why?"

"Because Rocky liked his creature comforts. Otherwise he wouldn't have stolen Cary's jacket. There's only one reason he'd take a low-paying maintenance job."

"Okay, I'll bite. Why?"

"He needed an excuse to be here. It had to be connected to the robbery."

Gus sighed. "I'm telling you to stay out of it."

Annie smiled. "Good. You're coming around to my point of view—that he was murdered because of the robbery."

"I didn't say that."

"You implied it."

He looked annoyed. "Watch the game."

"Come on, Gus, we need to talk about this."

"No, we don't . . ." He heaved a sigh. "All right, what do you want?"

"I could help. I'd be another pair of eyes and ears. You're Mike's uncle, fine. You live right across the lake, but everyone knows you're a cop. Fox Hill teachers and staff, even the kids—they'll never open up to you."

He drank coffee and thought about that. Finally, he

said, "Okay, if something's going on—and I'm not admitting anything—then two people are already dead. If you're not careful, you'll end up as number three."

"Have you got any suspects?"

"No, do you?" His tone suggested that anyone she pointed a finger at would have immediate grounds for a lawsuit.

"Not exactly," she admitted. "But think about this. You might have three murders on your hands."

He eyed her with disbelief. "You discovered another body you forgot to tell me about?"

"Funny. No. Last year a teacher was found dead at the foot of a staircase three stories high."

"Right, Stella Danforth. I checked it out. Consensus was she suffered a dizzy spell and fell. She was in her late seventies. The only surprise is how she managed to climb all the way to the top of those stairs in the first place."

"And?"

"And what?"

"Well, she could've been knocked unconscious, carried upstairs, and thrown over the railing."

"There's no proof of that. No witnesses, nothing. And there was nothing in the woman's background to make her a candidate for murder. We checked. No large bank deposits or withdrawals. She lived alone, was a dedicated teacher, liked gardening and playing bridge. Nothing that even smelled criminal."

"The last person you'd expect to end up like that," Annie concluded.

He frowned. "There's nothing there. Believe me, we looked."

But there had been a second's hesitation before he'd replied. Enough to make Annie suspicious.

Down below on the ice, the game had started. Skaters raced around, forwards passing the puck, getting knocked into the boards. The cavernous rink boomed and echoed with shouts and cheers: "Go, Big Red, go!"

Claudius leaned his head on Gus's knee and stared at him adoringly.

Annie told herself she wasn't in the least bit jealous. If Claudius wanted to make a fool of himself, so be it.

Back to the business at hand.

She decided to try another tack. "What about prints? Did they dust the railing?" she asked Gus.

"You're beating a dead horse. Everyone and his brother had access to that set of stairs. There was no point. Besides, it was an accident. The poor woman stumbled and fell."

"If she'd tried to grab the railing, her prints would have been there."

"If not, it'd mean she missed, which is why she fell," he said smugly.

Annie's spirits plummeted. It had seemed like a good idea.

"What about her job? Were there any complaints? What about her colleagues or parents?"

"Nothing turned up. Forget it."

This whole afternoon was turning out to be a waste of time, Annie decided. Gus wasn't cooperating. She should have gone home and baked bread for the Farradays' breakfast.

She had another idea. "I heard that Stella Danforth had very high standards. Maybe she stumbled across something illegal and refused to look the other way, so she had to be eliminated. Maybe she knew who'd robbed the library."

"There's no foundation for believing that."

"No? You jumped to the conclusion that she was old and feeble. She was in her seventies, but she was in good shape. According to Molly Houghton, Stella Danforth walked three miles a day. That's why her death was such a shock to everyone."

Suddenly, the rink exploded as everyone jumped up and started shouting.

Fox Hill had scored.

Annie tugged Gus's arm. Reluctantly, he looked away from the ice, and his jacket pulled back a little.

There was a service revolver clipped to his belt. She knew he wore a gun, but seeing it was a shock. He was off duty, yet still had his gun handy. This wasn't unusual; cops did it all the time. But even so, nothing was really off the record with Gus. Day or night, off duty or on, he was still a cop.

And she hadn't mistaken his hesitation a moment ago. He was definitely interested in her theory connecting Stella Danforth's death to the robbery.

Manchester Academy scored, then moments later, scored again. The rink rocked with shouts and cheers, boos and repeated yells of "Defense!"

Mike had let a left wing fake him out, walk in, and score.

Gus frowned. "Damn!"

"The bottom line is, you've probably got three murders, not two," Annie said firmly.

He let out an exasperated sigh. "You just don't give up.

All right, officially we don't have squat. But we're working on it. The whole business is speculative. If this gets out, it's my ass."

"I knew it! What do you know so far?"

"Not much," he admitted. "There's something funny going on, but exactly what, we don't know yet. We're working on it."

"So when are you going to arrest someone?"

"When we have proof."

"In the meantime people will go on dropping like flies?"

"No," he said sourly. "In the meantime, I expect your cooperation. Don't say a word to anyone about this."

"That's it?"

"Yeah."

She thought that over. Finally, they were getting some action, but Gus was tricky. He'd never blab anything really important.

On Sunday afternoon, she drove over to Fox Hill with Joey and his mother. Mrs. Chavez would help settle him in the dorm while Annie did some quiet snooping.

She didn't know what, if anything, she'd find out, but it was worth a shot.

The library's collection of historical letters, ephemera, and old journals was kept in a locked cabinet in the reference room. It was quiet as she sat down at the polished mahogany table. Outside, the sun was shining in a clear blue sky. Only a few students were hunched over their books on such a fine winter day.

She opened the old box of letters and sifted through the yellowed pages. In the middle, she found a letter written by Amos Franklin, dated 1804. He said that as a school-boy, he'd often stopped on his way home to read the inscriptions on the old gravestones.

By the time of the Civil War, much of the land bordering the school had been bought or taken over by local farmers. Some land had been plowed under, and in the manner of New England, nothing went to waste. Any stones dug up were put in fieldstone walls. The Wyndham graveyard vanished.

Later accounts held that fields bordering Fox Hill contained any number of stone walls. Part of the land was now an apple orchard, part sloped down to the lake and was used as football and soccer fields—and beyond that, more open land stretched uphill to a line of dark woods.

According to Franklin's letter, the original graveyard contained fifteen to eighteen stones and was located near two stone walls and a pumphouse. But the letter was yellowed and folded. In places, the ink was blotted and smeared. It might say powderhouse instead of pumphouse, Annie decided.

She put Franklin's letter aside and picked out another, dated 1900, from a local octogenarian. According to his recollections, the Wyndham family graveyard had been in a hollow between two stone walls that had run approximately ten yards in length, eight rods in width, by a fieldstone wall running parallel with an old wood road.

Over the years, the graveyard's location had been the object of much curiosity. Various citizens with an interest in local history had tried their luck at finding it—with no result.

The land in question was rough and sloping, with what

seemed to be fairly distinctive topographical features. Yet no one had found the graveyard in all this time.

Annie thought about that. Frost heaves and yearly mowing and reaping would have turned up bones if the graveyard had been anywhere near the soccer or football fields.

On the other hand, maybe not. Maybe by now so much time had passed that the bones had ceased to exist.

There was also talk in the letters of the possibility of the existence of an Abenaki Native American burial ground, far older than the Wyndham family graveyard. But this had never been proved—it remained a rumor.

Annie reread Amos Franklin's letter and decided one thing: If they hadn't found evidence of the graveyard's whereabouts by this time, then it had to be where no one had thought to look.

Maybe that ink-smudged word 'pumphouse' was actually 'powderhouse'.

Of course. The rosy old brick powderhouse was still there, big as life, behind Becker House, one of the oldest school buildings. Nobody paid the powderhouse much attention except on the Fourth of July, when the town draped the battered wooden door with bunting and the school band paraded past.

She sat back and thought about Patience. In the confusion of the past week or two, she'd been too busy to think about much of anything. Or maybe she hadn't wanted to go where some thoughts would take her, all the way back to prerevolutionary times when women had few rights and little voice. When a woman could be accused of witchcraft and poisoning her husband, tried, and hanged. These days such a thing was unthinkable, of course. Absolutely unthinkable.

Wasn't it? Then she thought about mob justice, lynchings, racial hatred around the world. Religious bigotry. Ethnic cleansing, wars, and terrorism. In a way things hadn't changed all that much. She sighed and decided she couldn't solve the world's problems. It was hard enough just dealing with Claudius.

After Mrs. Chavez was satisfied that Joey had settled in nicely at the school, Annie drove her home and spent the next hour doing something she should have done last week—washing the tavern's downstairs windows. The refrigerator needed a good cleaning too, but that would have to wait.

The phone rang. She threw down the squeegee and picked up the receiver. "Thurston Tavern."

It was Sgt. Choate calling to tell her that they'd picked up some kids in connection with vandalism. There was a good chance they were the ones who'd rammed her car off the road. They hadn't admitted anything, but it was early days yet. They'd been questioned, arrested on another vandalism charge—they'd been caught playing mailbox baseball, bashing mailboxes with a baseball bat—and released on bail. They'd be arraigned in court Monday morning, so if they were in the car that had tried to force her off the road, she probably had nothing more to worry about.

A short time later, Kirk phoned from the college psychology lab to let her know that he and Leah would be home around seven-thirty and to remind her to turn on the outside light over the tavern sign. It got dark early. If the

Farradays showed up after five—they'd gone skiing at
Sunday River—they might miss the driveway.

The third call was from Cary.

"Want to go out to eat? I was just sitting here and I said
to myself, I'll bet Annie hasn't even thought about dinner
even though it's way past four."

Annie said she expected weekend guests to return any
minute, but why didn't Cary come by for a bite? This
turned out to be a happy compromise. She chatted with
Cary for a few more moments, then hung up and turned on
the light over the sign out front.

Soon everything was ready—squash soup bubbling on
the stovetop, salad made, and calzones in the warming
oven. When Cary arrived, Annie had even lit candles on
the dining room table.

Cary looked around. "All by your lonesome? Where is
everyone?"

"The Farradays'll be back soon. Kirk and his sister,
Leah, will be home later."

"So what are we having for dinner?" Cary looked in the
soup pot. "Mmm, squash. I love it with sour cream, although maybe you could use yogurt instead. I don't want
to gain weight. I can hardly squeeze into my jeans as it is.
Where'd you get fresh squash?"

"The root cellar."

"Oh, yeah." Cary rummaged in her purse for a small
notebook. "Listen, you gotta hear this. I found it in the
paper the other day." Reading from the notebook, she
said, "Veteran's hospital nurse suspected in more than one
hundred and fifty mercy killings ... Loretta Minster."
Cary flipped the page and said with satisfaction, "My favorite serial killer. What a woman. She did her thing for

years and no one suspected. Luckily she's on trial now. The timing's perfect! I can fit her into chapter eight."

"No wonder hospitals make people nervous," Annie said. "How'd she get caught?"

"Everything's computerized. The hospital finally noticed that the death toll among patients had risen dramatically."

Cary served herself squash soup and made herself comfortable at the kitchen table, while Annie passed sour cream and parsley to put on top. She poured two cups of tea and sat down.

"It turns out," Cary said, "that our Loretta was on duty when one hundred and fifty patients kicked the bucket. What are the odds of that happening?"

"Not very good."

"Exactly. Loretta's goose is cooked. Her ex-husband testified that she tried to kill him, too."

Claudius, under the table, yawned and stretched luxuriously. Home and hearth. He drifted off to dreamland.

"Mmm," Cary said. "I'm starving. Pass the breadsticks and salad, please."

Annie complied. "What's new with you?"

"Nothing much. I finished chapter nine, but I'll have to go back and add to chapter eight." She paused. "I'm thinking of using trick photography to juice up some of the duller passages. Maybe juxtapose a shot of Loretta, the angel of death, next to a hospital bed. I could add a hypo and a bottle marked 'poison'. Not that there are any really boring passages," she added hastily. "It's just that some parts are . . . well, livelier than others."

"Oh." Gruesome, she meant.

CHAPTER
11

Annie woke Monday morning to discover a pair of brown eyes staring at her. Claudius planted a front paw on either side of her waist and licked her face. Time to get up.

"Cut that out!" She managed to haul him off and stumbled out of bed. The sun was shining, but for some reason she was beginning to feel a deep foreboding. Today she had to give that speech. What if all the three-by-five notecards she'd scribbled with her life experiences, both good and bad, contained nothing interesting? She decided she must have been out of her mind to agree to give the speech.

Downstairs, the kitchen was deserted, but a note on the table informed her that Kirk had gone to his college lab and Leah had left early to check a few places for the location of the missing graveyard.

Annie had too much on her mind, what with her speech looming on the horizon like a big black cloud, to bother about missing cemeteries.

Her spirits sank even further during breakfast. She prepared a fried-egg sandwich on burned, scraped toast for herself, and Claudius was to have kibbles. Lately he'd demanded gravy with his meals, and last night she'd dumped the last jar of roast chicken gravy on his kibbles. This morning, hoping he wouldn't notice, she poured warm water on his breakfast. He sniffed it and sat down, displeased.

"I'm sorry," she told him. "I'm not made of money. We all have to make sacrifices."

It was clear from his expression that if anyone made sacrifices around here, it wasn't going to be Claudius.

"Don't eat, then. Starve. I don't care." Reverse psychology, and it worked because, after a grumpy sigh, he polished off every last crumb.

She did the dishes, vacuumed, then perched on a kitchen chair and reviewed the stack of three-by-five notecards. Mentally, she began formulating excuses about a family emergency that required her to fly to New Zealand or Timbuktu, or maybe a sudden illness, a burst appendix or gallstones.

But such tactics would at best postpone the inevitable, and after a suitable convalescence she'd be expected to make good on the speech. Besides, she didn't have to hold forth on solving life's problems for more than half an hour or so. She could manage that, surely.

She wrapped a rubber band around the cards, turned around, and found herself practically nose-to-nose with Claudius. She hadn't realized he was still in the kitchen.

"This is my speech," she said, showing him the cards. "We're going to Fox Hill School this afternoon, and you'd better be on your best behavior. I mean it. Anything else you want?"

He gave her a long, reflective look.

"Oh, so you think my speech is terrible?"

He lay down, the bland expression on his face telling her he thought she'd do just fine. But she wondered. There had been a pause there; he'd definitely been evasive. If she hadn't been distracted by the top card again—surely she hadn't written: "Money isn't everything in life"; what could she have been thinking?—she'd have noticed Leah's VW Bug pull up the driveway.

Annie let her in. It had been love at first sight between Claudius and Leah. He rushed over to her now and generally made an exhibition of himself, wriggling all over with joy.

Leah put her bulging briefcase on the table and devoted herself to scratching his ears. "How are you, big boy?"

He was fine, but even better after five minutes of attention, after which Leah opened her briefcase and pulled out her notes.

"I checked out three possible locations for the Wyndham graveyard. No luck. The old Federated Church records were incomplete. There was a fire at the church some years ago. But the town hall has property deeds that go way back to the 1600's. I think that location on Powderhouse Road could be the right one."

Leah indicated a spot on the copy of the old property deed. "There's a stone wall here and here. The other side was Putnam farm land. Obidiah Putnam owned several hundred acres. Maybe he bought the old cemetery. I don't know. But I'll bet he dug up the stones, maybe moved the graves. Or maybe didn't bother." She raised an eyebrow. "Later this afternoon, Mike's meeting us there with his camera, right?"

"Yeah, and I'm bringing shovels," Annie said.

"Good. We'll need them." Leah folded up the plan and

put it back in her briefcase. "I'm going to write up my notes and make a couple of phone calls. I'll see you at Powderhouse Road around two-fifteen."

Several hours later, Cary was sitting at Annie's kitchen table, pouring a dollop of balsamic dressing over her salad. She had the day off and had dropped by for lunch. "How's the speech coming?"

Annie sighed. "I have thirty index cards covered with notes, but I think the whole thing will be a dud. These days kids don't want to listen to lectures."

"Then don't give them one," Cary said, forking up a bite of quiche. "Make it a conversation. Let them ask questions. Claudius will do the rest."

They discussed this knotty problem for another fifteen minutes, then Annie glanced at the clock and jumped up. "Hey, time to go. Mike and Leah are meeting us after the speech."

"What about the dishes?" Cary complained. There was half a quiche left, and she was still hungry.

"They can wait." Annie pulled on her jacket, then cleared the table and dumped the dishes in the sink. Meanwhile, Cary cut another slice of quiche and put it in a napkin. She'd eat on the way.

Leash in his mouth, Claudius was already champing at the bit by the back door. If Annie had any illusions about leaving him home alone, she had another think coming.

By the time Annie got settled in the Volvo's front seat with Cary beside her, Claudius was already in back, dancing around in anticipation.

They barreled down the road to South Lee and Fox Hill

School. The sun was shining in a clear blue sky. Annie put on sunglasses and glanced at Cary.

"So," Annie said, "what do you know about the old Wyndham family graveyard?"

"Just that it's missing."

"Leah thinks it might be on Powderhouse Road. Did you ever hear any talk at school about where the cemetery might be?"

Cary frowned. "One Halloween night we climbed out the dorm window and went looking for it. We should have done it in daylight when we could've seen where we were going, but it was the idea of it, you know? Patience Wyndham, the murderess. We'd loved to have found her gravestone, even if her body's not there. It would have been great!"

"Maybe we'll find it today," Annie said. Claudius had been very quiet in the back seat. She glanced in the rearview mirror.

He stared back, his expression enigmatic.

Hmm. His training had probably included sniffing for traces of dead bodies. His help might prove invaluable.

Cary glanced over at her. "Want to practice the speech, at least the opening? I'll listen."

"No, thanks. Actually," Annie admitted, "I'm going to talk about achievement. That success doesn't necessarily mean making the most money and coming in first all the time. People need to learn to value other things in life."

Cary laughed. "Are you serious? Fox Hill is all about coming in first."

"I don't care. This is something kids need to hear. It will work out really well." Annie hoped.

"How long is it going to be?"

"Half an hour," Annie said. Once she started talking about Claudius, his past and present career—skipping over the demoralizing bits such as when he'd gotten kicked out of the prison guard-dog program—the speech would all but give itself. She'd hardly have to do more than answer questions.

For some reason, kids loved Claudius. Maybe it was his lordly air, the arrogant way he had of looking down his nose at everyone.

Cary laughed. "Don't worry. One look at the Big C, and the kids'll think you're wonderful."

"Let's hope so. Otherwise, I'm in trouble."

Standing in front of the senior honors English class twenty minutes later, she shuffled three-by-five cards, swallowed hard, and decided to get straight to the point.

She introduced Claudius. It was perfectly clear he'd already bowled over the whole roomful of teenagers.

Lounging at her feet, lean, lithe, and powerful, Claudius epitomized nobility. He was lord of all he surveyed.

She plucked the lemons from lemonade card from the stack and began, "Sometimes what we first think of as adversity is actually a blessing in disguise . . ."

She went on to describe how she'd adopted Claudius, noting from the look on the faces of the teachers in the back of the room that they held highly traditional views about achievement. And what she was talking about didn't fit the bill.

Never mind. From the kids' reactions, her speech was going great guns. She was a rip-roaring success.

They sat, mesmerized, drinking in every word—laughing as she described the trials and tribulations of living

with Claudius. "He has a well-earned reputation as a bad
boy," she said. "When I call area boarding kennels, they
hang up at the mere mention of his name. He hates being
left home alone, so I take him with me most of the time."

"But weren't you scared of him at first?" a boy asked
after she'd invited everyone to come up and meet
Claudius.

"No, I knew he was special, right from the beginning.
He had integrity, character, and was somehow able to
communicate what he was thinking. I was never afraid of
him, but there were times when he drove me crazy. He believed he was the boss." And still did.

"No kidding, he was a real police dog?" another boy
asked.

"Sure. He even won a medal." She showed them the
medal and citation.

After fifteen more minutes of questions and answers,
Ivan Childress, the English teacher, hustled up to the
podium. "Thanks so much for coming, Ms. O'Hara. That
was certainly an informative talk. We're delighted you
and your dog could come today." He was already walking
them to the door.

"I had a wonderful time," Annie said as Cary came forward from the back of the room where she'd been sitting.
"Claudius enjoyed it, too." She had the distinct feeling
they were being given the bum's rush, but she was probably mistaken, and she did want to clear up one small
point. "The killers Claudius caught last year were totally
without conscience. What they did was a case of simple,
old-fashioned murder for gain. They planned to flee the
country and live where we don't have an extradition
treaty. Whether they'd have lived there happily ever after

is another matter. The woman had already killed two husbands for the insurance money. Eventually, she would
have insured her lover's life and killed him, too."

"Indeed. Well, that's really interesting . . . something to
think about." Ivan Childress pumped her hand.

Here's your hat, what's your hurry.

Moments later, Annie found herself out in the hallway
with Cary and Claudius.

Well, you couldn't please everybody all the time.

Outside the school, despite the brilliant sunshine, it was
cold and raw. Cary stamped her feet, pulled her muffler
around her neck, and trailed Annie and Claudius across
the street as Mike arrived, camera in hand. Claudius
forged ahead, and they all trudged back to the parking lot
to get shovels from the back of the Volvo.

"I've got four, one for everyone," Annie said, glancing
up in time to see Leah's VW pull into the parking lot. It
was two-fifteen. She was right on time.

A few minutes later, Leah was unfolding the copy of
the old property deed and saying to Mike, "If you're
lucky, you might even find the witch's skeleton. Part of it,
anyway. Just a joke," she added hastily when he frowned.
"Besides," she went on, "if we find the cemetery, any
graves will probably be in poor condition. Frost heaves
tend to bring up old coffins, and there have been cases,"
honesty compelled her to admit, "where people have actually fallen into old graves."

"But that's not likely to happen to us," Annie assured
him.

"Jeez, I hope not," Mike mumbled.

Leah looked around, getting her bearings, then indicated a stone wall in the distance. "Let's look over there. It will be sheltered, so the snow won't be as deep."

The old tumbledown stone wall stretched ahead through the trees. Leah, Mike, and Cary followed, shovels in hand, as Annie led Claudius over the wall.

Leah dug a few test holes, but didn't find anything interesting. Mike took half a dozen pictures and remained near the wall. Annie suspected he was still very nervous. He kept talking—something about his digital camera and how you wouldn't believe the detail he got in the pictures.

For the next half hour they worked their way around to the north side of the rectangle without finding anything. Leah dug another hole, then leaned on the shovel and sighed, clearly discouraged.

Annie glanced at Leah. Something about the slump of her shoulders rang a warning bell. "You're not giving up, are you?" she said.

Leah pulled herself together with a visible effort. "I'm just a little tired. There's still that area over by the trees to search." She moved forward, and Annie followed, scanning the snow underfoot. Here and there, she used her shovel to scrape snow away from a tree root.

Suddenly, Annie hit something hard with the shovel.

She bent and scraped away more snow with her hands as Leah, Cary, and Mike crowded near to look. "What's that?"

Leah bent to brush the last of the snow away. It was a large, flat stone. With everyone helping, they managed to turn it over. "Wonderful!" Leah exclaimed. "It's an old slate gravestone."

"There's a slate quarry near here," Annie said, excited.

Leah cleared the snow completely from its surface while Mike leaned over to snap a picture.

"What does it say?" Cary asked.

"Let's see." Leah scanned the letters chiseled in the stone. "'Welcome Death, Louis'—no, 'Louise'. That chipped space looks like a mistake. Well, it goes on. 'Louise Hawthorne, beloved daughter of James and Emily. Born January 6. Dyed April 23. She lives in the Lord'."

A border of tiny flowers had been chiseled at the bottom of the stone. At the top was a capering, grinning skeleton with the date, 1692.

Leah shook her head. "The grim reality of the seventeenth and eighteenth centuries meant nothing but herbal remedies, blood-letting, and leeches to fight diseases like scarlet fever, typhoid, and diphtheria. People died young, very young."

"This has to be the cemetery," Cary crowed, eyeing the stone. "Wow, we found it!"

"It looks like a discarded stone," Annie said, remembering the school history account of the '38 hurricane.

Mike frowned. "Why the skeletons and skulls?"

"These were Puritan times," Leah explained. "Hellfire and brimstone were very real to those people. The skull was a death's head. Sometimes the carvers added batlike wings to underline grim mortality and moldering flesh. Later on, around 1730, the skulls turned into angel heads. Supposedly, they depicted the soul's flight to heaven. There was a huge religious revival around that time called The Great Awakening, which emphasized the heavenly afterlife."

Cary shook her head. "There was a chance you wouldn't go straight to hell?"

"Depends on who you were. Those with big bucks put up tablestones, huge stone slabs on three-foot-high legs—the Mercedes of gravemarkers."

"I still don't understand what happened to the graves in the old cemetery," Cary complained.

"The farmer who owned most of the land beyond that wall may have appropriated this land too," Leah said. "Just pulled up the stones and plowed under any bones he came across."

"Ugh." Cary shuddered. "But why is this stone still here?"

"I don't know," Leah admitted. "Carvers usually threw the stones away when they made mistakes. If there is a slate quarry nearby, it would have been easy to get more stones. See, the top line?" She pointed to the chipped spot. "That's supposed to be an 'e', I think. According to town records, there used to be a sidewalk around here, and when the hurricane of '38 hit, it was destroyed. People would use whatever was handy to rebuild, perhaps even this discarded stone."

Annie nodded. "The school history mentioned someone, years later, digging in his front yard and discovering a stone like this. Dumped because the carver made a mistake. Look at this." She walked on, scuffling away snow and layered leaves beneath. "More stones, only these are smaller, cobblestones. Probably from the old road."

Leah looked around. "The Wyndham graveyard might be somewhere around here. According to the deed, it was between two fieldstone walls."

Cary pouted. "Well, where? This whole thing is getting old. I'm cold."

"There's another stone wall." Annie pointed through the trees. "Let's try over there."

"I can't feel my feet anymore," Cary complained.

"We don't have to do this, unless you want to," Annie said.

"Five minutes more," Cary retorted. "Then I've had it."

They walked over the ground, scuffling snow as they went. Annie didn't find anything, but Cary had more luck and uncovered another skull-topped gravestone. This one depicted the sorry end of Phenias Blood, aged sixty-five, struck by lightning in 1695.

For a few minutes, Cary showed renewed enthusiasm, but it didn't last. She was cold and hungry. This was a complete waste of time. Couldn't they leave now? "Why are we looking here, anyway? It's all overgrown, nothing but wild blackberry bushes and weeds. We found two gravestones. You said yourself it doesn't mean anything. They threw the stones away."

"I saw some letters about the old cemetery," Annie said. "They mentioned a location between two stone walls, like those over there." She pointed to the left and right.

This failed to impress. "Come on," Cary snorted. "There are a zillion stone walls around here. It doesn't prove a thing."

Claudius sat down and huffily scratched his ear.

He sniffed suspiciously.

"If we look long enough, we'll find it," Leah said with determination.

"Hunh." Cary wasn't convinced.

"Maybe we'll find Patience Wyndham's grave," Annie reminded Cary.

"Look, she died what, two—three hundred years ago, right? Who cares?"

"I do," Annie said. "Patience didn't have a fair trial. She was kept for months in unspeakable conditions. She was chained to the wall. You wouldn't do that to an animal!"

Cary shrugged. "That's the way it was back then. She was married to a rich old man who died. The cops or whoever was in charge—"

"Judicial authorities," Annie supplied.

"Whatever. Anyway, they looked to see who benefited from the old man's death, who inherited. And guess what—Patience was right there at the top of the list. She probably would have gotten away with it if she'd been more clever about giving him the poison."

Mike shook his head. "What if she wasn't guilty?"

"So what?" Cary retorted. She waved a hand. "A foot of snow on the ground, and we're wandering around looking for a graveyard nobody in his right mind cares about. If we were smart, we'd wait and do this in March after the snow melts."

Leah stiffened. "This is part of my thesis," she said coldly, "and it's important." She marched over to the wall and began clearing snow from one of the stones.

"Okay, here's a question," Cary said. "What's missing besides gravestones?"

Annie frowned. "What?"

"Wrought-iron gates and a fence. You always see gates and a fence around old cemeteries. Where'd they go?"

"If that farmer took the land," Leah said thoughtfully,

"he'd have taken the gates and fence and used them somewhere else. Even so, there might be some trace of the
fence left here." She moved a few feet, brushed snow
from another stone, then straightened in triumph. "Look at
this—a hole drilled into this stone!"

"Which means?" Cary raised an eyebrow.

"It could be where the gate was hung, or perhaps it's
where the bottom of the fence was anchored." Leah took
out a notebook and began sketching what she'd uncovered.

Claudius uttered a low woof.

The sun was going down, and Annie had a strange
sense of waiting, though she didn't know what for. The
area between the fieldstone walls seemed filled with com-
pressed memories of the long-ago dead. She was sure this
was the old graveyard.

Claudius started acting oddly, pulling hard on the leash.

"Stop that," Annie ordered, hauling him back.

He glowered at her, and she saw the worry in his eyes.
They were treading on old graves. The dead didn't like
that. Desecration, disrespect—whatever you called it, the
spirits were ordering them to get out. The fur along
Claudius's spine rippled and stood up. He growled.

There was an oppressive silence. It was dark here under
the trees, Annie thought. And cold.

Mike and Cary started walking toward Powderhouse
Road, leaving Annie and Leah staring at each other under
the trees. It looked as if the search was over, at least for
today.

"Well," Leah said, shrugging, "it's getting late. We
might as well go. I'll come back tomorrow." She put her

notebook away and crunched off through the snow after Mike and Cary.

Mike stopped to brush snow off the top of the stone wall, while Cary stamped her feet and shivered.

Leah peered closer at the wall, then turned back to Annie. "This is interesting," she said, indicating the top of the wall.

By now Annie had come up beside her and was brushing off the snow, as well. Most of the stones were granite, streaked with mossy lichen. Her fingers felt a sharp, straight edge under the layer of snow.

Nature didn't like straight lines.

This stone could be man-made.

Claudius growled louder and scrambled upright, yanking on the leash again.

"What's wrong with him?" Cary said, staring.

"Stop it! Heel!" Annie reined him in hard—by this time he was struggling to climb right over the wall. After a wrestling match, which she won by sheer willpower, he subsided by her feet with very poor grace. "And stay there!"

He heaved an aggrieved sigh.

"What's so interesting?" Cary demanded, peering over Annie's shoulder.

"Look at this!" She pushed aside the top stone, brushed off concealing layers of snow, and revealed a flat piece of black slate. The chiseled letters "Mary Wyndham" appeared under a hollow-eyed skull. "Virtuous Consort of Joseph Wyndham, who departed this life May 30, 1680, in the forty-fifth year of her age." Also listed were the names of her five young children, who'd died soon after birth.

"Talk about a hard life," Cary said thoughtfully as

Mike snapped a picture of the stone and Leah made a quick sketch.

"It must have been really difficult back then," Annie agreed. Her voice trailed off. She frowned, thinking. Something was wrong. Suddenly uneasy, she looked off to the right through the trees.

Something bright winked in the distance.

She stared, waiting for it to come again. Five, six seconds passed, then it winked again, a glittering flash of light, and was gone.

Something shiny—a mirror? Or was someone watching them with binoculars?

And if so, who?

The house through those trees belonged to Fox Hill. The old infirmary. It was a lovely old place, built on the slope of the hill, facing south.

Annie knew the old infirmary firsthand, having spent a week in bed there suffering from measles during her junior year. The second floor was a series of wide-windowed bedrooms facing a thick line of trees and the old powderhouse.

Cary was blowing on her freezing hands. Finally she said, "This place gives me the creeps. I'm out of here."

She turned and stomped off toward the road.

Claudius leaped up, tail wagging. Every inch of him was saying, *All right! We're leaving, and high time.*

Mike said, "So, are we all set?"

"For now," Leah said, putting away her notebook. She climbed over the wall after Mike.

Annie followed more slowly. Who'd bother peering through binoculars at three women, a boy, and a dog? It didn't make sense.

As they emerged from the darkness of the woods into the fading sunlight of Powderhouse Road, she saw a white SUV pull up nearby.

A gold-and-red seal on the side said: Fox Hill School Security.

A burly man wearing wraparound dark glasses and a black baseball cap sat in the front seat. He had a pudgy face, and a fringe of pale hair poked out beneath his cap. Beside him, a small poodle with a blue collar and dirty white fur yapped madly.

He shoved the poodle back, and Annie noticed that he was dressed all in black—shirt, jacket, and jeans. Was it a security uniform or a fashion statement?

"Shut up, Trixie," he snapped at the poodle. Eyeing Annie, he bared his teeth in what passed for a smile. "Hi. What are you doing roaming around the woods? This is Fox Hill School property. Do you have a legitimate reason for being here?"

Cary blurted, "We were just—"

"Taking my dog for a walk," Annie interrupted loudly.

Claudius cooperated by lifting his leg and annointing the SUV's left rear wheel.

The security man frowned but let that pass, while Annie chatted about her speech before the senior honors English class. She'd been nervous at first—well, she hadn't been trained in public speaking—but she was a Fox Hill alumna, and the kids had seemed to enjoy it.

What she really meant was: They had every right to be here, and if he didn't like it, he could lump it.

The name embroidered in white on his black jacket indicated that he was Harry Graham, Deputy. Deputy what, it didn't say, and they didn't ask. He was pleasant enough, paunchy, smiling beneath his wraparounds, but Annie noticed he'd checked them out thoroughly. He projected an air of lazily reined-in male power that could turn into instant action if he decided they were up to no good.

Meanwhile, Trixie was practically frothing at the mouth, yipping and scrabbling, trying to clamber over Harry's muscled forearm in order to throw herself out the window at Claudius, who was sitting between Annie and Leah, looking lordly and remote.

He woofed a greeting at Trixie and wagged his tail. Annie frowned and wondered when they'd formed this bond.

After another minute, Harry Graham drove off with a nod.

Trixie threw herself toward the rear of the SUV, leaping desperately, barking her head off through the window. Annie and the others walked back to the parking lot without further incident.

Pausing by the Volvo, Mike said he'd download his pictures and get them ready for his history project. If Leah or Annie wanted some, he'd make copies. He flashed an engaging grin and loped off toward the hockey rink.

With a nod and a wave, Leah climbed in her VW and drove off down the street. She'd be spending the next couple of days with a friend in Vermont. Instead of heading straight home, or even to the nearest Wendy's or Taco Bell, as Cary suggested more than once, Annie turned in the opposite direction, down Powderhouse Road toward the old infirmary.

They pulled up in front and parked. Annie let the engine idle and eyed the black-and-white sign stuck in the snow—Hapworth House. The headmaster's house.

So the infirmary had become the headmaster's residence.

Two cars were parked in the carriage house garage, a BMW and a Mercedes SUV. Nothing but the best for Dr. David Lawrence, PhD. Presumably he was paid a princely salary for his services—if school fees and tuition were anything to go by—and could well afford to blow forty or fifty grand per automobile.

Cary dragged the morning paper from her jacket pocket. A diehard Bruins fan, she checked out last night's game against Toronto. The Bruins had lost—even the new coach hadn't helped.

She flipped back to page one. "Hey, listen to this. They're really playing up Winterfest. The public is invited to take part in Fox Hill's annual winter festivities. The Snowflake Dance, downhill and cross-country ski races. The scholarship dinner and auction. Huh. Tickets to the dinner are fifty bucks. Nothing's cheap these days."

They drove downtown to the center of South Lee. Like most New England villages, it had been discovered by tourists and did its best to live up to expectations. The street was lined with old houses, a mix of residences and shops. The hardware store on one corner had a picket fence out front and a huge parking lot out back. A mini-strip mall contained a secondhand book shop located between a Greek pizza parlor and an organic health food store. Down the street were a country-and-western clothing outlet, a comic book shop, two dentists' offices, three banks, a Pick n' Pay supermarket, and three lawyers' offices.

Antique shops had sprouted like weeds, practically on every corner. Windows sported carefully arranged displays of baby carriages and white china tea sets, hutches with peeling paint, and what Annie suspected was reproduction pewter, probably passed off as the real thing.

She sighed. With all the competition, no wonder her shop was barely breaking even.

A big white banner was stretched across the street between the Congregational and Universalist churches. It proclaimed in two-foot-high letters: FOX HILL WINTERFEST! COME ONE, COME ALL! PRIZES, FUN FOR ALL!

"Everything looks so picturesque," Cary said, eyeing the snow-covered picket fence in front of the hardware store.

"Phony," was Annie's decidedly gloomy take on everything.

CHAPTER
12

"Mom says someone was askin' about you around Goss Lane," Joey said in between slurps of hot chocolate and bites of his burger with the works. "Any idea who it was?"

"No," Annie admitted.

It was a few days later. They were sitting in Smith's Sandwich Shoppe, a quarter mile from downtown Dover and the nearest place, except for the Parthenon Pizza joint, where a visiting parent/guardian could take a Fox Hill student for a square meal.

"Are you scared it's the murderer?" Joey wanted to know.

"No," Annie said, but he wasn't fooled.

"Huh, you'd think the cops'd be more on the ball about catching the guy. Wait a sec," he said suddenly, his curly black hair bobbing with detective zeal. "Next time I'm home I'll ask around and find out who it was."

"No," she said flatly. "You stay out of it."

His expression spoke volumes about lost opportunities. "Well, Mom says Maria Martinez drank a lot. Maybe her death was really just a hit-and-run after all."

"Maybe it was."

"But Mom says the big cop in charge the night Maria died came around askin' lots of questions the next day. He said you were run off the road by somebody. How come you didn't tell me?"

"I was busy. Besides, it didn't concern you."

"Huh. I coulda been in the car. Fact, I was. That's the night you brought me home."

She shifted uncomfortably. "I know what night it was." Why did she feel as if she were being grilled by an expert? He was just a kid, for heaven's sake.

"Of course, I don't wanna make you talk about something that's none of my business," Joey said, "but like I said, I could've been in the car, and almost was. So it involves me, sort of. Come on, I can keep my mouth shut."

"Keep your mouth shut?" she said. "Ha. You wouldn't know how if someone paid you."

He chomped his burger and thought a minute. "Yes, I would," he said. "But it'd have to be big bucks. They'd have to make it worth my while."

"That kind of thinking will only get you in trouble."

Mr. Pragmatic shrugged. "Hey, you gotta do what you gotta do. All I say is, sometimes people gotta do things they don't like."

"For a price. That's sad. You don't have to live like that. Moral principles should guide you."

"What's moral principles?"

"Knowing right from wrong," she told him. "And sticking to the right."

"Oh, yeah."

The radio on the counter was turned to a local talk show: Bill Gefert. Listeners called in with stories about the weirdest things they'd seen on the highway. One man from

Florida said he'd seen two huge alligators lying in a three-lane expressway. A cop on duty just sat in his car, waving traffic down the open lane. Did this go on all the time?

"Wow, did you hear that?" Joey said, examining the remains of his burger. "Wonder what a gator tastes like."

"I have no idea."

"You don't think gators could come up north? Tyler said some kid he knows bought a baby gator over Christmas vacation last year. His mother flushed it down the toilet."

"That's an urban myth."

"Yeah? What's that?"

"A made-up story that gets passed around until people actually believe it."

They finished eating, and she drove him back to school. He seemed to be happy. He was bright, and she was keeping her fingers crossed that he'd stay focused on schoolwork. He had so much promise—he was funny, clever, personable. Naughty now and then, of course, but that was normal.

Annie pulled up by the tavern's back door and went inside, then paused to listen. She always did that now, afraid that somehow the murderer might be in the house.

It was really terrible to be scared.

Claudius came running to welcome her home. She gave him a big hug and took off her jacket. Minutes later, just done feeding him—he'd pawed his bowl a few times till she got the point—the phone rang.

She snatched up the receiver. "Thurston Tavern."

It was Gus Jackson. He had news he'd trade for dinner at her place. "How about tonight?"

"Okay," she said cautiously, wondering if he'd arrested someone.

"Great." He hesitated, then said, "I'd love to have you over to my house, but it's still a mess. Mike's moved back to campus, but I haven't had time to get the place cleaned up."

"I saw Mike the other day. He told me he'd moved back to the dorm. We think we found the missing graveyard. One old slate stone had the Wyndham family name."

"No kidding? That's great."

"Mike took a lot of pictures, so he should have a great history project." Mentally, she was reviewing the food she had on hand. "By the way, we're having meatloaf."

"Good, I like meatloaf." He laughed. "Did you think I wouldn't?"

Claudius, comfortable on the rag rug by the kitchen stove, yawned and stretched, oblivious to Annie's ongoing troubles. She'd mentioned meatloaf, and he seemed to like the sound of that. His nose twitched with pleasure.

A short while later, by the time she'd whipped up a salad and set the table, Kirk arrived. She told him they were having company.

His gaze stayed on her face. "Chill out. You like Gus, so what's the problem?"

"No problem," she said, her voice carefully neutral. Then she admitted, "It's just that sometimes he drives me crazy."

Kirk smiled but kept his thoughts to himself.

Gus showed up soon after, and they sat down to eat. Kirk chatted about his class load and the responsibility of mentoring half-a-dozen grad students.

Annie put the coffee on. When she sat down again, she waited for a lull, then said, "So, Gus, what's the big news?"

"We decided to take another look at Stella Danforth's death."

"How come?"

"I told the headmaster, Dr. Lawrence, that we'd recovered one of the items stolen from the library—the miniature you found in Rocky Martinez's jacket pocket. Well, Dr. Lawrence remembered that he'd received an urgent phone call from Stella Danforth the day she died. She'd sounded very upset and demanded to see him. But he was on his way to the airport and said he'd talk to her when he got back. Unfortunately, that was the following Monday, and by then she was dead."

Annie nodded. "I'll bet she wanted to talk about the library robbery. She saw something suspicious and was going to tell Dr. Lawrence. That's why she was killed."

"We don't know that for sure," Gus said mildly.

"Come on," she scoffed. "It walks like a duck, talks like a duck. What else could it be?"

"Even so," he said, "we can't go around arresting people if there's no proof a crime was committed."

"Didn't you think it strange that an active woman in good health suddenly fell downstairs and died?" she asked.

"She could have had a stroke."

"What did the autopsy say?"

He sighed. "Okay, she didn't have a stroke, but she could've had a dizzy spell. That wouldn't necessarily have shown up in the autopsy, and it's possible that the call she made to Dr. Lawrence had nothing to do with the robbery. Maybe she wanted a raise."

"Only an idiot would believe that. The people who worked with her—"

"You questioned the school staff?" he demanded.

"Well, I said I would." Not exactly true, but close enough.

"Of all the—"

"What's going on here?" Kirk looked from Gus to Annie.

"I offered to help with the investigation," she said by way of explanation. "You'd think he'd appreciate a little help, considering that the cops have sat on their hands for twelve months."

"Jesus," Gus muttered.

She ignored him. "The day Stella died it snowed like crazy, and the main road was closed for hours. So the odds are if Stella was murdered, someone from the school did it. I questioned Pete Lanza and Marnie Pearson, and they acted suspicious."

"Why the hell am I not surprised?" Gus muttered.

"Pete claimed he'd just come back from skiing," Annie said. "It's just his word, though. Supposedly, he went over to Marnie's apartment, and they spent the night together, which isn't much of an alibi. They both could've slipped over to the library, pushed Stella down the stairs, and gone back to bed with no one the wiser."

"I see," Gus said. "What about motive?"

"I didn't get around to asking that," Annie admitted. She went to the fridge and took out apple crisp and heavy cream. After nuking the crisp, she cut three portions and set them down on the table. "I can't be expected to do everything."

They ate in silence. Gus looked as if he didn't trust himself to speak.

When Gus put down his fork, Kirk said, "Want another helping?"

"No, thanks. I'm full. And I'd better be going."

Annie, contemplating the disaster she'd just made of the evening—she and Gus had practically been at each other's throats—shoved her dish away.

Oh, well, so she'd made a fool of herself. Kirk had seen her at her worst before. Never mind Gus. Who cared what he thought anyway?

The fact that she did, she preferred not to think about.

She walked with him to the door.

He stared at her for a second, then put his hand on the doorknob. "It's started snowing again," he said.

She couldn't think of anything to say.

He opened the door. "I'll finish cleaning the cottage. We'll have dinner at my place soon. I'll call you."

Sure he would, she thought as the door shut and she watched him trudge through the snow to his car.

Probably her own life was in danger. It certainly had been the other night, and for all she knew, it still was. What had changed, really? The killer or killers could be anyone, even someone she knew. Evil hiding behind a mask of small-town friendliness. People she took for granted. The mailman, the plumber, customers . . .

But tonight was very much like any other evening at the tavern. Kirk finished helping her clean up, then said he had papers to correct and disappeared upstairs.

Claudius snagged some paper from the trash, and she wrestled with him over it. Finally, she managed to take it away.

"Keep out of the garbage!"

He woofed his defiance.

She glared, which had little effect on him. He had her number, that much was obvious.

She sighed and went up to bed.

The next morning was Saturday, the start of Winterfest Weekend. Kirk had already left for the college lab when Annie came downstairs to take Claudius for his morning walk.

Most Saturdays she opened the shop, but not today. She planned to spend the day at Fox Hill.

The cross-country ski race was scheduled for this afternoon. Not that she had any hope of winning, but the exercise would be good for her. Unfortunately, it was a costume race. Participants were encouraged to show up in fancy dress, or at the very least, in masks.

A few days ago, she'd dug out a carton of old costumes. Some were utterly hopeless. Moths had gotten into the fairy princess dress and cowboy hat and chaps, but the gypsy outfit hadn't looked bad. Washed and ironed, the flounced skirt and top had turned out pretty well.

She'd add bangles and a gypsy mask and black wig, then black out a front tooth. The only possible fly in the ointment would be maneuvering on skis while encumbered with petticoats, skirts, and an armload of clanking bangles. Well, the cross-country race wasn't as much about winning as it was about having fun.

Claudius meandered down the driveway, dog tags clinking in the crisp morning air. Annie, on the other end of the leash, was appreciating how the snow had turned the woods into a fairyland of white interspersed here and there with stark black tree trunks. It was half past ten a.m. and the sun was already almost halfway across the sky.

What was it Gus had said one morning last summer? She'd been a little depressed, and he'd bought her a cup of coffee at a downtown diner. He'd said, "You don't know how lucky you are." At the time it had seemed an odd statement. In retrospect, even odder.

She didn't know much about him. He'd been a Boston homicide cop in another lifetime. He'd been shot, a bad wound; then he'd changed jobs and moved to Lee.

Okay, he was a smart cop. He knew when to keep his cards close to his vest, when to bet, and when to fold. Well, suppose—just suppose—Rocky had really been mixed up in something big. Something to do with that stolen miniature. He'd had it in his possession when he died. It certainly seemed as if he'd taken part in the library robbery. If Gus knew this, if he had proof—well, how could she find out for sure?

She trudged back to the tavern and got into the gypsy outfit and her winter jacket. Then she dug out Claudius's costume and, after a brief battle, got it on him. He was a pirate with a beribboned black cap with skull and crossbones—with holes for his big ears. As a finishing touch, he wore a red-and-white striped shirt with a gold fringed sash.

"You look great!" she assured him.

His lip curled.

"Chill out."

He refused to look at her.

"Okay, have it your way," she said.

Without another word, she loaded Claudius and her cross-country skis in the Volvo and drove over to Fox Hill School.

When she arrived, there was nowhere to park. Cars lined the street leading from downtown Lee, and along both sides of Powderhouse Road. Crowds of people were already gathering for the start of the race.

By sheer luck she managed to squeeze the Volvo into

the lot by the powderhouse, jump out, straighten her skirts, and slide booted feet into her bindings. Poles in hand and Claudius by her side, she made her way down the street to the area behind the rink. Kids and adults were everywhere—clumping about on skis in brightly colored outfits of every size and description. John Wayne, Elvis, and Dracula were well represented, with at least a dozen pint-sized witches, Barneys, and Harry Potters. The store-bought costumes looked pricey, of course. God, she was getting cynical.

It was too nice a day for that. She was determined to forget her troubles and enjoy herself.

Gaily fluttering red-and-blue flags had been set up next to the sign-in table. There were refreshments on another, nearby table: coffee, hot chocolate, donuts, and cider.

Annie adjusted her scraggly black wig and dug out ten bucks for the fee. Molly Houghton grinned, put the bill in her metal box, and wished her luck.

Claudius, meanwhile, was busy trying to squeeze under the sign-in table. Annie hauled him out and ignored his sulking, gripped her poles, squared her shoulders, and headed for the starting point.

She hadn't skied this year, other than a few forays through the neighboring woods. Clumping around familiar terrain hadn't prepared her for competition.

She pushed off and headed downhill, the sound of her skis echoing like the wind as she slipped along the tree-lined course.

Lots of other, faster skiers passed her, all of them more determined than she was. Annie shrugged and fought back the urge to keep up.

His sash flapping wildly, Claudius padded along beside

her. He eyed the passing skiers wistfully. She told him that winning wasn't everything. He looked as if he didn't believe that for a minute.

At first she felt stiff, as if she'd already been working out for hours. Well, once she warmed up a little, she'd feel better. It was a lovely day, perfect for skiing. You couldn't ask for finer. The temperature had dropped last night. That, along with a spell of freezing rain, had coated everything with ice. Some tree branches had come down, but not many.

In the distance, she could see clear across the lake. The woods ended at a sunny slope; the Congregational Church steeple rose as if from a white carpet.

She slid down one hill and plodded up another, past innumerable trees, snow-covered stone walls, fields, and thickets. The wind sang in her ears. Her cheeks grew rosy with cold and exertion.

Claudius slogged on ahead, as if this were a forced march somewhere in the Arctic. Every few minutes, he turned around and gazed back at her. Beneath his pirate hat, he looked pained.

Huffing and puffing, Annie continued on. Forty-five minutes into the race, and she was wondering why she'd ever thought this would be fun.

The darned petticoats bunched up between her legs. Her wig kept slipping sideways. The bangles were driving her crazy, and she'd discovered muscles she hadn't even known she possessed.

All she could think of was somehow making it to the finish line. And lying down. Anywhere warm.

Another hill, this one steeper than any she'd come across so far. She groped her way up it. God, this was torture. She should have worked out weeks ago, gotten herself into shape.

It was too late now. She passed a big rock, misjudged the distance to her right ski, bumped into the rock, and swore.

A few yards away, Claudius sat down, looking glum. Annie felt like a failure.

This was ridiculous. It was just a cross-country ski race, no big deal. Why in the world did she have to meet Claudius's high expectations?

At the top of the next hill, the course split in two. A sign with a pointing arrow tacked on a pine tree indicated that the left-hand trail ended at Gibbet Hill, the downhill course.

Which meant she'd made it halfway through the race.

The sun shone brightly, the temperature rose, and she loosened her muffler.

The terrain here was steeper and tougher than the first half had been. The trail meandered through a steep ravine. There wasn't much vegetation, and the stunted, ice-shrouded trees leaned downhill. The rocky outcroppings were mainly slate. In fact, that old slate quarry was around here somewhere. Near a creek, if memory served.

She slowed and listened for running water, although the creek would probably be silent, shrouded in snow and ice. Hearing nothing but the sigh of the wind and the occasional crash of falling ice as the temperature continued to rise, she summoned up her failing energy and moved on.

What she needed was a breather and a pick-me-up. Why hadn't she thought to bring some liquid refreshment along? Water . . . or better yet, a bloody Mary with lots of vodka.

All she knew was that she hadn't been this tired in ages.

She labored up the next hill, then barreled downward into yet another ravine, breathing hard. All around her, the snow was deep, shadowed, with steep hillsides stretching upward. Except for the clank of her bangles and her loud panting, it was utterly still. Her mittened hands felt sweaty on the ski poles. She stopped, took off her left mitten, wiped that hand across her forehead, then put the mitten back on.

Claudius had raced out of sight over the ridge. She wondered where he was. Not that it mattered. She'd come across him sooner or later. Her shoulders began to slump from weariness.

What happened next came with no warning. She heard a booming *crack,* and a large tree branch crashed down high on the hillside.

Next she was aware of a low rumble, and on both sides, huge slabs of snow began sliding downhill like a runaway train. Straight at Annie.

There was nowhere to go, and no time to get there. She was trapped.

She tried to save herself by grabbing a nearby tree and hanging on for dear life. For a second she thought she'd be okay. Yes! And there was someone at the top of the ridge, watching. She saw a black mask and a flash of bright orange. . . .

Then she was torn from the tree and found herself tumbling over and over, crashing into rocks and trees, until she had no sense of what was up or down. There was nothing but snow everywhere. She was buried.

Silence and stillness followed. At first she was afraid to move, afraid to do anything that might set more snow sliding on top of her. Then common sense took hold. She couldn't breathe. If she stayed there, she'd suffocate.

Frantically, she worked her arms and legs, flailing around, trying to clear the area around her nose and mouth. God, she thought groggily, what a way to die. It was horrible.

She screamed. Saliva dribbled from the corner of her mouth. Downward. Gravity. At least she was more or less upright.

She screamed again and then, after what felt like forever, heard sounds. Scratching, determined digging. Someone was trying to rescue her. Thank God. That masked person she'd seen, that flash of orange.

Barking.

Claudius.

"Here, boy!" she shouted.

He kept on digging.

Seconds later, sunlight filtered down—he'd dug a hole deep enough to reach her.

He barked again and again as she worked to free her legs. Snow on his muzzle made him seem enormous, and she'd never been so glad to see him in her entire life.

There on the snow lay a scrap of orange fabric. Had he chased the person she'd seen and attacked him or her?

"Hello!" she shouted. "Anyone there?"

No one answered.

CHAPTER
13

When Annie finally thrashed around enough to dig herself free from the snow, she was completely exhausted and numb. She lay still and took stock of her body. She was wretchedly cold, but what else was new. Even with mittens, her hands were blocks of ice, and her feet felt as if they belonged to someone else.

She heard Claudius bark and felt him lick her face, his tongue sandpapery on her cheek.

Her brain felt sluggish, her eyelids were stuck together with icy snow, and her petticoats were torn. Her wig was gone. No loss there, but other than that, the race had been a disaster.

She was way out of her league. Why in the world had she thought a cross-country ski race would be no big deal?

And why hadn't she worn a second pair of socks?

Claudius, acting decidedly chipper, had ditched the pirate hat. He licked her face again.

"Enough, cut that out." She shoved him away and attempted to come to grips with her situation. Lying there wasn't an option. The temperature wouldn't stay above freezing for long, and hypothermia was bound to set in soon if she didn't move. Besides, she was getting hungry.

Claudius licked her face with renewed urgency.

Struggling upright—against gravity and her inclination to lie right there and die—she spent the next fifteen minutes floundering around, looking for her skis and poles. She finally discovered one pole some distance downhill. Both skis and the second pole were nearby, sticking out of the snow. At first glance, they looked undamaged, but of course that was too much to hope for.

The bindings were broken.

Something made her trudge back and pick up the scrap of orange fabric. If she found the son of a bitch who'd seen the avalanche and done nothing to help her, she'd skin him alive.

It was well past noon. The sun was starting to slide into the jagged treetops. A red-tailed hawk circled overhead, keeping a beady eye peeled for field mice.

Lugging the skis over her shoulder, she plodded through stands of snow-covered hemlock and spruce. Her breath arced a white plume in the brittle cold, and as her body warmed, her spirits lifted. All in all, it wasn't so bad. So her skis were broken. They could be repaired. Despite some aches and pains, she was sound in wind and limb. She was able to shuffle her feet forward, although her muscles burned with weariness and effort. Best of all, she would never, ever have to do this again.

The wind picked up. Heavy with the scent of pine, it barreled through the woods. Branches rustled, creaking with each gust, and ice fell everywhere, shattering on the snow, blazing diamonds.

By the time she'd crunched through the snow around

the far side of the lake and was making a beeline for the finish line, she was so hungry that she was dreaming of food. What she'd give for hot anything. Hot rolls, hot stew, a hot toddy.

The smell of woodsmoke, boisterous laughter, and brilliant red sparks shooting skyward—people were crowded around the roaring bonfire by the ice rink.

The end of the course. Praise the Lord. Annie would have been jubilant if she hadn't been so pooped.

Someone handed her a steaming mug of coffee laced with bourbon—trust Fox Hill to get their priorities right. And canapes: smoked trout, brie, stuffed mushrooms, garlicky tomato and ricotta bruschetta, and sardines on crackers, to name but a few. Eat your heart out.

Annie wrenched off her stiff mittens. She intended to eat whatever she could get her hands on.

Her fingers were so cold and stiff that she dropped more than she managed to cram into her mouth. Claudius made out like a bandit.

It seemed that the race had been over for a good half hour before Annie had appeared, galumphing through the snow like Godzilla. The English teacher, Ivan Childress, had won. He stomped around, silver trophy under his arm, Elvis mask drooping around his neck, receiving gushing accolades, while she downed another hot toddy and wished she'd thought to wear more fleece. Layers of fleece. Or better yet, down. Gloves, mittens, liner gloves, long johns, hat, pants, boots, socks. More socks.

The bonfire crackled and roared, the flames leaping a good fifteen, twenty feet high. Someone tossed on more logs, and she gravitated toward the warmth. She felt toasty, happy. She turned around, presented her backside to the fire, lifted her ragged petticoats, and began to relax. Ahh.

Cary appeared out of the crowd. "I looked for you out on the course. What happened? You finished dead last."

"No kidding." Little did Cary know how close she'd come to stating the bitter truth.

"You're out of shape. You need a decent exercise program." Cary put a hand on her hip. Her Barbie costume was still in one piece. Her blond wig and falsies looked just fine.

"Exercise nothing. I got caught in an avalanche. Every bone in my body hurts."

"My God, what happened? Where were you?"

"In that ravine near the old slate quarry. A branch came down with a huge crash—must have been because of the ice we got last night. The noise started a snowslide. Worst of all, there was someone else nearby on the ridge. I caught a glimpse of orange through the trees. Someone in a costume. I called for help, but the jerk skied off and left me there. Claudius dug me out."

"Jeez, that's terrible, but I'm glad you're okay." Cary eyed Claudius with skepticism. His red-and-white shirt was bedraggled. "What's he supposed to be?"

"A pirate. I don't know what happened to his hat." Nor did she care.

Claudius yawned. He was terminally bored. They weren't talking about food.

They were still discussing Annie's harrowing experience when Dr. David Lawrence came up and extended his hand to Annie. He was a big man with a firm handshake, hard blue eyes, and a clipped gray beard. He was dressed in a thousand dollars' worth of the latest Gore-

Tex ski wear. No tacky costumes for the distinguished headmaster.

"So you're the owner of the famous canine detective," he said, smiling. "I've heard all about you and your dog—Claudius, is it?—from the senior honors English class."

"The kids seemed to like him," Annie said.

Cary had wandered off to the food table, where several men crowded around her, and Annie came to the sensible conclusion that the Barbie costume had been one hell of a good idea.

While here *she* was, left to entertain the headmaster, whose trousers Claudius was sniffing assiduously. She pulled him back. "Sit!" For once he did as he was told.

"That's certainly a noble-looking animal," Dr. Lawrence remarked. "Or he would be, lacking his, uh . . . costume."

"He's supposed to be a pirate." Annie cleared her throat. "I'm helping the police in their investigation, and I wondered if you'd remembered anything more about Stella Danforth's phone call the day she died."

He frowned. "Why . . . no. Stella was upset. We talked awhile. But I told that to the police."

As he was about to walk away, their conversation having ground to an abrupt halt, Annie said casually, "By the way, where were you the afternoon Rocky Martinez drowned?"

"In my office," he blustered. "I've told this to the police, as well. I don't care to discuss it further!" He turned away again, then stiffened. He was staring at a knot of people on the far side of the bonfire.

Annie followed his glance. Molly Houghton and her husband, Carl, were both decked out as orange-juice cartons. Molly's was "grovestand-style," and Carl's was "homestyle." They both wore black masks.

Several other teachers milled about in varied outfits, ranging from simple to elaborate. Orange was a popular color. Touches of it were visible almost everywhere.

Annie tried to see if any costumes were ripped. If Claudius had dropped that bit of orange fabric now safely tucked in her pants pocket, he'd probably taken a bite out of the jerk who'd left her lying there helpless.

Unfortunately, from what she could see, all the costumes had taken a beating—no wonder, what with miles of tramping through the woods. Even if she found a match for the scrap of orange fabric, she wouldn't be able to prove it was the same person.

But she couldn't help looking around at several hundred tired and happy people who were laughing, eating calzones and hamburgers, and congratulating the triumphant winner, Ivan Childress, who was still showing off his trophy.

Sam McIntyre stood on the fringe of the crowd in an orange clown costume with big ruffled cuffs. His teeth were white and even against his ruddy tan. He was laughing at something Marnie Pearson was saying.

All too clearly she'd latched onto Sam for the night—maybe she'd dumped Pete Lanza. At any rate, she was decked out in a patchwork get-up as a pseudo bag lady. Well, it suited her. Black tights were stretched over her legs. Her multicolored ragged jacket rippled and fluttered as she gestured.

Really. She was gushing and posing all over the place. Clearly, Marnie thought she was something special. All those Saturday mornings rushing downtown to LaKeisha's new spa—having her hair done, getting pounds massaged off. Then the rest of the week, putting them all back on again.

Her husky laughter trilled across the bonfire. She leaned close to Sam, whispering a private joke.

No doubt she'd had a wonderful time out on the course, probably finished in the top five, Annie thought sourly as she turned away. Was she jealous? Certainly not!

And there, fifty feet away on the other side of the leaping flames, was Gus Jackson, of all people, deep in conversation with his nephew, Mike. They wore Venetian half masks, which they'd pulled loose.

Gus didn't look her way. Was he deliberately snubbing her? Well, who cared.

She selected a veggie burger from the tray of food. Stress made her hungry. Even worse, stress made her fat. The fight or flight syndrome. The body went crazy making fat cells in case you never got to eat again.

Annie's common sense fought with her high stress and lost.

She ate the veggie burger and two brownies, and felt better.

She selected another brownie. "Who won the downhill ski race?" she asked Dr. Lawrence, more out of politeness than because she was truly interested. The headmaster had been standing there, apparently lost in thought.

"Wh . . . oh, one of the students on the ski team. A senior. He won a scholarship to Dartmouth. Cum laude, a real scholar-athlete." He edged away. In moments, the crowd had closed around him.

Claudius sighed.

"Something bugging you?" Annie moved the brownie out of his reach.

He rolled his eyes.

"Don't you like Dr. Lawrence? Neither do I. He's a snob."

A half-dozen people passed by, headed toward the hubbub on the other side of the bonfire. Their boisterous laughter echoed. Clearly, they'd found fun and good times.

Neither of which appealed to Annie for the very good reason that she was exhausted. She'd better just go home. That decided, she dumped the skis and poles in the Volvo, stripped off the despised petticoats, and took Claudius for one last walk. On the way home she'd stop by the store and pick up some milk and bread.

Instead, as she drove past the library, she pulled over and sat staring at the building. A growing certainty made her turn off the engine and remove the key.

There was something she wanted to check. Leah had found a hole drilled in one of the stones on Powderhouse Road. She'd said it could be evidence of a wrought-iron fence. There might be some mention of the fence in one of the library letters, Annie thought. It wouldn't hurt to look.

The main reading room was deserted. Even the most studious bookworms were outside at the bonfire, chowing down and having a good time.

Annie's footsteps echoed hollowly on the wood floor as she entered the reference room. The glass case containing Amos Franklin's letters drew her like a magnet. She examined the wrinkled paper, slanting old script, and faded ink and found herself thinking that people didn't write like that anymore. Penmanship was a lost art.

A quick search of the nearest case produced what she was looking for: an undated paper in Joshua Barnes's own hand, showing that his tract of land on Powderhouse Road was bounded on the south by Obidiah Putnam's land, and on the east by Elijah Wyndham's land. So even before they wed, the elderly Joshua would have seen Patience on a daily basis.

Her sampler hung on the nearby wall. She'd worked it in the usual pale linen, the colors of the thread faded. It showed a view of Powderhouse Road as it had looked in the seventeenth century: the church with a tall steeple, the line of little houses, trees, tiny people. She'd even stitched three children playing, cows in a meadow, and a barking dog.

Down at the bottom, the aphorism in carefully stitched letters: "Look upon my labors. Summer's flowers bloom and die. Thus, o stranger, shall you and I."

Annie looked closer. Well, well. There between two stone walls was a tiny, fenced graveyard, and a small shed.

No expert on needlework, she still recognized most of the stitches. Smooth running stitches for vines and leaves, French knots for the stones, and very small knots for the dog's rough fur. Patience's name, date, and the aphorism done in wavering cross-stitches. The shed's narrow clapboard siding was done in tiny, diagonal satin stitches, and tiny black knots topped the fence.

The hole Leah had found drilled in that stone in the wall wasn't proof positive of the fence's location, but it was certainly interesting.

Patience had worked the sampler in the seventeenth century, when that fence had surrounded the old graveyard, and a shed like that would have stored bodies during the winter.

There was a real shed like that one near the powderhouse, where the grounds maintenance crew kept rakes, shovels, and other tools.

Until this past week, Rocky Martinez had been part of the maintenance crew.

How interesting.

Annie needed to take a look at that shed, for obvious reasons. The cops should have checked it out by now, but maybe they hadn't.

She had every intention of searching it, and if it was locked, she'd get around that, too.

Cary's cousin, George, was a locksmith. He owed Annie a favor, big time. Last year, he'd gotten married, and she'd supplied the reception dinner for the fifty-odd guests at cost: roast chicken, lobster tails, shrimp cocktail, baked Alaska—the works.

It was time to collect.

He'd lend her a set of picklocks, no questions asked.

She left the library, thinking hard. Powderhouse Road hadn't changed all that much, although the houses were now mostly school dorms.

Crossing the street, she noticed that the party by the bonfire was breaking up. The fire was dying down, and groups of people were heading for their cars.

Several hurried by as Annie led Claudius back to the Volvo. The next moment, she was taken completely by surprise. One second Claudius was walking along, minding his own business—the next he was airborne, growling, barking, in full attack mode.

Thank God she had a tight grip on the leash as he barreled into a knot of people. Pete Lanza dropped his armload of costumes and yelled, "Hey!" Taken by surprise, he tried fending the dog off with his forearm, while giving him a good kick in the ribs. Claudius managed to dance out of reach while Annie hauled him back.

"Stop it!" she shouted.

But Claudius was unbelievably strong.

"Stop it! Heel!" Bracing herself, she hauled him back. *Good grief. It was like trying to rein in a full-grown mountain lion.*

Miraculously, and as suddenly as he'd started growling, Claudius stopped. He stood tense, quivering, growling at Pete Lanza.

"I'm sorry," she gasped. "Are you all right?"

"You'd better keep that damn mutt under control," Pete said angrily. Another muttered curse, and he gathered up the costumes and walked rapidly away. There didn't seem to be much point in shouting more apologies at his retreating form. Pete wasn't in any mood to listen.

Annie drove home in a foul mood. Claudius lay quiet beside her in the front seat. As she switched off the engine, she said, "That's it. Life without parole. No more privileges, no treats, no more car rides. No nothing. And I'd like a full apology. No more kidding around. I mean every word. You know what you did was wrong, Claudius. Now go into the house and stay there."

He jumped out and headed for the back door, standing silently as she let him inside. Then he trotted off to the kitchen, head and tail held high to let her know he wasn't impressed with the big lecture. It was suppertime, and he expected to be fed.

Fine.

She closed the door, kicked off her boots, and dragged off her jacket, wishing things weren't such a tangled mess and that life would go back to normal—whatever that was.

A cup of tea, a ham sandwich, and three brownies later, she felt more like herself.

The answering machine was blinking. There were two messages. The first was from Kirk, indicating that he and Leah were driving to Boston and wouldn't be back for a few days. The second message was from Sam McIntyre. He wanted to know if she'd like to go out for a drink. It wasn't quite nine o'clock, but she was tired and depressed, and she called him back to say no.

Mrs. M. answered on the third ring with a brisk: "Yes?"

Annie explained who she was, and Mrs. M. informed her that Sam wasn't home. He was over at Fox Hill School.

Annie had already figured as much, but going into further explanation was beyond her right now. "Please tell him I called and thanks for the invitation, but not tonight."

"What?" Mrs. M. barked. She was a little hard of hearing.

Annie repeated the message until Sam's mother indicated she'd gotten the gist of it and abruptly hung up.

Claudius came out into the hall and dumped his food dish at her feet.

"Okay. Dinner, but no treats," she told him. She rummaged in the pantry and found half a bag of dog food he didn't like. She'd been meaning to give it the heave-ho, but in the circumstances he deserved it. In spades.

She dumped it in his dish, along with gravy made of wheat germ and warmed-up beef bouillon.

He eyed the mess with profound suspicion, then sat down and waited for something better to appear.

"Too bad," she told him. "We're living on a budget, and that includes you. Wheat germ tastes good." Big fat lie, but what did he know. "It'll give you bright eyes and a shiny coat."

He yawned. Obviously, he thought his eyes and coat were fine as they were, thank you very much.

"Couldn't you," she said sweetly, "just this once, eat what's put in front of you without an argument?"

He didn't move.

"Okay, suit yourself. I don't care if you starve to death." Leaving him to think it over, she took a rump roast out of the freezer for tomorrow.

Several couples had made reservations for an anniversary celebration. She had everything well in hand. The tavern was clean and neat, no piles of chewed this and that lying around, thank God.

Recently, in an act of sheer desperation, she'd bought a hard rubber Kong toy for Claudius. It had small holes in which to hide a treat, peanut butter or a tiny dog bone. So far, Claudius guarded it jealously, spending hours licking at the hole, trying to extract every last bit of peanut butter.

It kept him pretty busy, and he didn't have time to eat other things he'd shown an unfortunate predilection for, like the linoleum tile bathroom floor.

The telephone rang.

Annie answered, hoping it was a wrong number. She was too tired to deal with reality. "Thurston Tavern."

The voice was low, muffled, but she knew it was a man's.

"Do you want to know why Rocky Martinez died?"

"What if I do?" she asked cautiously.

"Then meet me tonight at Fox Hill School. And bring money."

"How much?"

"Two hundred."

"I don't have that much. I could get maybe a hundred—"

"All right. That's better than nothing."

"Where?" There was silence at the other end. Annie gripped the receiver with cold fingers. *"Where?"*

The voice dropped to a whisper, as if the connection was fading. "You know where."

"I don't! How would I know—"

"You know where. You were there the other day, searching in the woods."

"The woods?" She'd been with Leah, Mike, and Cary in the woods near the old powderhouse the other day. She'd seen the flash of what could have been binoculars.

"Ten o'clock. Come alone. I'll be watching." He hung up.

It was almost nine o'clock now and as dark as pitch outside. She replaced the receiver and sat very still, wondering what to do. By rights she should call the cops.

The red answering machine light was still blinking— an earlier call she'd missed. She pressed the button, and Mike's voice said, "Hi, Annie. Could you drop off some more notes on the graveyard? I'm in big trouble. Turns out the project is due Monday, so I really need them. I'll be up later. Uh, could you come up tonight? Thanks."

The machine clicked off as Claudius trotted in with his Kong toy. He lay down next to Annie's chair with a satisfied sigh. Absently, Annie patted his head, finding a feeble spark of comfort in the fact that it wasn't quite nine o'clock. She was safe and warm here in her own home. There was more than an hour to go before ten. She could spend that time deciding to call the cops, or at least Gus Jackson. The cops could show up and possibly nab Rocky's killer.

But Mike needed the graveyard notes tonight. She could kill two birds with one stone if she went to Fox Hill: help Mike and find out why Rocky had died.

Of course, she could call the police and still take the notes to Mike, but then she probably wouldn't find out anything useful.

Only an idiot would go alone. If she did as the caller demanded, she could be killed. That wouldn't do anyone much good. Who would take care of Claudius and the tavern?

She patted him on the head again. She could call Gus Jackson. His number was in the book. But was he home? And would he agree to let her rendezvous with her unknown caller? Or would his legal cop mind order her to stay home and let the boys in blue handle things?

They'd handled everything till now, and the result was zip. Nothing. Nada.

The man on the phone—*if* it was a man. It could have been a woman with a husky voice. Someone like Marnie Pearson, who happened to have a remarkably deep voice to go with her stump-like ankles. The caller, whatever his sex, said he'd be watching. It was an implied threat, of course. Maybe he thought she'd be so intimidated, she'd be scared silly.

And maybe he was right.

Suppose the caller didn't just have inside knowledge of

why Rocky had died. Suppose he'd actually lured him out onto the ice and killed him?

Or suppose she had it backwards? What if the caller was a witness who was too frightened to go to the cops? She tried to think of a reason that would fit—well, maybe he had his own troubles with the law and didn't want to get involved.

That made sense, sort of.

She actually picked up the phone book to look up Gus's number. And then . . . the person who'd called wouldn't show up. She knew that with certainty. *Because he said he was watching. Maybe he could see her right now, through the windows . . .*

She got up and drew the curtains, then sat down again. Kirk and Leah had gone to Boston, so she was basically all alone in the house. Except for Claudius.

The wind rattled a shutter outside. He turned his head, alert, ears pricked. After a moment, he put his head down on his paws and closed his eyes.

All too soon it was nine-thirty, then nine-thirty-five. Time to go, and she hadn't called the cops. Never mind. She take the graveyard notes to Mike, that's all. If someone happened to be up at the school, someone with inside knowledge of Rocky's death that he wished to tell her, fine. She could handle it.

Taking a deep breath, she padded through the house to the back door, then realized Claudius was right behind her. He stiffened and growled.

"Shhh!"

She dragged on her jacket and muffler, grabbed her notebook on the graveyard, and took one hundred dollars from the shop's petty-cash box. Then she let herself and

Claudius out. By the time she got the Volvo fired up and started down the driveway, she knew it was too late to turn back. Well, not too late. She could still change her mind and go back if she wanted to.

But why should she? She was just taking some notes to Mike, and Claudius was right there beside her. Everything was okay. She'd bet on Claudius any day, or night.

Of course, the caller, if he was the murderer, might well have a gun. In which case she might end up dead. Claudius, too.

Nonsense. With his police training, he knew how to handle bad guys with guns. They'd be fine.

For long minutes she didn't pass any other cars on the road. The headlights traced trees arcing overhead, branches laden with snow. Closer to the center of town, she saw a few trucks, then one or two cars cruise by. No headlights appeared in the rearview mirror. Nobody seemed to be paying her any attention.

When she got to Powderhouse Road, she had her first really bad moment. Most of the students and faculty were safely tucked up in their beds or at least relaxing in front of a TV set. At the far end of the street, a faint glowing ember indicated the site of the bonfire. The space in between yawned like a black hole. That's where she had to go.

She pulled over and parked near Wyndham Hall. The gnarled oak tree in front made her think of Patience, hanging gray-faced in death.

She wrapped Claudius's leash tight around her fist and walked quickly to the front door and rang the bell.

After a minute, the door opened. The dorm parent, Mrs. Keene, gray-haired and plump, said, "Yes?"

Annie produced her notebook. "Mike Rawlings needs this for a history project. I'm just dropping it off. Er, is he around?"

"Yes, but he can't have visitors. It's past nine-thirty."

"Oh, well, could you please give him these notes?"

"Certainly."

Annie handed them over, and a moment later the door closed.

She was sorry she hadn't had a chance to talk to Mike. Now it was too late.

Well, it wouldn't hurt to go down the street a short way, she thought. Seconds later, with the help of her pocket flashlight, she was walking past the hockey rink. Just ahead lay the fieldstone wall behind which she suspected lay the mortal remains of Elijah Wyndham and his family. Not Patience, of course. God knew where the chopped-up bits of her body lay buried.

She climbed over the stone wall while Claudius leaped over effortlessly. The snow here was scuffled. Of course. They'd searched here for a good hour or so the other day.

Behind her, the old powderhouse sat still and remote in the cold moonlight. Quaint-looking, red brick by day, by night it loomed huge and windowless. The slate roof looked black. She knew the door was around the other side, by the small shed where the school maintenance crew kept their tools.

She stood in the shadows of a big maple, carefully looking in every direction. There was no sign of life, not a sound. No movement other than a slight wind that set nearby icy branches rattling.

She glanced at her watch, surprised at how calm she felt, and took a deep breath. Just about ten p.m. Well . . .

Claudius lifted his head, sniffing the night air.

The snow crunched under her feet, echoing under the trees as she emerged from the shadows almost as if someone were following her. She spun around, stomach knotted, but saw nothing.

Thank God.

Claudius whined and nudged her leg.

"Quiet!" She looked around, terrified that he'd seen someone. She stared everywhere and saw nothing. She turned the flashlight toward the looming powderhouse. Dead leaves rustled in the wind.

They walked to the end of the wall—Claudius, nervous by now, was trying his damndest to clamber over the wall on the right. She hauled him back. "Stop that!"

Suddenly, and for no discernible reason, Annie was terrified, her heart pounding like a drum, so loud that it was all she could hear as she scrambled over the wall after Claudius.

They rounded the far side of the powderhouse and stopped dead. Panting hard, she stared in disbelief.

The door was open.

The interior of the building yawned blackly.

No way was she going in there. Not on her life.

For long moments, she stood paralyzed, unable to move a muscle. She didn't know what she'd expected to see, but certainly not this open door.

Only a complete idiot would go in there.

She took a step forward almost before she knew what she was doing. Claudius, head down, growled softly.

And then, down the street, a car engine roared to life and headlights flared. The car started forward with a screech of tires.

That did it. She turned and ran back to her car, with Claudius dragging her the last few feet. Rounding the hood, she yanked the door open and Claudius leaped in. She was right behind him, locking the doors as fast as she could, fumbling for the keys. Finally finding them and managing to insert the ignition key, she got the engine started.

The other car was almost upon them now, racing down the street.

She heard a popping noise, like a firecracker, and her rear window disappeared in a shower of glass.

He was shooting at her!

She shoved Claudius down and floored the accelerator. The Volvo roared out of the parking lot and down the street. As her pursuer careened after them, another shot was fired. Lights sprang on in nearby houses. Windows flew open, and people started yelling.

She reached the bottom of the hill, spun the wheel hard left, and took off toward the edge of town. Fifty yards ahead, a road led off to the right. She took it, thanking her stars it was plowed. Frantically, she tried to think. She knew this road well, and maybe her pursuers didn't.

It was a slim advantage but better than nothing.

She roared on, taking a curve in the road, and the car behind her disappeared. The hill to the right was known as Gibbet Hill for a good reason.

She shuddered, hunched over the wheel, and pressed on the accelerator. Several old Colonial houses set behind picket fences very close to the road flashed by.

To her horror, car headlights appeared behind her. She put on a burst of speed, so busy looking in the mirror that she didn't notice the Volvo was swerving sideways. There was a bang and a shudder as her side mirror lopped off a wooden pineapple on a gate. Then she swerved back onto the road.

Behind her, she heard a crash, then a window flew up. Shouts echoed. A quick look in the rearview mirror showed that a section of the picket fence had collapsed on the hood of a dark van. A man's tall figure leaped out and pointed his arm at her. More shots were fired, and then he disappeared from view as she whipped around the next corner.

She bent down and concentrated on driving straight to the police station, where she ran inside and told the first cop she saw that shots had been fired at her on Powderhouse Road.

The cop happened to be Sgt. Choate, not exactly her favorite person. This wasn't Annie's day.

"Is Gus Jackson around?" she gasped.

Gus wasn't there. What else was new? He was never around when she needed him. She didn't know whether to laugh or cry.

"Gus went to the scene of a bad accident on Route 150," Sgt. Choate said. "A tractor-trailer slammed into a pickup truck and turned over. There were multiple injuries. We may have to fly the pickup truck driver to Manchester." He handed her a cup of coffee. "You look like you need this. A couple of black-and-whites will check out the school. Let's get your statement down."

She sipped coffee and managed to calm down a little, although her handwriting was pretty shaky as she wrote out exactly what had happened: the phone call she'd received, her decision to go to the school to deliver some notes to a student, then seeing the powderhouse door wide open, and the shots fired.

This was something Sgt. Choate couldn't ignore.

He read her statement, asked her several questions, then rushed from the room. A short while later, flashing lights appeared outside the window, and with sirens wailing, two police cars roared off down the hill in the direction of the school.

She drank a second cup of coffee. When the squad room radio down the hall erupted in a prolonged burst of static, Sgt. Choate went off to check developments. One look at his expression when he returned over an hour later and Annie knew they hadn't found the man who'd shot at her.

"Several people heard shots," Choate explained. "We found the broken fence, so that part of your story checks out, too. But the van is gone, and the guy got away. We'll do a more comprehensive search for evidence in the morning. Maybe we'll come up with shell casings and get a fix on the gun. Meantime, why don't you go home? You look beat."

Annie nodded. She was completely done in.

"Sure you can drive?" he asked.

"I'm okay, thanks."

It was nearly midnight when she finally arrived back at the tavern—with two squad cars trailing along to make sure she got there safe and sound. The officers checked to make sure no one suspicious was lurking around before they bid her good night.

All she wanted to do was crawl into bed, but Claudius had to do his business.

"Hurry up," she muttered.

Somewhat grumpily, he complied, and she pulled him inside, shutting the door and locking it, then setting the alarm.

She crept upstairs and fell into bed. Claudius padded soundlessly behind her and took his customary place at the foot of the bed. He put his head down on his paws while she curled into a fetal position and wondered why she still felt so cold.

Sunday morning, Annie woke to a sunny day. A sleepy glance at the clock indicated it was after nine o'clock. She'd overslept. She sat up, yawning widely.

Lord, she felt stiff. And she had a lot to do today.

First things first. A shower, clean clothes, and coffee. That accomplished, she pried her eyes open long enough to let Claudius out into the side yard and whip up a couple of fried eggs and toast.

After breakfast, she called Cary and told her what had happened last night. Cary was by turns astonished, horrified, and furious that she'd missed all the excitement. Then Annie called Gus Jackson. This call was much harder to make. She had to admit how stupid she'd been.

"I heard about what happened," he snapped. "For God's sake, can't you stay out of trouble?"

"Come on," she said. "What did you expect me to do? Stay home and screw up a chance to find Rocky's killer?"

"You're lucky you're not lying on a slab downtown!"

"Hey, I wasn't the one doing the shooting!"

"I read your statement. You were out of your mind, taking a chance like that. Every patrol car we could spare checked out Powderhouse Road and the school. They found the smashed fence, but the driver got the van going and took off before we arrived."

"I made a mistake, I admit. But at least I flushed the killer out—"

Gus hung up on her. It was half an hour before he could bring himself to call back. During that time, she fed Claudius and got busy preparing the rump roast for the anniversary dinner.

"Promise me one thing," Gus demanded when she answered his call.

Annie held her breath. She didn't like lying. She especially didn't like having to lie to a cop. She crossed the fingers of her left hand behind her back. "What?"

"Promise you won't do anything like that ever again. If this guy calls again, you call me or the station at once. Understand?" He interrupted her reluctant mumblings. "No if's, and's, or but's. Got that, Annie?"

"Okay."

"I'll have a car drive by the tavern a couple of times a day," he snapped. "They'll check in every hour on the hour. So don't try anything cute."

A thought occurred to her. "There might be a clue they missed. What if I drive up later on this afternoon—"

"Not on your life!"

"It's broad daylight!"

"I don't care if it's high noon! You got that?"

"Whatever. Look, I've got Claudius. He's better than any two-legged bodyguard."

Big sigh. "Just do as you're told for once."

An hour later, as he had promised, a black-and-white drove by and the phone rang. Annie looked out the window. The cops had a cell phone. She told them she was fine.

They nodded and drove off, and she called Cary's cousin, George, and told him what she wanted. With some reluctance, he agreed to come over with the lockpicks.

He was still complaining when he parked in her driveway. If anyone found out he'd loaned her the picks, there'd be hell to pay. But she insisted she'd be careful. No one would find out, and she'd return them by nightfall.

George grumbled something about knowing damn well he shouldn't trust a woman, that they'd both end up behind bars, but he finally went back to his truck.

Morosely, he slid the key in the ignition, while down the street, the black-and-white drove by.

The two cops stared at the red truck with LOCKSMITH emblazoned on its side. They slowed.

"Don't look at them," Annie cautioned. "Look at me. We're having an innocent conversation." She gave a jaunty wave at the cops, who nodded and sped off.

"George, I have an idea," she said thoughtfully.

"What?" he demanded, his voice heavy with suspicion.

"How about giving me a ride to Fox Hill School and back. Forty-five minutes. I just want to check something out."

"What?"

"A shed. We could take Claudius with us." It was a clever bribe, since George happened to be a dog person.

In no time at all they were barreling along the road to South Lee. George was resigned. Annie was pleased that things were going her way, and Claudius was delirious, since the side window was open and he was breathing in a million fascinating smells.

George slowed at a corner, and she said, "Drive faster. We don't want him to see us."

"Him? Who's him?" he demanded.

How to explain? The same "him" who'd murdered Rocky and his sister, Maria, and probably, at least as far as Annie was concerned, Stella Danforth a year ago. The same "him" who'd set up the powderhouse ambush in the dead of night.

But she hadn't mentioned the shooting to George and didn't intend to. Her life was complicated enough already.

CHAPTER
14

At her direction, George pulled over and parked in the lot behind the administration building. The plan was simple. They'd get out: George, professional-looking in overalls and carrying his bag of locksmith tools, and Annie, taking Claudius for a stroll. They'd go up the old powderhouse, unlock the door, and look around. Not that she really expected to find anything suspicious, but the door had been open last night. The killer might have left footprints, something to point to his identity.

That done, they'd check out the shed used by the maintenance crew. Annie had no idea what they'd find, but she was sure they'd find something.

They arrived at the powderhouse without incident, and George tried the doorknob, which refused to budge.

"Locked," he said, as if that was that and they might as well leave.

"So unlock it," she hissed, looking around to see if anyone was watching.

So far, so good. Students walked along the snowy paths. No one seemed to take an undue interest in what they were up to.

As for Claudius, he sat frowning and sulking. Obviously, he thought they should be taking a walk, not just standing around.

George selected a pick and stuck it in the lock, twiddled it around for a second, and popped the door open.

They were in.

The interior of the powderhouse was dim and smelled musty. The building was fairly small, maybe twenty feet square, with a vaulted roof. Shelves lined the walls and seemed to hold nothing more exciting than lawn fertilizer and weed killer.

If there was dust on the cement floor, Annie didn't see any. And no footprints.

George looked around bored. "Done?"

"I want to look in one more place." She wasn't sure how he'd react. After all, she'd mentioned unlocking one door, not two.

His reaction was decidedly negative. "I ain't got all day, Annie. You said one lock."

"Lobster tails," she said. "Roast chicken. Baked Alaska. If you'd gone anywhere else, you'd have paid through the nose."

"Okay, let's go," he said with a sigh, picking up his bag.

The shed wasn't far, built into the side of a small hill. It had a large door, stained brown, and a shiny new Yale lock.

Now, that was surprising, Annie thought as George bent once more to his task. *A new lock?* Why? The shed had been here for more than two hundred years.

George worked the pick and the lock clicked open. He straightened up, looking at her. "All set. You know, if you had a steady boyfriend and a decent love life, you wouldn't be wasting my time with this shit. How about I introduce you to this guy I know. He's got a steady job, doesn't drink—well, not much, and then only on weekends."

"I'm fine, thanks." She stood holding Claudius by his leash. She waited, strangely reluctant to go inside. There was a lot at stake. If they didn't find any clues, she was fresh out of ideas.

Claudius was waiting, too, although not quite so patiently. Finally, he took charge—well, someone had to—and scratched the door with his paw.

"Okay already," she muttered and pushed the door open. She didn't see anything unusual: a lawn mower with a grass catcher. A snowblower. Rakes and shovels hanging from wall pegs, and a tool bench.

It smelled of motor oil—several cases of oil were stacked in the corner. Like any other tool shed, there were shelves with cans of assorted nails, nuts, and bolts. Screwdrivers, hammers. Electric drills, and saws.

Actually, the shed could have used a good cleaning. Some trash had been tossed in one corner: a crumpled fast-food bag, an empty pizza box, a piece of cardboard.

Annie picked up the cardboard and found that the other side was covered with blue velvet. Interesting.

Something moved in the opposite corner. A field mouse. It scuttled away and disappeared in a hole in the wall.

She put the cardboard down and let Claudius take up the slack on his leash. He roamed around, sniffing the hole where the mouse had vanished. Losing interest, he headed for the tool bench and stopped, quivering. He looked at her and barked.

"What's wrong with him?" George muttered.

"I don't know . . . something's under that bench." She bent down and peered in the shadowy darkness. She could just make out a bulky, rectangular shape, and reached in and pulled it out. A duffel bag. Upon examination, she discovered it was empty except for a discarded pack of Marlboros.

Claudius sniffed the cigarette pack and then the duffel bag, still growling. Suddenly, he dug deep in the stitching, and when he looked up, something tattered and white was dangling between his teeth. She put her hand out. "Give."

Obediently, he released the bit of paper.

"Good boy."

It was half of a Boston parking ticket, dated three weeks ago. By now, the bag's owner had probably taken care of the fine.

Even so, they took the duffel bag and relocked the door. George said, "What the heck does an old duffel bag matter one way or another? Somebody probably left his hockey gear in the shed."

"It's not big enough. It's not a hockey bag."

It started to snow again as they got into George's truck. They'd been gone more than an hour, but Annie had left a note on the back door, "Gone grocery shopping, be right back."

A perfectly normal afternoon chore, and with any luck the cops would buy it.

When she showed up with no grocery bags, they might have second thoughts, but she decided she'd cross that particular bridge when and if she came to it.

George turned the key in the ignition and nothing happened. "I've been having trouble," he said with a sigh. "Damn starter." He turned the key again. This time the engine coughed twice and turned over before it died.

"Damn!"

Annie knew better than to interrupt a man in the middle of car troubles. She kept herself occupied, thinking.

The best place to hide something was where no one would expect. Like milk in a refrigerator or hay in a haystack. Not that hiding an empty duffel bag was a big deal. Someone had tossed it under the workbench.

Not the bag itself, but what it had once held.

Eventually, George managed to coax his engine into turning over, and they drove back to Lee. When they got to the tavern, the cop car was parked by the back door.

"What the hell is this?" George said, frowning.

"We had a robbery scare the other night. Turned out to be nothing, but the cops got carried away. Listen, could I borrow the picks for a day or two?"

"Why?"

"I might want to check that shed again."

"Don't let anyone know you've got 'em." He handed them over.

"Thanks." She stuffed the picks in her jacket pocket.

Itching to leave, he'd already shifted into reverse, so she got out of the truck, taking Claudius and the duffel bag with her.

George wasted little time roaring off down the driveway, and she approached the two cops, who eyed her expressionlessly.

She wasn't fooled. That blank look masked an officious police mentality. They'd noted the absence of shopping bags. One empty duffel bag didn't count. Where were the milk and eggs?

"Hi," she said.

They nodded. One was blond, one dark-haired, both big and beefy. The blond smiled, pretended to aim his forefinger and thumb at her and said, "We saw the note on the door."

"Yeah," his partner agreed. No smile.

They both eyed the duffel bag.

She didn't owe them an explanation, she told herself. It was a free country. If she went out to buy groceries and came back emptyhanded—so what?

"Wouldn't you know," she said, "I couldn't find any cilantro. Hard to find this time of year."

"Really?" said the dark-haired cop. "I bought some the other day at Pick n' Pay."

"Oh, well, I went to a little organic food store. They usually have everything, but no luck today."

At this point, tail wagging like mad, Claudius galloped up and attempted to lick the cops to death.

With a great deal of difficulty and considerable embarrassment, Annie dragged him into the house.

By the time she got the door shut and dumped the duffel bag, the cops had taken off. So much for the boys in blue.

Claudius made for the kitchen. He lapped up what water there was and banged the bowl until Annie refilled it. Finally satisfied, he curled up on the rug by the stove.

She made tea and mulled over what to do next. Common sense said "Hand the duffel bag over to Gus and let him take it from there." Not that that would do a damn bit of good if someone, the killer, were watching the tavern.

Of course, she might be wrong. The duffel bag might have nothing to do with the murders.

So now what? she thought. Was she supposed to just sit here, waiting for that homicidal maniac to take another potshot at her? If he was hanging around, watching her, then he'd seen her drive off with George in his red truck and an hour or so later come home again.

Or he could have followed them—a disturbing thought. Lulled into a false sense of security by George's presence, she'd forgotten to check the mirror. A dozen thugs could have trailed them to Fox Hill and back, and she'd have been none the wiser.

Talk about stupid.

Well, it was over and done with. There was no use worrying about it. She had dinner to prepare and half-a-dozen paying guests on the way.

Several hours later, the guests having departed, well fed and happy, Annie turned off the outside light and locked up. As she cleared away the dinner dishes, she decided to phone Gus.

She got his answering machine. Big letdown. She'd practically worked herself to a frenzy over the duffel bag.

She hung up without leaving a message.

To tell or not to tell, that was the question. Sharing what could be crucial evidence seemed a no-brainer, but Gus's track record in divulging anything meaningful in return was dismal. If she handed over the duffel bag, she'd never hear about it again.

She wasn't Wonder Woman. There was only so much she could do alone. Three people were dead, and nobody seemed to care, despite hints from Gus about an ongoing investigation which so far hadn't produced a single suspect.

Things were getting definitely scary—she'd been run off the road, ambushed, and shot at. And what were the cops doing? Questioning her about groceries, for heaven's sake.

Gus wasn't stupid. Maybe the best thing would be to lay her theory out in detail. He'd have to give her a fair hearing.

She dialed his number again, and this time he answered. "It's me," she said.

"Where are you?" Suspicion deepened his voice.

"Home. I have something you should see."

"What?"

"Don't get mad." She told him about checking the shed and what she'd found—the duffel bag and Boston parking ticket. She did not tell him about George's lockpicks, which even now were burning a hole in her jacket pocket.

Then she had to endure a tirade about her duplicity, sneaking past the cops, committing God knew how many felonies.

"Two counts of B and E, for starters," Gus snapped. "The powderhouse, plus the shed. Then there's removal of evidence. Obstructing an ongoing investigation. I could go on. You're in real trouble, Annie. I could come over there and arrest you right now."

She sliced herself a piece of leftover chocolate cake. Stress definitely made her hungry. "Do you want to see the duffel bag, or what?"

It seemed that he did. Ten minutes later he was banging on the back door. Claudius barked and ran around in excited circles, and she let Gus in.

"You're looking pretty chipper for someone who just might end up in the slammer before the night's out," he said sourly.

"Baloney." She handed over the duffel bag and parking ticket, then cut him a piece of chocolate cake.

Claudius sprawled under the table, sniffed Gus's boots, and chewed the laces very carefully.

"Someone stalked me in the cross-country ski race," Annie said. "I can't prove it, but I bet it was the same man who shot at me last night."

"Anyone else see this mysterious stalker?"

"Well, no." So much for that.

She started to reach in her pocket for the piece of orange fabric, then forgot all about it as Gus unzipped the duffel and said coldly, "You ruined any prints, and there's no chance of retaining the chain of evidence. If this ties in with whatever the hell's going on at Fox Hill, it's completely useless in court."

"But if I hadn't searched the shed, you wouldn't have the bag at all."

"We'd have checked the shed sooner or later. We'd have found it." He shrugged. "It's probably nothing anyway."

"Yeah? Maybe they'd have removed the bag by the time you searched the shed." The way she figured it, she was ahead on points.

"Hmm, this might be something." Gus examined the parking ticket. "Boston. We'll run it down. Probably nothing. Anything else you want to talk about?"

"No." Why should she tell him everything? As usual, dealing with Gus was a one-way street.

Why did she persist in thinking he'd ride to the rescue like John Wayne?

That wasn't what happened in real life. Look at the six o'clock nightly news. People got shot, stabbed, and otherwise done in all the time, and what was the percentage of cases solved? Less than twenty percent—that dismal statistic she'd picked up from The Learning Channel.

Most real mysteries weren't solved by the cops. So what possible reason would she have to put all her eggs in that particular basket? None.

Gus finished his cake. His mouth curved into a smile. "How about a truce? Got a date to the dance tomorrow night?"

There was something about his smile . . . She felt herself melting, but was damned if she'd let him know it. She dithered. If she asked "What dance," she'd look stupid, and there was no point in lying. "No."

His smiled widened. "So, do you want to go?"

"Okay."

"Good. Pick you up at seven. Thanks for the cake. How about getting me a plastic baggie?"

She found one, and he slipped the ticket inside, then gazed down at his shoes and the half-eaten laces in amazement. Then he grabbed the duffel bag and, muttering to himself, he left.

She watched his car disappear down the driveway and thought about truthfulness and honesty. Men always made such a big deal about little white lies—like borrowing a set of lockpicks and keeping it a secret. . . .

The next day, for mysterious reasons known only to Gus and the Lee police department, the cruiser no longer drove by the tavern every hour on the hour. Well, Annie thought a little huffily, that was fine with her. It made sneaking around unnecessary. If the urge to detect anything overtook her—for instance, if she felt like going back to the tool shed at Fox Hill—she'd just jump in the Volvo and take off.

Unfortunately, the rear window needed replacing, so she dialed up Glass-2-U, who promised to get the job done within the hour.

She washed the kitchen floor, did the laundry, and dusted. Glass-2-U was as good as their word and showed up to replace the window within forty minutes.

She spent the next few hours in the shop. Not many customers. A few browsers, and one woman who couldn't make up her mind between lace napkins and a hooked rug. In the end she bought an old kitchen scale.

By noon, Annie came to the conclusion that she deserved the rest of the day off. She'd clean up clutter in the barn. Or just sit and read a book.

But Claudius drove her nuts, running from window to window, barking at everything that moved outside. By one-thirty, she couldn't sit still.

Okay. Make a list of suspects.

She drew a line down the middle of a yellow pad and wrote the names of everyone she could think of who was even remotely connected to Fox Hill School.

Dr. Lawrence headed the list, and why not? He was the headmaster. She scribbled the rest of the faculty and staff: the Houghtons, Pete Lanza, Marnie Pearson, and others on the left side of the line. The right side—motives, clues—remained embarrassingly empty. She'd put down the names of the three victims and a possible motive for their deaths.

Money. Vague, but human nature being what it was, money was a sure bet—or at least something of great value.

She looked over the faculty and staff. Harold Graham, the security guy, had shown up the afternoon they'd searched the woods behind the powderhouse, right after she'd seen the flash of light—probably binoculars.

He could have stuffed them under the front seat. She'd been so busy watching his yappy poodle, she hadn't noticed anything else. He merited a closer look, but not directly. If he knew anything, he'd never tell her. No, she'd pump someone else. Someone who worked at Fox Hill, who saw him every day.

As it happened, she knew one of the women who cleaned the school, Martha Valladares. Martha had a weakness for antiques and every few months browsed around the shop and bought something inexpensive. She wasn't the type to offer gossip that might endanger her job, but if Annie could soften her up with something, maybe she'd talk.

She dialed Fox Hill, and the switchboard connected her to housekeeping.

"Martha Valladares?"

"Yeah." Sounds of the phone being dropped. "Sorry, this is Martha. What do you want?"

"It's Annie O'Hara. Remember your asking me to look out for a cruet set? I happened to pick one up the other day." With the suggestion that she'd let it go cheap, she lured Martha to a local watering hole for a drink—Slattery's.

Half an hour later, Martha slid into a booth near the

back window, and since Annie said she'd pay, ordered a Scotch.

Annie stuck to lite beer and placed the cruet set on the table. In no time at all they struck a bargain, and Martha beamed.

"Come here often?" Annie asked, sipping her beer.

Claudius, under the table, laid his head on Annie's feet.

"A few times a week," Martha said. "It's a good crowd."

Annie nodded.

"South Lee's a nice town. Expensive, but what place isn't these days."

Annie agreed. It was tough, all right.

Claudius yawned.

Martha rambled on about the cruet while Annie got a ten-dollar bill from her wallet, at the same time letting the scrap of orange fabric fall onto the table.

Martha motioned to the waitress and ordered a double. "What's that?" she asked, eyeing the orange material.

"The craziest thing," Annie said. "I took part in the cross-country race at Fox Hill. A man was stalking me, and my dog got a piece of his costume. This is it."

"Good heavens." Martha picked it up. "Hey, it's got a tiny pattern, little flowers, you can hardly see them."

"Do you know Harold Graham?"

"Harry? Yeah, he works in security at Fox Hill."

"I wonder if he's the same man who's dating a friend of mine," Annie lied glibly. "He lives in a downtown apartment."

"No, Harry Graham's got a trailer over on West Street. Overflow Fox Hill staff housing. They hired a lot of new teachers and staff last year. Had to set up a couple of trailers. Harry's the last one on the street."

"Oh, he can't be the same guy."

Martha had a second scotch while Annie worked the conversation around to Stella Danforth's untimely death. "I think Stella's death is connected to Rocky Martinez and his sister, Maria. Rocky's dying in the lake was no accident. I don't care what the cops think."

Martha nodded. "Strange, his walking out on the ice like that. I saw him that afternoon, an hour or so before it happened. I'd just come to work. He was in the parking lot, talking to Sam McIntyre. Don't think they saw me." Martha returned her attention to her glass and drained it. "Who'd have guessed Rocky would be dead before nightfall?"

Annie frowned. Sam hadn't said anything about seeing Rocky the afternoon of his death.

It probably wasn't important. They were bound to run into each other all the time since they both worked at the school. On the other hand . . .

"Well," she said, "it is odd—three people dead in such a short time. Don't forget that Stella died a year ago. I think that's when it all started. She was in terrific shape for her age. Why would she suddenly fall down a familiar set of stairs? She was murdered. Nothing else makes sense."

"I wonder if Stella had a premonition she was gonna die," Martha said.

"Did you talk to her that day?"

"Yeah, I was working late, washing the hall floor in the administration building. She came in, acted funny, nervous. Maybe even frightened, now I think about it. She had this little poodle, Trixie. She was crazy about her. Bought her all kinds of toys. You name it, that dog had it. Someone at the school adopted the dog after Stella died. Yeah, she was definitely not herself that day—maybe that's why she fell. She could have tripped."

Harry Graham's poodle was named Trixie. He must have adopted her.

"I don't think Stella tripped," Annie said thoughtfully.

"So there's a maniac on the loose? Come on." Martha laughed.

Annie glanced out at the street. Meeting Martha had been a bad idea. She didn't know anything, or if she did, wasn't about to admit it.

Annie eyed her wristwatch. Almost three o'clock, and she still had a lot to do. Figuring out what to wear to the dance tonight, for instance. Something warm, sexy.

Did she own anything wearable that fit that criteria? A slinky black dress with spaghetti straps? No, she'd freeze.

She sighed, glanced out the window again, and spotted Tubby O'Connell walking along the sidewalk. Well, well. Why wasn't he back at his funeral parlor, counting all the money he'd made lately?

His eyes met hers and slid away. Suddenly, he turned around and headed across the street toward Fox Hill—of all places.

She frowned. What was he doing up at the school? *And there had been something definitely phony about Tubby's body language. She would swear he'd known she was in the bar. He'd been spying on her.*

But why would he—

Martha eyed Annie's empty glass. "Having another?"

"Uh, no, I have to drive home."

"Be careful. It's gonna ice up again when the sun goes down."

Annie dropped another ten on the table. "I've got to go. Just remembered something I have to do."

Taking Claudius, she hurried out the side door, which led to an alley. It stretched gloomily toward a narrow side street. Fox Hill was just around the corner, and she knew that Tubby drove a little blue sports car.

It took only seconds to get the Volvo started. She drove two blocks, then pulled over to the curb across from the school gates and waited.

As she sat there, Claudius jumped up in front and pressed his nose to the windshield. He let out a tentative woof or two, and she told him to cut it out. The idea was to avoid attracting attention.

He lay down, disgusted, while she stared out the window and hoped it wouldn't get dark too soon. She had no intention of missing the dance, but she was very curious about what Tubby O'Connell was up to. Why had he been following her?

Sure enough, the little blue sports car whipped through the gates, Tubby's blond hair and glasses visible behind the wheel.

He paused, then eased into the flow of traffic and roared off toward Gibbet Hill Road.

Annie followed seconds later, hoping he wouldn't notice. Not that the Volvo stood out, but you never knew. Maybe she should have confronted him right there in the street, but she didn't know anything for sure.

Someone had murdered Rocky, and when his body had been hauled out of the lake, Tubby O'Connell hadn't seemed particularly disturbed. In fact, he'd said something about Rocky's being a damn fool. At the time she'd thought it callous and cruel, but maybe it was more than that. Maybe Tubby had known Rocky was a thief and that he'd stolen the miniature from the library.

Tubby drove on, seemingly intent on his destination. Two cars remained between them as they paused at a traffic light. It turned green, and he roared off up the hill. As far as she could tell, he didn't know she was behind him.

Where could he be going? The gas station or possibly back to work at the mortuary? No, they were both in the opposite direction.

She drove along, feeling smug. This wasn't so hard—routine detective work.

When both of the intervening cars peeled off onto side roads, Annie let the sports car pull ahead. Not much traffic right now. She drove along, enjoying the ride as the Volvo took the curves with ease. Tubby slowed to thirty. Annie braked. There weren't any other cars on the road now. One look in the mirror, and he was bound to notice her.

Suddenly, he put on a burst of speed and rounded a corner, tires squealing. She sped up, too, and saw his brake lights flare as he turned onto a narrow side road.

He'd spotted her. Or had he? She couldn't decide, then thought, what the heck, and swung after him.

Angry with herself for being careless—maybe if she'd been more cautious and stayed farther back, he wouldn't have seen her—she careened along beneath low-growing birch and pine bent over with the weight of ice. A few saplings had snapped and lay across the road. As her wheels bumped up and down, she stared out the window and realized exactly where she was—on the north side of the old slate quarry, and very close to Baxter Creek.

She slowed, looking for a place to turn around. The hell with Tubby O'Connell, whatever he was up to. Who cared. She had no wish to get involved in something ugly and possibly dangerous, here in the middle of nowhere. If Tubby knew about Rocky's illegal activities, odds were he wouldn't tell her anyway.

Abruptly, the road rose, and she pressed the accelerator. From her vantage point at the top of the rise, she saw the creek roiling down below. The black water looked deep and dangerously high, nearly to the top of its banks.

Claudius stood up and growled low in his throat.

The road became rough and rutted under the snow. Although it had been treated with sand and salt at some point, it was still practically impassable. If Tubby was maintaining forty-five, his sports car must be taking a terrible beating.

Then, just ahead through the trees, she noticed a weathered gray shack at the end of a side road. A sagging wire fence enclosed the area, probably part of the old slate quarry. A rusted sign creaked in the wind: KEEP OUT.

The padlock on the gate was broken. The gate was open.

She pulled in. It was wide enough to use as a turn-around, and there were recent tire tracks. Tubby's.

She turned off the motor, rolled down the window, and listened. The sun was going down, and the glare was blinding. She peered through the snow-streaked windshield, wondering where Tubby had gone.

Claudius whined. She scratched his ears and told him everything was okay. But it wasn't.

Following Tubby had been a really dumb idea. She

hadn't accomplished anything sensible. She was miles from anywhere, and since she'd forgotten to recharge the batteries again, her cell phone was dead.

Well, no good would come of sitting here. She started up the engine and drove on. Five minutes more, then she'd turn around and go back to town.

The road curved sharply, heading downhill to a bridge. Running water lay ahead—Baxter Creek again.

As she rounded the curve, she almost slammed into Tubby's little blue car right there at the edge of the bridge.

Claudius jumped up and growled, and Annie gripped the wheel with hands that shook.

It was obvious what had happened. Tubby had been going too fast. He'd spun out of control and hit the guard rail. There was no sign of him, so she turned the engine off again and listened. Nothing, just the sound of rushing water.

Wondering what to do, she got out with Claudius and walked up to the sports car. The left rear tire had blown. The car wasn't drivable unless he had a spare, and even then, probably not. The front end was smashed in—the radiator had taken the brunt of the damage. Steam was escaping.

Wherever Tubby was, he'd need a ride back to town. Okay, good Samaritan that she was, she'd forget other matters until they returned to civilization.

But there was no sign of Tubby. His car motor had been turned off. The key was gone.

The sun was sliding slowly west. It had grown colder, and the wind had picked up. She headed toward a weathered shack set deeper into the woods. Maybe Tubby thought he'd find a phone there, the idiot.

Then she heard him yell, his cry so full of fright that for a second her heart seemed to stop. He was somewhere ahead, in that desolate area near the side of the shack, where the creek water flowed deepest. The remains of a wooden sluice box angled upward to the shack's second floor. The whole thing looked precarious. The end supports had rotted away, and broken boards spilled into the fast-running water below.

He screamed again. Obviously, he was in serious trouble. She unclipped Claudius from the leash and pointed toward the shack. "Go, boy! Find him!"

As Claudius raced off, she followed cautiously. The middle of the road was a sheet of ice, so she kept to one side.

Claudius barked from the far end of the shack. He must have found Tubby. She yelled, "Hey, Tubby?"

"Help! Help me!"

She grabbed a broken board—maybe he'd need something to hold on to. The snow was deep here in the unplowed area leading down to the creek. The snow came in over the top of her boots. Her feet were soon freezing.

Walking was exhausting; she couldn't move fast. Claudius kept barking, and Tubby kept yelling—sounding more panicked by the second. She stumbled, almost fell, and had to lean one hand on the side of the shack. The old boards groaned, and she worried that the shack would collapse on top of her at any second. But walking farther to the left was impossible. The snow was just too deep.

She made her way around to the back and stared. Good Lord, Tubby had evidently fallen through a rotted platform in the old sluice structure and plunged downward into the swollen creek. She could see his head and shoulders just above the water line.

Claudius, at the edge of the broken platform, was barking like crazy.

"Get that damn dog off me!" Tubby shouted, slipping lower in the water even as she watched. A rotted board he was clinging to snapped suddenly, and his head disappeared below the surface.

"Don't move!" she cried. There was a horrible creaking noise, Claudius barked a few more times, then a tense silence fell.

She held her breath.

"Get over here, you bitch!" he screamed. "For chrissakes, don't just stand there! Get that dog off me!"

"Shut the hell up! I'm doing the best I can!" The board she was holding wouldn't do any good. It wasn't long enough to reach him. She wondered if there were any longer boards on the other side of the shack. Maybe near the front.

Despite Tubby's incessant screams and threats of what he'd do when he got his hands on her if she didn't get Claudius away from the hole, she turned around and went back the way she'd come. One of them had to stay calm, and it looked like she was it.

With considerable difficulty, she managed to tear a few good boards loose from the siding. Even so, she wasn't sure they would be long enough. Well, they'd have to do. There just wasn't anything else.

She lugged them back to the broken platform and knelt, stretching the longest straight ahead across the opening, wedging it as firmly as she could. "Grab hold of this."

Claudius kept dashing back and forth, barking and in general getting in the way.

"Stop it!" she ordered.

He sat down with a sigh of disgust.

Annie ignored him. She had more than enough to deal with. Tubby was still yelling like a stuck pig, and the sun was slipping below the treetops. Soon there'd be no light at all, and then what would she do? Well, she could drive the Volvo up here by the shack and leave the headlights on, but the terrain was hilly. She doubted the lights would reach the back of the shack where Tubby was trapped.

She crawled forward on her hands and knees until she could lean over the hole he'd fallen through. He was neck deep in the fast-flowing creek, desperately hanging on to the board she'd extended and glaring up at her. "Jesus, you took your time! That dog damn near killed me!"

"He did nothing of the sort. You want me to help you— then shut up."

Resentfully, he inched higher, holding on to the board with one hand, steadying himself. She'd placed the other boards as best she could, making a temporary, and very shaky, platform for him to crawl up onto.

He grunted and strained higher, pulling himself painfully out of the water. He sagged and almost fell. "I can't—"

"Yes, you can. Grab my hand. I'll help pull you up."

Claudius crawled closer, and she shoved him away. "Cut that out!"

"What—what'd you say?" Tubby shrieked.

"Nothing, just grab my hand."

He reached up toward her outstretched fingers, grabbed

on, and almost pulled her down with him—he was no
lightweight.

"Wait, not so fast!" She braced herself and wrapped her
free arm around the edge of the bottom of the sluice box
supports. They creaked alarmingly, but held.

It took him four or five minutes to crawl out of the gap-
ing hole to safety, then he collapsed, looking like a
beached whale, his clothes soaked and torn. His hands
were bleeding, and his face was filthy and streaked with
sweat.

He eyed Claudius and shivered.

"Get that dog away from me!"

"He won't hurt you if you do exactly what I tell you."
Annie took off her jacket and lay it around his shoulders.
"Come on, we'll go back to my car." She didn't look at
him again until they arrived at the Volvo. She put Claudius
in back. Tubby climbed in front, and she switched on the
headlights and drove back to the gate in the fence.

"Goddamn it!" Eyeing the wreckage of his car as they
drove by, he was all but apoplectic.

Annie turned the heater on high and headed back to
town. "You knew I was following you."

"Yeah, so what."

"Why did you turn onto this back road? Did you think
I'd end up in the creek? Was that the plan?"

His eyes shifted uneasily. "I was just trying to lose
you."

"That's why you came up here?" She didn't believe it.
Not for one minute.

"Yes," he insisted. He shook himself, as if trying to
throw off what had happened. "Look, I made a mistake.

No big deal. I wrecked my car, went to look for a phone to call a wrecker, and fell in. That's it."

No matter what she said, he refused to change his story. He wrapped his arms around himself under her jacket and leaned back.

She drove the dark miles to town in silence.

When they arrived at the funeral parlor, she pulled into the lot next to the garage. Something was going on, and Tubby was up to his ears in trouble. "Three people are dead, Tubby," she told him. "This afternoon you almost made it four. What are you up to?"

"Nothing," he snarled. His eyes slid away from hers. "You're crazy!" Without another word, he practically threw her jacket at her and stomped up the path to the house.

She backed out of the lot and roared off down the street. She was annoyed, not only with Tubby for being such a jerk, but also with herself. If she'd gone straight home, none of this would have happened. Tubby would still have his expensive little sports car, and she wouldn't have frozen feet, bruised hands, and a soaked jacket.

It was hardly an auspicious start to a lovely evening.

When she got back to the tavern, she ate a piece of cake and drank a cup of tea, dumped the dishes in the sink and discovered that while she'd been relaxing, Claudius had kept himself occupied by chewing the newspaper.

She counted to ten, then cleaned it up, fed him, and let him outside. When he came in, he sat down and waited, head high, eyes gleaming.

"You don't deserve a treat."

He glanced at the nearby basket. *Antiques* magazine lay on top. He gave her an innocent look.

Enough was enough.

She stalked upstairs to shower and change, keeping an ear cocked for sounds of chewing, ready to dash downstairs and put a stop to whatever mischief Claudius might be up to.

When she stepped from the shower and dried off, she was feeling more like herself. She had every right to an enjoyable evening. She'd wear that little black dress, look her best, and the heck with the consequences.

The hem of the dress came to her knees and swung when she moved. It looked as if it had cost a fortune, but she'd picked it up at Marshall's at half price. Sheer black stockings, three-inch heels, and a lovely old garnet necklace completed her outfit. If Gus wasn't impressed, he must be dead from the neck up.

When she went downstairs, the carpet was strewn with cotton batting, what looked like the remains of her Garfield bedroom slippers, and more chewed-up newspaper.

Claudius was nowhere to be found.

She picked up the tattered newspaper and gave it a good long look. Damn. He'd found *Antiques Weekly*, her favorite. Well, she'd just have to get along without this week's copy.

Keeping her temper was practically impossible. Concentrate on positive reinforcement, she told herself. Ignore negative behavior.

For two cents, she'd wring that canine's neck.

This wasn't rocket science. Claudius was smart. Not fifteen minutes ago, she'd told him to be good, and he'd deliberately found something else to destroy. Why?

She pondered this question. The possibilities were endless. He wanted attention. He was lonely, stressed. Well, whoop de do. So was she, but did she chew the carpet and every issue of *Antiques Weekly* she could sink her teeth into? No.

Immediate action was called for. She stalked to the kitchen. Where there was food, Claudius wouldn't be far away.

He was under the table, faking complete innocence. His tail banged on the floor.

"You're not to eat newspapers or my slippers!"

He yawned.

"Bad boy! You are not to eat *Antiques Weekly*, or this either!" Annie shook the furry orange Garfield under his nose.

He grinned and licked her hand.

She tried again, twice more. He leaped up, put his paws on her shoulders, and licked her face all over.

"I love you, too. Well, we'll have to work on it," she told him, making a feeble attempt at dignity. "You have to meet me halfway. You have to try and be good."

His tail wagged a mile a minute.

Wordlessly, and hating herself for being weak, she got down a box of beef-basted bones and handed him one. Then she went back upstairs to wash her face and reapply her makeup.

When Gus arrived, she put on her coat and went outside to his car with a sense of having been bested by an expert.

Meanwhile, Claudius was glowering out the back door. He knew she was leaving again, without him.

In the car, Gus turned on the radio. Aretha Franklin at the top of her form.

"You look terrific." He sounded as if he really meant it.

"Thanks." With Aretha demanding respect and Gus paying her compliments, Annie began to feel better.

"How'd your day go?" he asked. Ordinarily it was the most innocent of questions, but not tonight. When she didn't answer right away, he shot her a sideways glance. "Anything going on I should know about?"

She hesitated. Maybe she should tell him about this afternoon, and Tubby O'Connell's odd, threatening behavior, but what would that accomplish? Gus would tell her she'd been an idiot and to mind her own business.

"I don't think so," she said. "At least not yet. What about the duffel bag and the parking ticket? Did you find out anything?"

"No. Look, how about a truce for the night? We'll concentrate on having a good time."

"Why not? I don't bite."

"You sure about that?"

"Don't get your hopes up."

He grinned. "That sounds downright promising."

CHAPTER
15

The evening passed all too soon for Annie's liking. Gus turned out to be a pretty fair dancer, and she had a good time. Sam was there, with Marnie Pearson on his arm, looking extremely pleased with herself. Tonight her eyes were unbelievably blue. Contact blue, in fact. Not that Sam seemed to mind.

Well, so what.

Cary was almost decent in her red dress, and Zack Henderson, her date, couldn't keep his eyes, much less his hands, off her. But she didn't seem to mind.

While they were grouped around the bar, Annie caught Sam alone for a moment and said, "Someone said they saw you talking to Rocky the afternoon he died. Did he mention that he was meeting anyone?"

"Let me think . . . No. We only talked a minute. He gambled heavily. Said he needed to pay off a debt. I told him I couldn't help. I saw him talking to Pete Lanza in the parking lot about a half hour later. They looked like they were both pretty hot under the collar." Sam glanced at Marnie, several feet away, freshening her lipstick.

Just then, she looked up and shot Annie a withering

look. "I'm thirsty, Sam. How about getting me a drink?" Marnie whined.

Annie gave up trying to talk to Sam alone. She decided to call him in the next day or so. Maybe there was something else he could remember about his conversation with Rocky. Any clue, no matter how small, was useful.

Toward the shank of the evening, the music became slow and dreamy, and she floated around the floor in Gus's arms, lost in a romantic fantasy.

He held her closer and kissed her cheek. Her heart thumped like mad. Then his pager beeped, and he groaned and pulled away.

He checked the message. "Damn, bad timing. I've gotta go. Something's come up downtown. Do you want to stay—or I could drop you off."

She decided to go home.

Standing on the tavern's back step, Gus gave Annie a quick embrace. He said he was sorry. He said they'd have to do this again.

She let herself into the tavern feeling cheated.

No sign of Claudius, which was odd. "Claudius?"

A distant "woof" came from the other end of the house. The living room. He woofed again. Something was definitely wrong.

Annie walked down the long hall, wondering what was the matter, and found him stuck in the living room wall.

He'd chewed a refrigerator-sized hole in the plasterboard, probably trying to get at a mouse.

She got him out and cleaned him up. He wouldn't look at her. The mouse must have gotten away.

Big sigh. Maybe Kirk could help her repair the damage. A few pieces of plasterboard, spackling, paint.

"You're not to chew the wall ever again," she told Claudius. "Do you understand me?"

Questions were definitely not the way to get through to him.

"Okay, no chewing the wall. Period. I don't care if an army of mice run up and down all night long. Leave them the hell alone!"

He eyed her expressionlessly, and she went to bed.

Tuesday morning she tracked Pete Lanza down at Dunkin' Donuts. He was sitting in a back booth, wearing his old army jacket over jeans and a loose flannel shirt. He was drinking coffee, hunched over the sports section of *The Boston Globe*.

She bought a bag of assorted donuts. Pete looked up when she sat down. His hair was sleep rumpled, his eyes bleary, but he still had that surfer look.

He said irritably, "What do you want?"

"Have a donut."

He reached into the bag and selected a Boston creme. Munching, he mumbled, "Thanks. Not to be rude, but I'm busy."

"Okay, I'll make it quick. Someone said they saw you talking to Rocky Martinez the afternoon he died."

"So what," he muttered. "I talk to lots of people."

"What did you talk about?"

Pete hesitated, then said, "No big deal. It was just past noon. I was on my way to lunch. I was surprised to see him. Usually, he plowed the roads early and left if it wasn't snowing. That day it didn't start snowing until later on, around two p.m."

"And?"

"He said he needed money. Claimed he had to get out of town. I told him, hey, we all need money."

"After he died, did you tell the cops?"

"What for? It isn't a crime to need money." He laughed. "If it was, we'd all be in the slammer."

"Did you give him any?"

"Jeez, I hardly knew him. I saw him around school, cutting grass and plowing the roads. Whatever."

"Rocky was in the army," Annie said, eyeing Pete's jacket. "Was he in your outfit?"

Pete looked annoyed. "No."

"Did he mention anything about gambling debts?"

"No, but maybe that's why he needed to take off. I didn't give him anything."

Annie didn't believe him. "Come on, how much did you give him?"

"Christ . . . okay. Twenty bucks. It's all I had on me."

"He couldn't have gotten far on twenty bucks. Did he say why he had to leave town?"

"No, just that he had to leave."

"When he died, you didn't think your exchange was worth mentioning to the cops?"

"Hell, I'm not nuts. I don't want trouble. I talk to the guy for a couple of minutes, and what happens? He ends up dead. His death was an accident. No big deal. I didn't want to get involved."

"The person who saw you talking to him said it looked like an argument."

"Yeah, well, your pal's a liar. Sure, Rocky was upset at first when I told him no. He said he needed money real bad. I felt sorry for him, so I gave him twenty."

They weren't getting anywhere. Sam had said they'd

appeared to be arguing, but maybe Pete was telling the truth and Rocky had gotten upset when he thought he wouldn't get any money.

Annie changed gears. "What about Stella Danforth? Did you hear anything after she died? Maybe that some- one had a grudge against her?"

"Christ, you still harping on that?" His voice had a tone she couldn't place. Boredom, and something else . . . yes, as if he expected an accusation. He selected a jelly donut. "Look, I liked Stella. I went to the funeral and paid my re- spects. Her sister and brother came from Vermont. Nice people. There was a pretty big turnout, considering. Fox Hill staff, a bunch of people from town. She taught here for years, had a lot of friends. She was a good teacher, re- ally cared about the kids. We used to sit and talk some- times." It was surprising how much he knew about Stella. As he chewed, he rambled, his voice gaining confidence. "She was easy to talk to. Interested in life, know what I mean?"

Annie nodded and wished she'd known Stella Dan- forth. "What about Maria Martinez?"

He shrugged. "Rocky's sister. I heard about what hap- pened. Too bad. Still, it's not a bad way to go."

Annie nearly choked on her donut.

"Well," he said, "at least she didn't suffer."

Annie had another donut and waited. He talked about the difficulties of teaching math to kids who didn't know their asses from their elbows and explaining this to par- ents who were even dumber.

"About Rocky," she said. "Did he mention trying to get money from someone else?"

"No, but there was something . . . yeah, while we were

talking, a couple of cars drove by. All of a sudden, Rocky looked scared. He grabbed the money out of my hand and took off toward the hockey rink."

"He saw someone that frightened him," Annie said thoughtfully. Not Martha Valladares—someone else. Interesting. "Maybe we'll talk again, Pete."

He laughed. "Yeah, let's talk about something more cheerful next time."

She left the rest of the donuts with him and drove up to Fox Hill.

Claudius, in the car, had sniffed her hands and knew all about the missing donuts. He lay down on the front seat and brooded about lost opportunities.

Let's see, she thought, driving slowly down West Street behind the school. Harry Graham's trailer was supposed to be at the end of the row of temporary housing.

She parked behind the hockey rink, where she had a clear view of the cluster of trailers. Four were visible beyond a grove of trees and some overgrown bushes drooping with snow.

A dark-haired woman in jeans and a blue-and-white checked wool jacket emerged from her trailer and began shoveling her steps. A black Volkswagen stood in her driveway. She lived next door to Harry Graham.

After putting the shovel away, the woman locked up her trailer, got into the Volkswagen, and drove away.

Annie waited, and Claudius took a short nap.

Harry Graham's SUV was parked outside the last trailer. About ten minutes later, he came out with Trixie. He was dressed in jeans and a heavy jacket with a fur collar. They walked around while Trixie took her time about piddling. At long last, she squatted by the back of the trailer and did her duty. That done, he loaded her into the SUV and roared off in a cloud of blue exhaust.

He was barely out of sight down the street when Annie grabbed Claudius and hotfooted it over to his trailer. Who knew how long he'd be gone? If she was going to search the place, it had to be now or never.

The door was locked, but she didn't even need George's borrowed picks. Using a credit card, she popped the door open in no time. The trailer was warm, hot even, and smelled to high heaven. Too many beers, fried onion rings and greasy hamburgers, and cigarettes. Not enough fresh air. Dirty clothes were scattered around—battered sneakers and a pair of jeans dumped on a khaki jacket—girlie magazines and old newspapers everywhere. Thick dirt coated the stove top.

She opened the fridge while Claudius poked around in the overflowing trash bin. The fridge smelled worse than the trailer. Judging by the meager contents, Harry Graham had a taste for mustard, Miracle Whip, and ketchup. A broken egg had coagulated and dried near the crisper drawers.

The sink was full of dirty dishes. The kitchen cabinets were white, the paint flaking. He'd laid in a year's supply of beef stew, baked beans, potato chips, and salsa.

A bowl on the floor said TRIXIE in red. A dog bed in the corner was decorated with flounces and ribbons. It even had a heated cushion. Annie suspected Stella had bought them for her dog before she died.

Claudius sniffed the dog bed and bowl with great interest, whined a little, then wandered back to the trash.

A pad on the table was covered with scribbled numbers and cryptic jottings. Harry was either into gambling big time or figuring the stock market. On the counter were a bowling trophy, a few cans of dog food, a bag of dry food, and a box of pills for dogs in heat. Some sort of preventive for canine pregnancy.

A chest of drawers held underwear and socks. Two drawers were empty, and two pairs of jeans and a couple of old sweatshirts were stacked on the closet shelf. A red windbreaker on a chair—size XXLL, with *Fox Hill* beneath the left lapel. She checked the pockets. Empty, except for a book of matches, some betting slips, and a crushed pack of Marlboros.

She ran a hand under the mattress on the sagging bed and looked under the sofa cushions. Nothing. A real search by someone who knew what he was doing, Gus Jackson for instance, would probably turn up something, she thought morosely.

She turned around as Claudius trotted up with a scrap of cardboard in his mouth. He'd dragged it out of the trash. His tail was wagging.

"Give." She held out her hand, and he dropped the cardboard between her fingers. "Good boy!"

He sat down and waited.

Well, well. The cardboard was covered with dark blue velvet, and similar to the piece she'd seen in the shed. Interesting. There'd been an empty pack of Marlboros in the shed, too.

She locked up the trailer and went home. What did she have? A few clues, but they must add up to something. If only she could put the pieces together in a way that made sense.

She made calzones and a fresh garden salad for lunch, while Claudius prowled around, growling uneasily. He kept starting at something she couldn't see or hear. Something was bothering him.

She decided to watch TV, an F.B.I. drama. Cops and robbers. Dialogue she didn't have to pay attention to. Her brain would do its thing and make sense of what she knew so far, and if that didn't work, she'd take Claudius for a long walk.

Later on, halfway through, the two thieves were discussing a planned bank job. Dressed in camouflage gear, they were shooting tin cans in a swamp. The F.B.I. agent describing the action said, "Harper and Livoli had been highly trained by the army. Harper was a sharpshooter. Neither had adjusted to civilian life. They craved excitement and danger."

Annie stared at the screen as the puzzle pieces began to fall into place. It couldn't be true. It was horrible, inconceivable. But what if it was true? She jumped up and ran to find last week's newspapers. Maybe she was lucky and Claudius hadn't eaten all of them.

Thank goodness—Tuesday's paper had covered the story, although by then it was old news and had been buried on page ten, below the fold. Barely a paragraph in length, an update about the Boston jewel robberies. No new information, just a rehash of the bare facts. But she knew. Rocky had probably been mixed up in that. Along with Harry Graham? That blue-velvet-covered cardboard, which could have been part of the lining for a jewelry salesman's case. She let the paper fall in her lap and sat very still.

Claudius, lying on the couch by her side, yawned, stretched, and scratched his ear, then trotted off to the kitchen.

My God.

What should she do now? Call Gus and tell him what she suspected? Maybe he'd already figured out the who, what, where, and why. But so far he wasn't talking, and wasn't likely to—at least not to her.

Three people were dead. That much was certain.

Dr. Lawrence had said Stella Danforth had called his office, clearly upset, on the night she died. Maybe she'd discovered that Rocky was a thief. Hours later, she'd been disposed of by the simple expedient of being shoved down a steep flight of stairs. She'd died almost instantly. She'd had no time to cry out, or if she had, no one had heard her.

Rocky had been more difficult to get rid of. A young man, strong, already fearful, he'd been lured onto the icy lake. The murderer or murderers had gone to a great deal of trouble to make it look like an accident.

Maria's death had been hurried. They hadn't had time to come up with a foolproof way to kill her. They'd simply run her down in the street. Crude, but effective. Well, they'd been lucky. In a worst-case scenario, Maria might have survived and fingered her killer, but she'd died without regaining consciousness.

So the killer or killers had parked a few streets over, then returned on foot to mingle with others in the neighborhood and gawk at the so-called accident.

At which point, Annie had arrived.

The timing had been crucial and unfortunate. Once the killer, already nervous, saw Annie—with her reputation for crime-solving—he'd jumped to the conclusion that she was on to him.

No doubt about it, Annie had a lot to think about. She

got out her suspect list and looked it over. It was decidedly unpleasant not to trust people you knew, even slightly.

She couldn't get out of her mind the fact that three people had died violently. She dialed Gus's number, but he wasn't home. Damn. She was jumpy, on edge. And no wonder, what with everything she'd been through lately.

Compelled by an impulse she couldn't deny, she searched the book shelves for last year's Fox Hill alumni report. Faculty and staff were listed, along with head shots. She flipped the pages. Yes, there was Rocky—skinny, beaky-nosed, with slicked-back hair and close-set eyes. She wondered why the school had hired him. She wouldn't have trusted him an inch.

She turned several pages until she found Stella Danforth. The yearbook had gone to the printer's just before her death. She was listed as professor emeritus of history.

She'd been white-haired and slim, with an easy smile that reached her eyes. She had a sensitive mouth, slender nose, and expressive face. Although over seventy, she'd looked much younger.

If Stella Danforth could part the veil of death and speak, what would she say?

Annie tried to see through Stella's eyes. What had she known that had set off that deadly chain of events? Something she overheard or saw? Had Rocky shown the miniature to someone? Had he asked how much he might get for it in Peterborough?

Probably Annie would never know for sure. "But I'm going to get whoever killed you," she told Stella's photograph.

She put the yearbook away and sat for a long time

thinking about what she should do now that she had a pretty good idea why three people had been killed.

Her first reaction had been to call Gus, but he wasn't home. Hardly a surprise. Men were never there when you wanted them.

What in the world should she do?

Staying home, doing nothing, wasn't an option. It was too unnerving, waiting for the killer to strike again. She had to do something, anything.

She'd go back to Fox Hill. Maybe she could talk to Dr. Lawrence about her suspicions. Everything seemed centered on the school.

This was Kirk's night to work late in the psychology lab. She scribbled a note for him, which she dropped on the Queen Anne desk in the hall on the way out.

When she got to Fox Hill, she found that Winterfest activities were still in full swing. Tonight there were the last of the outdoor events: hockey games and the snow-sculpture competition.

Students, faculty, and doting parents streamed up and down Powderhouse Road and admired the snow sculptures in front of the dorms. Imagination and a lot of hard work had gone into each work. A fire-breathing dragon with a lashing tail. A castle with a moat and drawbridge. Snoopy and Charlie Brown playing hockey.

The kids in Wyndham Hall had won first prize with a sculpture of three witches stirring a cauldron.

The amazing thing, Annie thought as she led Claudius away from the cauldron—he'd started lifting a leg—was that the kids had done all this in such a short time. The sculptures had been finished in just two days.

Claudius was always grumpy when he didn't get his

own way. He shook his head and walked along indignantly as Cary appeared at Annie's elbow. "Hi, what do you think of the sculptures? Aren't they terrific?"

"Amazing."

"The witches look so lifelike," Cary said. "Down to the warts on their noses."

They paused in front of a horse and chariot driven by a lumpy Roman who looked like a gladiator.

White, of course. Snow was white. But there was something red smeared on the edge of the chariot. Blood. Quite a lot of it. Cary hadn't noticed, and Annie stared at it stupidly for some seconds, feeling light-headed. *Someone was lying in the chariot.*

A man, curled on his side . . . Dr. Lawrence. The blood was seeping from a wound on his temple.

Annie felt hot, then cold.

Claudius lunged forward, growling.

She hauled him back. She should call for help. Scream. Instead, she felt frozen. It took an enormous effort as she reined in Claudius again—he sniffed the chariot suspiciously. "No!"

At the same time, Cary spotted the body and shrieked, "Oh, my God—it's Dr. Lawrence!" Pandemonium ensued. Claudius began to bark and howl, people came running, an ambulance and three cop cars pulled up.

Gus Jackson arrived, looking grim. He noticed Annie and said tiredly, "Trust you to find another body."

Annie shrugged. It wasn't her fault, and this time, luckily, it wasn't even a corpse. Dr. Lawrence had suffered a serious blow to the side of his head, but he was still breathing when he was loaded into the back of the ambulance and taken away to the hospital.

Something to be grateful for.

Winterfest came to an abrupt end. It was hours before
the scene around these sculptures returned to normal.

While she was being questioned by Gus and another
cop, whose name she didn't catch, Annie tried to tell Gus
about her suspicions. But they weren't based on hard evidence. They were circumstantial, based on instinct, and
hard to put into words. She'd barely opened her mouth
when another cop came running with the news that Dr.
Lawrence might be regaining consciousness.

"Sorry," Gus said. "Talk to you later." He jumped in his
car and roared off toward the hospital.

Annie made her way back to the parking lot where
she'd left the Volvo. The other cop cars drove away. Cary
had gone off with Zack Henderson. Annie was left with
Claudius.

She didn't want to be alone, not now—not considering
where her thoughts were leading her. She wanted answers,
and she wanted them now. She exhaled a deep breath,
overwhelmed with anger and sadness. She decided to
drive over to Sam's. But first she'd use the library telephone to call the police. She'd tell Gus to meet her at
Sam's.

The female dispatch officer who answered said Gus
was downtown at the hospital, but when he called in,
she'd be sure he got the message.

"It's about that homicide case he's working on," Annie
said. "Tell him to send a couple of squad cars to Sam
McIntyre's house on Wamesit Trail."

"If this is an emergency, why didn't you dial 911?"

"Look, I haven't got time to explain," Annie said im-
patiently. "I'm at the Fox Hill School library. The police

department number is listed by the phone. What does it matter which number I used?"

"We don't like the non-emergency line tied up with frivolous calls."

"Dammit, this isn't a frivolous call!"

The dispatcher waited a moment, then said expressionlessly, "I'll give Gus the message."

Annie slammed the phone down and went out to the Volvo. The drive didn't take long. Sam's car was parked in front of the house. No sign of Gus or any police cars.

She pulled over to the curb and, taking Claudius along, started up the front walk. Then she noticed a light in the garage and pushed the door open.

Sam was in the corner by the workbench, cleaning something. There was a bowling trophy on the bench. It looked like a twin to the one she'd seen in Harry Graham's trailer. Sam whirled as the door creaked open. "Wh . . . oh, it's you."

There were a hundred questions she wanted to ask, but her tongue seemed to be stuck to the roof of her mouth.

He frowned. "You okay? You look sort of—"

"I'm fine," she managed. "Just tired. I've had a bad couple of hours. I found Dr. Lawrence." Sam was tense . . . that look on his face . . . He was dressed in army fatigues.

"Jeez, I heard. Must have been a terrible shock. What happened?"

"Someone hit him in the head and stuffed him in one of the snow sculptures." She knew it had happened, but it still felt unreal. She stared at him. Claudius, by her side, began to growl.

Sam had moved slightly, and she could see what he'd

been wiping down. It was a hammer. The cloth he'd used was streaked red. Not bright red. Some hours had passed, and the color had dried to a brownish red. But it was blood.

Sam saw the knowledge in her eyes.

She took a step backward, then another, but as she turned to run, he lunged for the door and got there first. A gun was in his right hand. He grabbed her arm with his left.

Claudius growled low in his throat, and Sam said, "Keep the mongrel under control or I'll shoot him."

"You wouldn't dare."

"Want to risk it?" He laughed. "Poor Annie. You should see your face. You walked right into my parlor."

"I figured out what was going on." That was partially true anyway. "I want to know why," she said. "You owe me that much."

He considered that for a moment. "I guess it won't hurt. It's not as if you'll be around to tell anyone. We were all in the army reserves together—Tubby, Harry Graham, and me. I've known them for years. We were tight. Real close. I don't expect you to understand. Anyway, we served in Bosnia and hooked up with Rocky Martinez over there. When we came home, everything was a drag. No excitement, no thrills, and no easy money. So I came up with the idea of robbing jewelry salesmen. Tubby, Harry, and Rocky followed my orders. We were raking in the money, and life was exciting. I got off on the adrenaline rush. I was in control. It was like old times. It was great."

"Well, if it was so great and you enjoyed it so much, what went wrong?"

"Rocky started making trouble."

"That's what I thought," she said. "For a while I wondered if Pete Lanza was involved. He wears an army jacket."

"No, Pete was never part of it. He was in the National Guard, not the reserves." Sam lifted an eyebrow. "I'm impressed. You figured out most of it. Still, it won't do you any good. We're going for a little ride."

She stared at him, sickened. Why had she ever thought his Southern accent attractive? It dripped with menace.

His smile was faint now. "Any more loose ends you'd like tied up?"

She swallowed hard. "Why kill three people?"

"Stella Danforth got nosy. One night last year, we were storing the take from a Boston jewelry heist in the old shed. It was perfect. We'd used the shed before. Then she comes by, walking that damn dog. She sees us." He shrugged. "Next day, she starts asking questions. She was going to Dr. Lawrence. We had to get rid of her."

"Why kill Rocky?"

"As I said, he made trouble. The damn fool wanted a bigger split. Said he needed it now. I told him later, as we'd agreed, after we'd fenced the jewels. We couldn't spend the money right away, not for months—till the heat died down—but he wouldn't listen. He got mad and took a swing at me. I blocked the punch and hit him hard. His head snapped back and slammed into the side of the car. Sounded like an egg cracking. I knew he was dead."

Annie took a shaky breath. "How did he end up in the lake?"

"At the time it seemed like a good idea." He gave another shrug. "Hey, I couldn't leave him lying there in the parking lot. It was snowing hard, but someone might have seen us together. So I drove to the other side of the lake, dragged him out onto the ice, and dumped him in. Then I drove to work and resumed my regular shift on the ambulance."

The air around Annie seemed colder. She felt sick. "You knew you'd get the call when it came in."

"I was counting on it. If by some miracle he wasn't quite dead, I'd finish the job with no one the wiser." He shook his head. "You made a lot of trouble for me, Annie. Too bad. I really liked you."

"You're crazy—you killed three people!"

"Actually, Rocky took care of Stella Danforth. Then he made trouble—we got into a fight. I hit him a little too hard. It was an accident."

"And Maria? Was that an accident, too?"

"Hardly. She found out about the robberies. Rocky kept a miniature he took from the library. I told him it was dangerous, but he needed money and said he was going to sell it at some two-bit antique show. He got drunk and showed it to Maria. She wanted a cut to keep her mouth shut, so we had to get rid of her, too."

The cold horror of it took Annie's breath away. "To kill for so little reason—"

"Be serious. Rocky wasn't satisfied with a quarter of a million bucks. That would have been his cut. If he'd kept to the bargain we agreed on, everything would have been fine. All he had to do was lie low and live on his normal salary. When enough time had passed, I would have fenced the jewels in Canada. The past two years we robbed half-a-dozen jewelry stores. That's a lot of money." Sam continued in his warm Southern drawl, "Then you got caught up in it. Rocky was a creep, a loser, but I was sorry about you. I liked you. But one thing led to another. Harry tried to run you off the road, but that didn't work. Unfortunately."

"So you tried again in the cross-country race."

He nodded.

"You *shot* at me—that's what set off the avalanche!"

"Bingo. I borrowed Harry's rifle and missed. Never was much of a shot. And that damn fool dog of yours ripped my costume. I got rid of it and dumped it in a pile of drama department costumes. I didn't dare go near you after that. The dog had my scent. So I told Harry to lure you to the school the night of the cross-country race. He was supposed to kill you, but he missed. He's always been a pretty good shot—" Sam broke off as a car roared down the street.

It was the Fox Hill security SUV.

For a second, Annie's heart leaped. Harry Graham couldn't be the only man on the force, and surely Gus and a couple of Lee police cruisers would be arriving any minute.

But when the SUV pulled over and the door opened, Harry got out, frowning. "Christ, what the hell's goin' on?"

"A minor complication," Sam said.

"Yeah, well, we ain't got all day. No way this bitch is gonna keep her mouth shut, so what are we gonna do?"

"We take her across the lake. An accident, like Rocky."

Harry looked worried. "Hey, is that a good idea? Two in a row? I don't know—no way the cops are gonna buy it."

Sam shrugged. "Can you think of anything better? No? Then shut the hell up."

Annie struggled desperately against Sam's grip. Claudius growled, and Sam shoved the gun hard into her side. "Cut it out or I'll shoot the damn dog."

"Harry's right," she gasped. "You won't get away with this. No one will believe it!"

He jabbed her again, harder. "It's not the same. Rocky was an accident, I told you. He was drunk."

Annie shivered. Her side ached, and she could barely keep Claudius under control. He was snarling and jerking at the end of the leash.

But if she let him go, Sam would shoot him.

Maybe there was some way to get the gun away from him, knock it out of his hand . . .

Sam was talking calmly, as if murder were an everyday event—like gassing up his car.

He was a sociopath.

She said, "You don't really believe you'll get away with a fourth murder. You don't care. You like killing."

He grinned. "Well, practice makes perfect. I don't count Dr. Lawrence—who, by the way, saw me with Harry's rifle after the cross-country race and started asking awkward questions. I told the old boy he was imagining things—it was just a stage prop from one of the school plays—but he didn't believe me."

A sharp yipping sound suddenly came from the SUV. Trixie.

Harry looked around nervously, and Sam snapped, "Jesus Christ, shut that stupid dog up!"

He dragged Annie to the back of the SUV and yanked open the hatchback. His face was hard, his eyes like chips of ice. "Get in or I'll shoot the dog right here and now."

Annie didn't move. She couldn't. Every muscle in her

body felt paralyzed. Sam glared at her. For a few seconds no one said anything, and Trixie jumped into the back seat and peered out, stubby tail wagging. She'd spotted Claudius, her Romeo.

Claudius stiffened and barked.

Annie grabbed his collar tighter. "Hush!"

Harry's hands were bunched into fists. "Stay there, Trix." His gaze swiveled back to Sam. "I don't like it. If you shoot, someone will hear. Besides, the cops know her. We'll never get away with it."

"Don't be a fool," Sam said coldly. "The cops are a bunch of jerk-offs. They'll drag her body from the lake and do the usual autopsy. Accidental death. I'll dump the effing dog in, too. It'll look like she went out onto the ice after him. We'll be in the clear."

Annie had a terrible feeling he was right. Their deadly plan would work. A few years earlier, a woman had died in similar circumstances. She'd ventured onto thin ice after her dog, fallen in, and died.

Annie tensed and wriggled. Sam put the gun to her head.

"Get the hell into the SUV!"

Harry stomped his feet in the snow and mumbled, "If we get outta this, I'm gonna quit. I got more than enough to live on for a coupla years. I can't stand this."

Sam shoved Annie forward again.

"All right," she said, desperately trying to think of something, anything . . .

Trixie barked, and for just a second, Sam was distracted by the little poodle's yapping. In one desperate move, Annie let go of Claudius, reached up and grabbed the hatchback and in the same instant slammed it down on Sam's arm.

The gun flew out of his hand, and she yelled, *"Get him!"*

With a blood-curdling snarl, Claudius leaped.

The next few minutes ran together in Annie's mind like a video on fast-forward. She saw Sam's twisted face, distorted with rage and fury, then she lost sight of everything except Claudius's slashing jaws, his lunging body, and terrible growls. He attacked with disciplined savagery and didn't let go.

Sam never had a chance.

He staggered backward, falling into Harry, and they both tumbled to the ground with Claudius on top and in control.

Annie screamed at the top of her lungs.

At first she didn't think anyone heard. Then a window flew open, and Mrs. M. poked her head out. "What the hell's going on?" she shouted. "I've had it!" She slammed the window down, and Annie fervently prayed that she was dialing 911.

Moments later, there were several shouts, and a neighbor came running. Annie yelled for someone to call the police—there was always the outside chance that Mrs. M. had lost interest and gone back to watching TV.

Annie tripped and fell over Harry, who was moaning and holding his bleeding arm, and went down amidst all the fighting and yelling.

She struggled to her hands and knees, ran to the SUV, and found the jack handle in the back. She whacked Harry in the head, and he stopped moaning. At the same time, she shouted at Claudius to keep attacking Sam, and for once he did as he was told.

Moments later, a pair of police cruisers with strobe lights flashing and sirens blaring came whipping around the corner and swerved to a stop at the curb. Gus Jackson had arrived.

CHAPTER
16

"Start at the beginning," Gus said. "Talk."

It was an hour later. They were in his office.

"You won't like it," Annie said. "It all started, at least as far as I was concerned, with a dog named Trixie." Gus heaved a sigh, and she went on, "I'm sorry, but that's what happened. Trixie was passed from hand to hand in the year after her mistress, Stella Danforth, died. A few people at the school tried to keep her, but for one reason or another, it just didn't work out. Molly Houghton said her husband, Carl, was allergic to dogs. Then Harry Graham—one of Stella Danforth's killers—ended up adopting her dog. He didn't realize that Trixie hadn't been fixed, and she came into heat.

"One afternoon, she was in his truck when he drove by the tavern. Claudius caught the scent and took off after them. That's when he ran away. He tracked them all the way to Fox Hill and, I suspect, had his way with her. Days later, Molly Houghton spotted him and locked him in her barn. When I came to pick him up, he led us to the lake and Rocky's body. Maybe Claudius heard what happened on the ice that day. He was locked in the barn and couldn't have seen Rocky being killed, but he must have sensed something was terribly wrong. When I showed up at Fox Hill, Sam, Tubby, and Harry were already nervous. They'd decided they had to get rid of Rocky's sister. They ran her down, and I showed up on Goss Lane just minutes later. I was taking Joey Chavez home, but they didn't know that. Sam had read newspaper articles about Claudius and me. He decided I was investigating Rocky's murder and the Boston jewelry heists. That night they panicked and tried to run me off the road. It was supposed to look like an accident."

"They weren't very successful," Gus said. "Go on."

"They tried again during the cross-country race. Sam hid on the ridge with a rifle. He shot at me."

"And missed."

She frowned. "The avalanche almost got me. Claudius saved my life. Then they found out I was alive and must have figured third time lucky. They'd hidden the jewels in the shed. The day Mike, Cary, Leah, and I searched the woods near the shed, looking for the old Wyndham grave-yard, they decided they had to act fast. Harry drove up and confronted us, and things went downhill from there. Leah, Cary, and Mike were with me, so he didn't dare try any-thing then. They moved the jewels, then Harry called me up later and told me to come back to the school at night, alone."

"And, stupidly, you did just that."

"I thought I'd flush them out." It sounded lame, even to Annie's ears.

Gus glowered at her. "We picked up O'Connell and re-covered the jewels. They were hidden in a casket at the fu-neral parlor. You *dated* Sam McIntyre? Are you nuts?"

"I thought he liked me." She shrugged. "We only had one date. After Claudius attacked him during the ski race, Sam didn't dare ask me out again. He was afraid Claudius knew he was up to no good. Uh, what about Dr. Lawrence? Is he going to be all right? What's going to happen to Trixie?"

"Dr. Lawrence has a concussion, but he'll be okay, and Marnie Pearson said she'd adopt the dog. Don't change the subject."

Much later, Gus ran out of questions and drove Annie home. He waited until she let herself inside before driving away.

She closed the back door, unsnapped Claudius from the leash, and looked around.

Everything appeared to be normal. The telephone answering machine light was blinking like crazy. She had all sorts of messages, but she'd had enough for one night. If anyone wanted to talk to her, they could wait until morning.

She gave Claudius a biscuit and made coffee. Every muscle in her body ached as she got the brandy from the cupboard over the fridge. She dumped a shot in her coffee. It went down like burning silk. She sighed and slowly began to recover.

Claudius lay on the rug, contemplating Annie, and chewed his biscuit. She suspected he was pretending it was Harry's arm.

She straightened up the kitchen and went around the tavern, turning off lights. Upstairs, she brushed her teeth and climbed into bed.

Down in the damp, dark cellar, the furnace chugged into life. The tavern creaked in the wind, and she decided to count her blessings. Thanks in no small part to Claudius, she was alive and well at home. So the tavern needed a new coat of paint and the floors sloped every which way. So she fought a never-ending battle with dust-balls and spider webs. Right now, tucked up in bed, covered with her grandmother's old velvet and wool quilt, she was safe and sound.

Everything was all right.

Claudius lay down at her feet, stretched luxuriously, and settled his muzzle on his paws. He closed his eyes.

She smiled and scratched his ears, knowing he had his own thoughts to keep him happy: The bad guys in jail, a bone, a warm bed, and herself to bamboozle . . . what more could any dog want?